Silver...

HAVE ...
OF 56 ...

OF

EROTIC DOMINATION

If you like one you will probably like the rest

A NEW TITLE EVERY MONTH
NOW INCLUDING EXTRA BONUS PAGES

Silver Moon Readers Service
c/o DS Sales Ltd.
PO Box 1100 London N21 2WQ

Silver Moon Books Inc
PO Box 1614 New York NY 10156

*Distributed to the trade throughout North America by
LPC Group, 1436 West Randolph Street, Chicago, IL 60607
(800) 826-4330*

If you like one of our books you will probably
like them all!

**Write for our free 20 page booklet of extracts from
early books - surely the most erotic feebie yet - and,
if you wish to be on our confidential mailing list,
from forthcoming monthly titles as they are published:-**

Silver Moon Reader Services

PO BOX 1100 London N21 2WQ

or leave details on our 24hr UK answerphone
0181 245 0985
International acces code then +44 181 245 0985

<u>New authors welcome</u>

www.silvermoon.co.uk
www.thebookshops.com/erotic

PLEASE SAVE ME!
by
Dr Gerald Rochelle

Don't miss our web site: www.silvermoonbooks.com

1

Barbara stood in the lift smoothing down the lapels of her black suit jacket. When it stopped, a tall man in a cashmere overcoat pushed in front of her and tossed a magazine into the waste basket as he left. She glanced down and saw the front cover; it showed a naked woman, gagged and tied down to a bench being whipped with a leather belt. Barbara did not know why, but she picked it up and hurriedly stuffed it into her briefcase. She went straight to the ladies toilet, locked herself in a cubicle, sat down on the toilet and began to flick through the pages.

Barbara looked at the cover again and was transfixed by the look of fear on the woman's face. She was glancing back with wide, blackened eyes and straining against the ropes that held her tightly onto the bench. The leather belt was hitting her slender buttocks heavily and there were red stripes across her flesh from previous blows. Barbara, her hands shaking with a strange excitement, turned the page and saw a picture of woman bent over a man's knee. She was wearing a white blouse and her white panties had been pulled down around her ankles. Her bottom was beautifully rounded and reddened and she was stretching her arms out in pain as the man's hand smacked down hard.

Barbara felt herself tingling and turned to the next page. It showed a young dark-haired woman tied to a wooden chair. She was facing forward and her ankles were drawn in tightly by ropes against the chair legs. Her hands were tied behind her and her shoulders were pulled back stiffly. Her breasts were quite large and a leather whip was being brought down onto them fiercely. The woman's nipples were red and hard and there were red marks across her breasts, stomach and thighs.

Barbara felt frightened by the pictures but she could not resist the prickly heat of excitement that was running through her. She leant the magazine on the floor and bent her bottom upwards off the toilet seat. She lifted her black skirt and took hold of the sides of her white panties. She pulled them down to just above her knees and felt a breath of cool air fan across the warm skin of her buttocks. She sat back down on the seat and picked up the magazine again.

She opened it and went to a picture of a woman, completely naked and tied fast by ropes to a rough wooden post. Her arms were pulled tightly behind the post and her ankles were secured to each side of its base. She had a leather ball stuffed into her mouth and two leather straps which led from it were pulled tightly across her cheeks and secured to large nails driven into the sides of the post behind her head. A fully-dressed black man was kneeling at her feet and licking her cunt with his long slurping tongue.

Barbara rested the magazine on her knees and let her fingers slip down the front of her stomach. She poked them into the tight mass of black pubic hair that curled tightly at her groin and forced them down until she found the crack of smooth skin at the front of her fleshy cunt. She opened it a little and inserted one of her fingers. The petals of her outer labia folded back and revealed the wet inner folds. She ran her fingers along their glistening, moist surface and leant back on the toilet seat so that she could open her legs wider. Her panties pulled tight against the outside of her knees and as she felt the wet inner leaves of her cunt she also felt the tension of the material of her panties pulling hard at her skin. For a moment, she imagined she was tied up and being violated against her will like the women

6

in the pictures, then, shocked at what she was thinking, she pulled her fingers away and took up the magazine again.

It folded open at two pictures. On the one side there was a dark-haired woman bent over on all-fours with two men holding the upper parts of her thighs so that her knees were slightly off the ground. She had a rope around her neck and it was pulled tight to a metal ring in the ceiling. There was a man kneeling in front of her and he was forcing his cock into her mouth. The woman's elbows were barely touching the ground and she was holding onto the thick base of the man's cock in an effort to stop herself being strangled by the rope. Behind the man were several others, waiting in a line for their turn.

The other picture showed the same woman but now she was being held out on her back, the rope had been taken from her neck and there were angry red marks where it had cut into her flesh. She had obviously been beaten and she looked limp and dissipated. There were two large cocks stuffed into her mouth and she was struggling for breath as they plunged deeply into her. There was a man between her legs and he was holding her buttocks up high and thrusting his cock into her arse. Her stomach and thighs were glistening with semen and it ran freely down the sides of her face. Her eyes were dark and heavy-lidded and she looked terrified by her ordeal.

Barbara rested the pictures on her lap and pushed her finger further down between her fleshy crack. Her cunt was wet and open and when the tips of her fingers found her clitoris, it was engorged, hard and throbbing. She squeezed it between her fingers gently, then, seized with a strange desire, she pulled it until it hurt. She cried out softly and as she stared deeply into the pictures of the tortured woman she felt the hot energy of orgasm running through her body. She pulled at her clitoris even harder and held onto it as she plunged two fingers of her other hand eagerly into the wet flesh of her cunt. She pushed them deeply into her warm vagina and she lifted herself off the toilet seat as an unstoppable and rapid orgasm pulsed jerkily through her. She threw her head back as it flushed all over her tingling skin and she banged her head against the wall as she felt the muscles of her vagina contracting tightly onto her wet, dripping fingers. She held herself rigid for a moment, then she released her clitoris and cried out in relief as the magazine fell to the floor of the cubicle.

Barbara came out of the toilet looking flushed and dishevelled. She went to her desk, still feeling hot and wet and pushed the magazine into a drawer. As she sat down she felt the fleshy edges of her wet cunt sticking to the flimsy material of her panties.

Barbara was very attractive, but three years working as a clerk in an old-fashioned accountants' office in South-West London had made her rather prim and shy. She always dressed in a dark suit and white blouse, and she wore only light make-up with the faintest tinge of rouge and a small amount of black eye shadow. Usually, she tied her dark hair up in a pony-tail but today, because she was late getting up, she had forgotten and it hung freely in swirls around the carefully ironed collar of her blouse. She was looking for an elastic band to secure it when Mr Simms, her boss, called from his office.

"Barbara! Bring in the Portman file would you? Mr Portman is here early."

She picked up a blue file from her desk and hurried into his room.

Mr Simms was about forty but looked younger. He was tall and elegant with slightly greying hair and always wore a dark blue suit. Barbara liked him and she was often flattered by his attention or compliments. He leaned forward over his leather-covered desk.

"Ah Barbara. Sit down. I see you have left your hair loose today, it looks nice."

She squirmed down onto the seat, hanging her head slightly in embarrassment as she felt the moisture from her cunt still sticking to the material of her white panties.

"This is Mr Portman."

Barbara turned and saw that it was the man in the cashmere coat! The man who had left the magazine in the lift! She flushed with embarrassment.

He looked straight at her as if he knew that she had been looking at the pictures. She felt her face going red and she bent her head, letting her hair fall forward to try and hide it. His stare followed the neck-line of her blouse and fixed on the buttons that pulled it tight just above the embroidered edge of her white bra. Aware of his gaze, she lifted herself up on the chair and squeezed her shoulders forward in an attempt to draw the lapels of her jacket across the front of her blouse. She felt flustered, hot and very uncomfortable.

"This is Barbara," said Mr Simms, "she's been looking after your affairs."

"Enchanted," said Portman as he stretched out his hand. "Just call me Portman."

She reached over and took it nervously and he looked deeply into her eyes. She was struck by his dark good looks and only when she felt a sweatiness between their hands did she pull away.

The meeting went on for about an hour. Every time Portman asked a question Mr Simms asked Barbara to answer and every time she answered Portman stared hard at her. She felt as if he was hypnotising her because the more he stared the more she wanted to look at him. Feeling uncomfortable, she crossed her legs and noticed him glance up and stare at her knees. She smoothed her skirt down over the fronts of her slender thighs then bent forward and picked at a bit of fluff that clung to the side of her right calf.

"Enchanting," he said as he watched her, and she flushed bright red.

When he got up to go, she stood and took his hand again. He held it for a long time and bent his elbow to draw her closer to him before finally releasing her. As she watched him go she looked down and saw that her jacket was open and the top button of her blouse had come undone. Hurriedly she buttoned it up before collecting the file and returning to her desk.

Mr Simms spoke to her later in the day.

"This Portman seems to have a very complicated business: travel expenses all over the world, rents for property in God knows how many counties, agents fees and cash flying about everywhere. I hope he's not a villain!"

Barbara just smiled and got on with her work.

At five o'clock she closed her desk drawer, shouted good night to Mr Simms and left the office. It was getting dark outside and was already cold so she pulled the lapels of her jacket up around her neck and hurried out onto the pavement. She noticed a large black car parked against the kerb outside the entrance; there were two men sitting in the front and another in the back. As she turned to make her way to the tube station the man in the back of the car opened the door and shouted to her.

"Are you Barbara?"

Barbara was surprised and when she looked over to the man she did not recognise him.

"Yes," she said hesitantly.

"Good, can we have a word?"

Barbara was a little nervous but did not think anything

could happen so close to the office so she walked over to the car. The man got out of the back seat. He was tall and dressed in a black suit and his hair was long and black and pulled back into a heavy pony-tail.

"You're Barbara, you met Portman today, yes?"

"Yes, yes I did. What do you want?"

"Portman would like to see more of you."

Barbara suddenly felt frightened and took a pace back from the man but he stepped forward and grabbed her arm.

"I said Portman would like to see more of you."

Barbara pushed at the man with her other arm but he grabbed that as well. A wave of panic flooded through her.

"Let me go!"

The man took no notice and pulled her towards the open door of the car.

"What are you doing? Let me go!"

She struggled to pull away again but he was too strong and before she could scream out or get anyone's attention he pushed her into the back seat, jumped in beside her and slammed the door.

"Let me go!" she shouted as she made a grab for the door handle.

The man clutched her hand and pulled her away. She looked up to the office window and caught a glimpse of Mr Simms staring down into the street, then the man seized her shoulders and threw her back onto the seat.

"Go!" the man shouted and the car sped away down the street into the deepening darkness.

2

The man with the pony-tail sprawled lazily across the back

11

seat. Barbara squeezed herself against the door, trying to keep as far away from him as she could. Her heart was beating fast and she felt her cheeks flushing with fear. The man looked across at her.

"Nice tits, really nice tits."

He leant across and pushed his hand into the top of her blouse. She could not believe what was happening. She was terrified and tried to push him away.

"Get away! What are you doing?"

"Feeling your tits, what do you think I'm doing?"

He pushed his hand further inside her blouse and cupped one of her breasts in his palm. He lifted its weight then squeezed it hard. She cried out and tried again to push him back but he was too strong.

"Very nice. Now let's feel the other one shall we?"

He drew his hand roughly under her other breast and squeezed that even harder, then he reached his fingers up and pinched her nipple. She cried out again but as she tried to pull away he squeezed it harder. It hurt terribly, sending a deep stinging pain into her breast and causing her to gasp for breath. She could not pull away.

"Very nice," he said once again, pushing his face in front of hers, "very nice indeed."

He pressed his mouth against hers and started to lick around her lips with his tongue. She pulled back and turned her face away but he stared at her angrily and, pulling his hand out of her blouse, grabbed her face and turned it back to him.

"Don't turn away from me you bitch!"

He started to kiss her again and this time, no matter how much she tried to turn away she could not. He ran his tongue around her lips and then probed it inside her mouth, licking her tongue and the insides of her cheeks. She could not stop him and let him probe her mouth until it was wet

12

and sore.

Then the front passenger turned around to see what was going on.

"Leave her Ramon, you fucking Spanish animal! We've had no instructions about her yet. You'd better not spoil the goods!"

"It's only a bit of fun Carlo."

Ramon pulled back and Barbara gasped. Her blouse was undone and her bra was pulled down on one side exposing her breast. She reached down to button it up but Ramon grabbed her hands and laughed as she fought against him. She started to scream.

"Keep the bitch quiet can't you?" said Carlo.

Ramon clasped his hand across her face but she twisted away and screamed even louder.

"For fuck's sake Ramon, keep the bitch quiet!"

Ramon sat back for a second then grabbed the front of her white blouse and tore it. It ripped easily and he took the panel of material, wound it up like a rope and pulled it across Barbara's screaming mouth, forcing the sides of her cheeks back as he pulled it tightly. Then he stretched the two ends behind her head and tied them firmly. Some of her long hair caught in the knot and she snorted and gasped in pain but because of the tight-pulled gag she could no longer scream.

Her eyes widened in fear and she started to throw herself about frantically. Her tongue pressed against the back of the gag and she thought she was going to be sick. Ramon grabbed her blouse again and this time ripped the front of it completely apart. Her left breast stood out nakedly from her exposed bra. Its pale flesh was reddened by his rough handling and the nipple that he had squeezed so hard stood out prominently. Then he rolled her over on her front across the back seat and pulled her arms behind her. She gasped and fought for breath but he took no notice as he wound the material from the blouse tightly around her wrists, forcing her face-down and almost sitting on her.

Barbara stared into the leather of the seat and felt the hot pressure of Ramon's body on top of her as she bit into the gag, terrified and ashamed. Her hot breath condensed against the shiny surface of the seat and she felt its wetness against her burning cheeks. She did not know what was happening. She could not believe it. She was being abducted but she did not know by whom. All she knew was that they had mentioned Portman. But how could that be? He was a client at the office. What was going on? She felt faint and wanted to cry but she was too terrified to make a noise.

The car drove on through the darkness, stopping every now and again at traffic lights or at a road junction. When it stopped, Barbara hoped someone would see her being held captive in the back and come to her rescue, but no one did.

She buried her face deeply into the leather seat and closed her eyes, hoping that when she opened them again she would be safe. She felt Ramon lifting himself off her and she felt relieved and could breathe more easily but when she tried to get up his hands thrust hard against her shoulder blades and forced her back down again. She felt his hands grabbing her hips, his long fingers curving around them and digging into the edges of her stomach, then she felt him lifting her hips away from the seat. He was very powerful and with her hands tied behind her back it was impossible to resist.

He raised her hips off the leather seat and the weight of her body fell even more heavily on her face, which was already buried deeply into the seat cushion. She felt smothered and panicky and fought for breath. She felt his hands pulling at the hem of her skirt and she wriggled frantically, but it only helped him pull her skirt up. He slid it up her thighs until he exposed the tops of her black stockings. He paused for a moment and stared at her.

"Very nice!"

Then he continued pulling her skirt up slowly. He drew it past the tops of her stockings and revealed her black suspender belt. One of its clasps had come undone and the stocking top was pulled down almost to the inside of her knee. Finally, he drew the skirt up high enough to expose her white panties. They were squeezed tightly between her buttocks which stood out round and full against the black lines of the suspender belt.

"Very, very nice."

She felt the coolness of the air as her bottom was exposed and she squeezed her buttocks together in an attempt to protect herself. Ramon let go of her skirt and ran his hands over her buttocks. She felt the heat from his large palms as he massaged her tightened muscles. He started to probe his fingers in between them, pulling at her white panties as he prised at the edges of the flimsy material. She felt the cool air again but this time against the exposed flesh of her cunt. She went onto a frenzy of writhing and wriggling and even when he grabbed the sides of her hips again she did not stop. For a moment she thought she could break free from his grip, then she felt a searing pain across her bottom.

Smack!

His hand smacked down hard across her buttocks and she was thrown forward in pain and shock.

"Stop wriggling!"

Then another hard smacked came down fiercely across her stinging buttocks.

Smack!

"Stop wriggling!"

She tightened her muscles as the pain of the second smack tore through her. She felt so shocked and afraid. She had never experienced being smacked and she did not know how much she could stand. She was petrified and lay still with her face buried into the leather seat cushion. She held her breath for as long as she could and when she could hold it no longer it burst from her mouth in a loud, snorting gasp. She felt spit dribbling across her chin and lay as quietly as she could in the hope that he would leave her alone.

"That's better, now let's see what we've got here."

He grabbed the tight material of her white panties that was creased between her buttocks and ripped it downwards. She gasped with the shock as she felt them coming down over her thighs. Without letting them go, he ripped at them again. They came down to just above her knees and his fingernails left red scratches along the pale insides of her thighs. He put his hands back to back and thrust them between the tops of her thighs, forcing them apart and revealing her cunt. She could not resist him. She felt his hands forcing her legs apart and she felt the terrible exposure as her cunt came into view and the painful tightness of the material of her panties as it dug into her skin.

He released her for a second but only to hoist her hips higher. She gulped as he forced her thighs apart again then, without stopping, he poked his fingers between her legs until they touched her pubic hair. He grabbed it roughly and pulled at it hard. The pain was intense and she let herself move towards his hands to relieve it, but that only caused her bottom to go even higher and her cunt to be even more exposed to his probing fingers.

She wanted to beg to be released but all she could do was snort and gasp and dribble down her chin. He grabbed her pubic hair again, pulling at it hard and forcing her to lift her buttocks and expose her cunt fully to him. He extended his fingers towards it and, starting at the front, ran them slowly along her crack. She felt the warmth of his finger tips and held her breath, terrified by what he was doing, as he ran them back again, letting them glide along the inside edges of her outer labia. When he got to the front, he pressed his fingers against her clitoris. She let her breath out and immediately gasped for more, holding it in again and squeezing her eyes up tightly. She felt the dribbling spit running freely beneath her chin and onto her neck.

He pressed harder against her clitoris then drew his fingers away and she let her breath out again but this time allowed herself to breathe in more easily. She felt his fingers again, touching the front of her outer labia and starting to run eagerly along the pink edges of her cunt, gliding softly along the moistening edges and peeling her labia apart. He was not pressing his fingers in, nor was he pulling her flesh apart, it was just the touch of his fingers, and the terrible exposure, that were causing her labia to separate. His fingers ran along the full length of her crack and her labia peeled apart wetly. She felt shocked and desperately embarrassed. When he reached the back of her cunt her outer labia were open and engorged and glistening with moisture. He stroked them again and their wetness allowed his finger to slide inside. The swollen edges of her cunt opened widely and exposed the pink flesh of her inner labia, wet and warm and dilating wantonly under his searching touch.

Barbara could not believe what was happening, she felt so ashamed, so humiliated and yet this man's touch was causing her cunt to open wide and run with wetness and desire. She buried her head deeply into the seat in an attempt to hide her embarrassment but she did not try to pull away from Ramon's probing fingers.

He ran his fingers along the edges of her cunt again. The swollen folds of her outer labia poked out between her open thighs and the moisture on them glistened in the street lights. She felt him start to put his finger into her cunt; it went in deeply without stopping and, as she pulled away shocked and distraught, his finger came out.

"Open it up bitch!"

A hard smack landed across her bottom.

Smack!

"Open it up you fucking bitch!"

Smack! Smack! Smack!

He wrapped his forearm underneath the front of her hips and lifted her bottom higher. He pulled her across his lap and started smacking her hard.

Smack! Smack! Smack!

"This should make you think twice about pulling away from me!"

Smack! Smack! Smack!

The pain was terrible. It felt as though her bottom was being burnt, but it served to make her realise that she dare not resist him and she relaxed her muscles, allowing her reddened bottom to ease back up under the steady pressure from his arm.

He parted her labia again and thrust his finger deeply into her cunt. This time it went right in and she gulped noisily against the gag as she felt it filling her. He twisted it around the edges of her vagina then started pushing it up and down, slowly at first, but then quicker and harder. As he pushed his finger harder into her cunt her head and shoulders were forced down painfully against the leather seat. Her face was squashed against the smooth cushion and spit ran freely from her mouth and spread over her cheeks. He kept plunging his finger into her cunt and her neck hurt as she was forced harder down until she could hardly breathe.

Then she realised that her bottom was rising up to meet his thrusts, that she was matching his forceful finger with equal pressure. She felt disgusted with herself but did not stop, keenly lifting herself higher and opened her buttocks to get more.

"The bitch likes it! Here, how does that feel?"

Ramon thrust two more fingers inside her and she gasped as the pressure widened her cunt even more. Suddenly, he stopped and relaxed his grip on her but she did not lower her bottom. She kept it high and continued moving rhythmically as though his fingers were still plunging deeply inside her.

Ramon turned and knelt behind her. He undid his trousers and pulled out his cock, it was stiff and long. He held it in his hands and placed the throbbing glans next to the swollen edges of her cunt. She felt a surge of heat as it touched her flesh; she had never had a cock. It sent burning shivers through her body and she raised her bottom to try and wrap her cunt around it but he held it away, taunting her with it. She lifted her bottom more and drew her knees up to get it even higher and open her exposed cunt even more. She wanted it filled, she was burning with a need to be filled. She had pushed her own fingers inside her cunt and Ramon had just done the same, but she had never had a cock in there and now she could feel its heat and she wanted it desperately.

Her neck was aching and spit was running in streams from the edges of her mouth and she groaned and slavered as she lifted her bottom even more. She felt a surge of heat passing through her; it started in the soft flesh around the edges of her cunt but quickly spread around her clitoris then surged deeply inside. It exploded high up in her vagina and her whole body shuddered and jerked as the climax engulfed her. She could not breathe, she lifted her bottom even more and her face flushed hot and red. She tensed up tightly, driving the seizure deeply through her pulsating veins, then suddenly the breath burst from her and she screamed a muffled, gurgling scream of desperation as her orgasm released itself like water from a burst dam.

Barbara collapsed and fell crookedly back onto the seat. Her face was burning with heat and she felt depleted and used. Carlo turned and, with his arm draped casually over the seat-back, shouted to Ramon.

"Ramon! Leave the bitch alone! We're nearly there."

3

The large black car drew up in front of a black-brick apartment block. Ramon dragged Barbara out of the back door and hauled her in through the entrance of the imposing building. Her blouse was in tatters and open at the front, her bra was half-pulled down and her left breast was fully exposed. One of her stockings had come undone from her suspender belt and it hung down around her calf and her white panties were wound up in a tangle and pulled tightly just above her knees. Her skirt was still pulled high and her pubic hair was just visible as she stumbled across the pavement, her mouth still tightly gagged and her hands pulled up and tied behind her back. Her long black hair was tangled in swirls around her face which was wet from sweat and reddened from the chaffing against the leather seat of the car.

Ramon dragged her roughly into the entrance hall and, with Carlo and the driver following, they made their way to the lift.

"She looks a bit of a sight," said the driver.

"Yes, what a fucking slut eh Vic? What have you been doing to her Ramon?" said Carlo.

Ramon sniggered and pulled roughly at Barbara's arm. Her eyes widened with fear as the lift stopped and she was marched out.

"Here Carlo, give me a hand," said Ramon, pulling Barbara's arm while she struggled and pushed at him with the other.

Carlo grabbed hold of her free arm and together they marched her into a large office. They both released her at the same time and she fell to the floor in a heap.

"Ah, you've got her then! Get her up, let's have a look at our new beauty."

Ramon and Carlo grabbed her arms and dragged her up off her knees. She stared in shock at Portman as he strode across the office towards her.

"Quite a prize," he said as he leant towards her and lifted her chin. "Yes, quite a beauty."

Portman circled Barbara, looking up and down her trembling body. He reached forward and put his hand roughly between her legs. She drew back in fear as he ran them up the insides of her thighs and grabbed the flesh of her still-wet cunt.

"Ah, I see that our little beauty finds this exciting!"

He pulled her outer labia wide and slipped his fingertips along the wet crack of her cunt.

"Very nice! I hope you have not been messing with her Ramon!"

Ramon looked down at the floor and did not reply.

"Right, get her washed and cleaned up."

He turned to Barbara and looked in her eyes.

"If you can be quiet I will let them take the gag off. Can you be quiet?"

Barbara felt so nervous and shaky that she could not move. Portman grabbed her chin and squeezed her cheeks tightly.

"I said can you be quiet?"

Barbara tried to nod but she could not move because he was holding her chin so tightly. She tried to shake his hands away so she could reply but he took it as a refusal.

"Can't do what you're asked eh? I think we will have to teach you a lesson before we can go any further. This is the lesson, if you can't do what you're asked then you will be made to do it anyway. Get that?"

She tried to break free from his grasp again but again he took it that she was refusing his order.

"Bend her over boys. She needs some punishment!"

He released his grip on her chin and she gasped noisily, trying to show him that she was prepared to be quiet, but it only seemed to make him more angry.

"Bend her over boys, it's a while since I've given a beauty like this a good spanking. Let's see how she takes it."

Ramon and Carlo grabbed Barbara's arms and bent her forward. She tried to resist but it was impossible and she fell heavily onto her knees. She tried to shout out but she still could not open her mouth enough and she spluttered and choked as Ramon pushed the back of her head down until her face was forced against the tiled floor.

Portman went behind her and looked down at her. Her hands were writhing in their bonds and her skirt was high enough to see the dark recesses of her cunt. He grabbed the hem of her skirt and folded it onto her back. Her bottom was completely exposed and the wet folds of her cunt were squeezed between her taut thighs. Her white panties were still wrapped tightly just above her knees.

"Lift her arse up Vic!"

Vic grabbed her under the waist and heaved her bottom

as high as it would go.

"Very nice indeed," said Portman leaning over Barbara's back. "Now let's see if you can learn a bit of obedience. Keep a good hold on her boys!"

Portman bend down behind her and raised his hand above her tight-stretched buttocks.

"This will teach you to do what you're told!"

He brought his hand down hard.

Smack!

"Now, that's just the first, does that make you feel like following my instructions?"

Barbara was thrown forward by the power of the smack but Vic hoisted her bottom up again and held her securely.

Smack!

This time he did not let her go at all and the weight of the smacking hand fell fully on her buttocks. She wanted to yell out but she could only gasp and dribble.

"Not hard enough eh?"

Smack!

This one was harder and she felt its terrible sting penetrating her flesh.

"More?"

Smack! Smack! Smack!

Barbara's face was pressed hard against the floor and waves of sickening pain ran through her. She felt Vic lifting her bottom even higher and she felt completely exposed and terrified.

Smack! Smack! Smack!

Portman's hand came down heavily and this time it smacked across the exposed flesh of the edges of her cunt. The pain was unbearable, she wanted to scream for mercy, she wanted to promise to do anything she was ordered, she wanted to beg for forgiveness, but she could do nothing except suffer.

"Enough? Has that taught you to be obedient?"

Portman leant forward and put his mouth by the side of Barbara's ear.

"Be quiet! That's what I'm teaching you. Be quiet!"

He reached behind her head and loosened the gag.

"Be quiet! Or you will get more punishment."

He loosened the gag even more and let the knot fall loose. For a moment she kept it tightly between her teeth, then she opened her mouth and it fell away, wet and bitten, to the floor. There was a moment's pause then suddenly she let out a terrible scream, howling like an animal and screeching wildly until it was stifled as Portman clasped his hand across her mouth.

"You've not learnt your lesson have you?"

Barbara shook her head violently. She wanted to tell him she would be quiet, she wanted to tell him she did not mean to scream, she wanted to plead for mercy. She did not think she could bear any more and tried desperately to break free and tell him that she would do anything he said, but the more she tried the more he tightened his grip.

"Carlo, she needs more, see what you can do."

Portman kept his hand across her mouth as Carlo went behind her.

"Lift that beautiful arse up Vic, I can bring her to heel," said Carlo, taking his jacket off and rolling up his shirt sleeves.

Vic lifted Barbara's bottom until her knees came off the ground. He wound his arm tightly under her waist and hitched her up until she lay, still struggling, across his knee. He grabbed her white panties and tore them down roughly to just above her ankles.

"Right bitch! You'll do what you're told after this!"

He bent slightly and rested his hand across her reddened buttocks, rubbing it slowly across the smooth cheeks then

24

drawing it high above his shoulder. There was a pause and Barbara held her breath, not knowing what to expect, then his hand came down and smacked across her bottom violently.

Smack!

Barbara's breath was knocked out of her and the stinging pain made her body rigid with a convulsion of agony. Portman's hand clasped tightly across her mouth as she was thrown forward and she shook her head to try and dispel some of her suffering.

Smack!

Carlo spanked her so hard she thought she was going to pass out. She went rigid again and when she tried to breathe she could not because Portman's hand was so firmly across her gaping mouth.

Smack!

The pain was terrible. Her bottom felt on fire. The blow was so heavy that it threw her forward and the stinging pain was so intense it ran right through her and seared her innards. Portman put his mouth close to her ear again.

"Are you going to be quiet now?"

She could only just hear him above her snorting and gasping and she tried to break free of his clasping hand so that she could breathe and tell him yes. She wanted to get on her knees and beg him to believe her. She wanted to hang onto his feet and promise to be quiet forever as long as he would stop her punishment. She was so desperate to be heard.

"Still not ready eh? Give her six more Carlo and don't stop until she's had them!"

Carlo lifted his hand again and brought it down.

Smack! Smack! Smack!

Barbara was struggling with all her energy but it was running out fast. She felt unconsciousness sweeping

25

through her and a sickening giddiness made the room spin before her staring eyes.

Smack! Smack! Smack!

She felt the tension going out of her body and she dropped limply over Portman's knee. Her eyes were wide but everything was going dark. She did not even have the strength to gasp for breath.

"Let's try now shall we?"

Portman pulled his hand away from her mouth and she felt a trickle of air flowing across her tongue. His hand was covered in spit and he looked at it in disgust them turned and wiped it across her red buttocks. She was aware of the coolness as his hand rubbed across her sore flesh but little else.

"Are you going to be quiet now?"

She could not speak.

"What did you say?" he asked tauntingly. "You need some more spanking?"

She tried to speak but she only dribbled.

"Carlo!"

Barbara quivered with fear and spoke shakily.

"Yes," she said, "yes, I promise to be quiet."

Portman wiped his hand again on her red bottom and stood in front of her.

"Say it again bitch! Are you going to be quiet?"

"Yes, yes, I promise."

"Call me Sir!"

"Yes, I promise to be quiet Sir. I promise."

"And you will do anything you are told?"

She did not reply.

"I said and you will do anything you are told or do you need another spanking?"

"Yes, yes Sir, I will do anything I am told."

"Perhaps a fucking is what you need?"

"Oh please, Sir, please, I've never been ..."

"What! You've never been fucked? Is that what you said? You've never been fucked?"

"Please, Sir, please, I've never been ..."

"Say it bitch!"

"Please, Sir, I've never been fucked."

Portman jumped up excitedly and sat down behind his desk, laying his hands out onto his knees and smiling broadly.

"This is better than I thought. A virgin! What a prize! This is one for the Ringmaster. Take the bitch for a wash and I'll go and fetch him. Vic, you can drive me. I think the Ringmaster will be very pleased with our little virgin. And you two, whatever you do, don't you dare spoil the goods."

4

Ramon grabbed Barbara's arm and pulled her up. She stood shakily, swaying from side to side and fearful at what was going to happen next. Her face was reddened by the gag and the pressure from Portman's hand. Her mouth was dripping with spit and her eyes were moist and blackened with tear-smudged eye shadow.

Ramon pulled at her arm and dragged her across the office into an adjoining bathroom. She could not walk because her panties were too tight around her ankles and she stumbled and shuffled as he pulled her impatiently. Still holding onto her, he leant across the bath, put the plug in and turned on the water. Carlo came in and she shuddered with fear as he approached.

"My God you're a filthy little slut!"

Barbara felt ashamed and hung her head. Carlo reached

27

forward and undid the clasp that held her skirt at the waist. It fell down around her ankles. She stood in front of him, her jacket fully open and the tatters of her blouse barely covering her bra which was now pulled down below both her breasts. Her white panties were tight around her ankles and her hair was tousled and wet and stuck to her spit-smeared face.

"Down on your knees slut, we need to get you clean."

Barbara knelt down at the side of the bath. She waited quietly to be told what to do next and watched the water splashing into the bath. Carlo lifted her knotted hair and pulled it.

"This first."

He grabbed her hair tightly, forced her head forward and plunged it into the water. She coughed and choked then managed to pull herself back, gulping deeply for breath.

"Don't want to get clean eh?"

He pushed her head into the water again. She spluttered frantically as this time it was held under. She opened her eyes and could see the bubbles bursting from her mouth. She struggled against the pressure of Carlo's hand behind her head and finally her released her. She gasped frantically, unable to get enough breath to stop her panic, then she was forced down again until she thought her lungs were going to explode.

Then suddenly she was pulled to her feet and she threw her head about in confusion as the two men ripped her jacket and blouse off, then yanked at her bra until it broke free. Ramon lifted her feet one by one, took her panties off and threw them in a heap with her other, tattered clothes. Ramon and Carlo lifted her up and held her above the water before dropping her heavily. The water splashed over the side as she fought to keep herself upright. They laughed as she tried to pull her legs up to stop herself slipping under the water, then they started scrubbing her. Ramon used a long, wooden-handled brush and Carlo used a flannel. They rubbed her skin roughly as she sat in the bath trying to cover her breasts with her arms. They laughed at her efforts to try and stop them as they probed between her legs and wiped around her breasts. When they had finished they dragged her out and she stood dripping wet with soap bubbles sticking to her hips and breasts.

"Pretty little thing isn't she?"

"I wonder what she fucks like?"

"You'd better not let Portman catch you fucking her. You know what he said, he's gone for the Ringmaster and you don't want to cross either of them."

Barbara shivered with cold and wanted to ask for a towel but did not dare.

"He'll never know, keep the door closed. Go on!"

Ramon went to the door and closed it quietly.

"Bend over bitch! Let's see what that beautiful cunt fucks like."

Barbara felt terrified but did not dare move.

"Please," she said shakily, "please, let me go, please don't do anything more to me. Please let me go."

"Stupid fucking bitch! You've seen the last of your freedom for a long time, probably forever. You'd better get used to plenty of fucking because that's what's in store for you from now on. Plenty of fucking and lots of other things as well! That spanking was only the beginning. I expect you'll soon wish that a spanking was all you were getting! Now bend over!"

"Please don't, please ..."

"Carlo, leave her! Portman will find out and then we'll be in for it."

"But the bitch needs to get used to it, she needs some

practice or she'll be no use to anyone. What do you think bitch?"

Barbara hung her head and, as she dropped her arms to her sides, she saw how much her hands were shaking.

"Please let me go, please, please don't do anything to me, please."

"Bend over and shut up!"

Barbara was petrified with fear and just stood, naked, dripping wet and shivering with cold.

Carlo grabbed her by the shoulders, turned her around and forced her to bend over the side of the bath. She felt unable to resist and allowed him to manipulate her as he wished. She knelt against the side of the bath, her hips pressed against the edge and her arms stretched over the steaming water to the other side. He put his hand between her shoulder blades and pushed her forward. She grabbed hold of the other side of the bath to stop herself falling into the water.

"If we can't fuck your cunt then we'd better try your arse. Open your legs bitch!"

Barbara was too afraid to disobey but she was now shaking so much that she could not do what he said either. She felt terrorized and frozen with fear and stared down into the water hopelessly, wanting to cry and plead to be released.

"I said open your legs, let's see what I'm going to fuck!"

Still she could not move.

Carlo picked up the long, wooden-handled brush and without any warning brought the broad wooden side down across her bottom.

Smack!

Barbara grabbed the shiny edge of the bath and fell forward. She started to yell but he smacked her with the brush again with such force that it knocked her forward and her face went into the water.

Smack!

She screamed in pain and bubbles flooded around her face. She pressed her hands against the side of the bath and in desperation raised her face above the water. She gasped and choked and tried to wriggle free, taking her hands off the edge of the bath and swinging round.

"Please, please, let me go ..."

"Ramon! Come and hold the bitch!"

Ramon came over and leant over the bath. He grabbed her wrists, pulled them together and pressed her hands hard against the edge of the bath. Carlo put his hands between her thighs and prised them apart then grabbed the cheeks of her bottom and parted them, revealing the swollen, pink edges of her cunt and the dark, tight ring of her anus.

"Beautiful! Really beautiful!"

He leant forward and put his face in between her buttocks. He licked his tongue out and touched the edges of her anus and, as she felt the sting of his touch, a strange thrill ran through her.

He leant back and smiled, then he undid the zip of his trousers and pulled out his cock. It was fully hard and he ran his fingers along its length, squeezing the shaft and engorging the throbbing glans even more. He pointed it towards her cunt and laid it against the wet folds of her outer labia. He pressed his hot cock against them and they peeled back easily but he did not press it in. He ran it along the silky petals of her cunt, then lifted it away and pressed it against the ring of her anus. She started panting and gasping for breath when she felt the heat of his cock against her and the strange thrill she had felt from his tongue turned into a wave of fear as the engorged glans forced hard against her tight anus.

"Please, please ..."

"Shut up bitch! Ramon! Duck the fucking bitch if she can't be quiet."

Ramon grabbed Barbara's hair with his free hand and pulled her head high above the water, then her forced downwards and plunged her head under the water. He held it there for a few moments then pulled her out gasping and dribbling water from her open mouth.

Carlo pressed his cock harder against her anus until the it began to open. Barbara felt the heat of his cock on its inside edges and gasped as Ramon tightened his grip on her hair and her face was plunged into the water again. She held her breath and kept her eyes open and when she was released she gasped loudly.

Carlo's cock pressed further inside the edges of her anus and she felt the tight muscle opening and letting it in. There was nothing she could do to stop it and her eyes widened with fear as it began to fill her. It felt huge and she was terrified at the thought of it going inside her, she could not imagine that her tight anus could open enough to take its thickness. He pressed harder and it slipped in further. She gasped as it went in and her face was pushed into the water again. This time she knew what to expect and she lay face-down, holding her breath and waiting to be released. She felt Carlo s cock going even further. She could not believe what was happening as the tip went inside and its heat ran deeply into her arse. But now she did not think of breathing, all she could only think of was the cock that was sliding so easily into her arse. All she could feel was its ribbed, veiny surface pulling at her sensitive innards and her anus dilating to receive it.

Then her face was out of the water and she breathed deeply, but this time, while she was taking in breath, she was waiting to be pressed down again. She felt anxious until Ramon forced her down and she waited, face-down and wide-eyed in the warm water of the bath.

Carlo's cock went deeper inside and she felt the ring of her anus tightening around the thick shaft. The heat inside her was tremendous but now she felt herself pushing onto his cock. She felt her buttocks lifting higher and opening wider to make it easier to get his cock inside. Deeper it went and its heat radiated inside her whole body, filling her with desire and a longing for more.

Her face was lifted out of the water and she gasped one long breath then held onto it expectantly. But Ramon was not quick enough for her and she plunged her head back down without any pressure from his hand. She forced her head deep into the water and concentrated on the cock that was still sinking itself inside her, then she felt it stop and realised that it was all the way in. She could feel Carlo's balls against the wet edges of her cunt and she pushed against them hard, urging his cock to go further.

He pushed a bit deeper then stopped, unable to get it in any further. Barbara pushed against it and realised there was no more to take. She drew away, feeling the tight pressure of her anus against the hard veins of his throbbing cock, then she pushed back again and felt the shape of his glans pressing against the inside edges of her arse. She pushed again and again drew back and found herself moving rhythmically, searching out every feature of his pulsating shaft and squeezing it against her tender flesh.

Then her head was pulled out of the water but she did not take a breath. She wanted to hold onto it and feel only the hard cock fucking her arse. She did not want to think about breathing, she only wanted to think of Carlo's cock buried inside her so she pushed her head back into the water, pulling against the pain as Ramon tried to hold her back by her hair. She forced her head deep into the water and resisted all his attempts to get her out.

She started fucking the cock hard and then, before she could enjoy it more, she felt a surge of heat penetrating her innards. She felt a wetness soaking inside her cunt and a burning heat inside her arse. She squeezed down onto the cock, sucking at it and desperately trying to keep it all inside her. She dragged at it, and fought to keep it in, but the heat was too great, it flooded up though her and her buttocks opened and she fell forward as the unbearable strain exploded inside her. She felt her bottom lifting higher and she felt the surge of semen bursting from the end of the hot cock but everything was lost in a turmoil of images as she felt herself falling and drowning and finishing with the most tremendous orgasm. She flopped down in the water still holding her breath then, barely conscious of what was going on, her head was lifted out of the water and after a few moments, and much against her will, she gasped for breath.

She began to come round. Her head was spinning to start with but as she came to she realised her arse was empty; it was hot and burning at the edges but it was empty.

"More, please, more," she whimpered.

Ramon got behind her, took his cock out and plunged it in. Her arse was open and soaked with Carlo's semen and Ramon's cock ran in to its base in one hard thrust. Barbara gasped as it filled her and took in just enough air to allow her to plunge her face back into the water. She bit down hard onto her lips and started fucking the cock. This time it was easier because of the hot spunk that still ran inside her and she slid up and down it frantically. She fucked harder and bit her lips harder and held her breath then, as she felt the surge of spunk running up Ramon's cock she bore down onto it ferociously.

She squeezed her arse around it and felt his semen flowing up the shaft. She could feel it coursing towards his engorged glans then she tightened up as much as she could and felt it spurt deeply into her. Still she held her breath and still she fucked the cock but she could not hold back another tremendous orgasm. She knew she wanted to breathe and this time she felt desperate for air, but she wanted to feel the spunk and she wanted to feel her own body enveloped in the building convulsion that was overwhelming her. She fucked and held on for as long as she could. She felt every drop come out of his cock then suddenly her lips burst open and, even though her face was still under the water, she gasped for breath.

She choked and threw her head high to get breath but there was no air to breathe and she felt only water burning her throat and running into her lungs. She gasped and choked wildly and then began to scream in panic. Water ran from her mouth and she threw her head from side to side, fearful of never breathing again. Her orgasm was still flowing through her body and she could still feel the hard cock pulsating with its last remains of spunk, but she knew somehow she had to fight for air. Finally, she got a proper breath and fell onto her hands, shaking, panting and overwhelmed with pleasure but still fucking at the dissipated cock that was still inside her arse.

When Ramon's cock finally slipped out she felt a coolness between her legs and immediately became aware of her humiliation. She could not believe what was happening to her. She could not believe that she had been abducted and beaten and now she could not believe the pleasure that she had gained from having her arse fucked by two men she had never seen before. She reached down and felt her cunt, it was warm and wet and she ran her fingers around it and caressed her swollen outer labia as they ran with droplets of sweet-smelling moisture. She felt her clitoris, it was hard and engorged, and a deep tingle ran through her as it quivered against her finger-tips. Her desires started again, but a noise startled her and she turned around in fear as she heard Portman shouting at the door.

"What the fuck have you been doing?"

"Only her arse boss, honestly, only her arse."

Barbara looked up at Portman in the doorway. His face was red with anger and behind him stood a tall, dark figure. She squinted to see more clearly as the figure stepped forward into the bathroom. His black hair was scraped back tightly from his sallow face and his eyes were dark and penetrating. He was dressed in a black leather jacket, tight black leather trousers and a black shirt. His jacket was embroidered with silver sequins, he had a silver clasp around his neck and his calf-length leather boots had silver studs running up their sides.

"Is this the beautiful virgin?"

"Yes Ringmaster," said Portman.

"She doesn't look much of a virgin to me!"

"Only her arse Ringmaster, honestly, only her arse."

The Ringmaster looked down between Barbara's thighs; semen was still running from her anus. He reached down and prised the tops of her thighs apart. He pressed his finger into her cunt and she gasped.

"Maybe," he said uncertainly.

"Honestly Ringmaster, only her arse."

The Ringmaster paced around Barbara as she kneeled against the edge of the bath. He felt her buttocks, pinched the skin of her arms and cupped her breasts in his hands. He lifted her chin in his hand and looked closely at her face. He squeezed her cheeks to expose her teeth and rubbed his fingers inside her lips. He tossed her hair about in his hands then raised some of it to his face and sniffed it. He went again to her buttocks and looked at them closely.

"Have you beaten her?"

"Only a spanking."

"How did she take it?"

"Very well, it certainly made her do what she was told. I think she could take a lot more as well."

"But look," said the Ringmaster indicating her dripping anus, "this is not what you promised, it's going to affect the price. You are going to have to take less than we agreed."

The Ringmaster and Portman looked at each other tensely for a few moments then they both grinned.

"It's a deal."

"Good," the Ringmaster said calmly, "I'll take her straight away, oh, and if I were you I'd get rid of those two."

Portman turned to Ramon and Carlo.

"You're finished," he said angrily.

Barbara cowered against the edge of the bath, naked and shivering with cold as Ramon and Carlo argued with Portman. In the end they left, slamming the door behind them, swearing and cursing and promising to get even. The Ringmaster handed over some money to Portman and they shook hands.

"Always good doing business with you," said the Ringmaster. "I think this little bitch will be a fine addition to my little circus. Oh, by the way, what's her name?"

"Barbara, she was a clerk in an office."

"Barbara eh? I will enjoy taking a hand in her training myself. Come on Barbara, get up, I have to leave tonight."

5

Barbara was not even allowed to get dressed. The Ringmaster tied a thin rope around her neck, reminded her that if she screamed or yelled she would be beaten, then dragged her out of the room and into the lift.

He paused for a moment at the entrance then dragged her across the pavement on the leash. She felt so humiliated as she was pulled towards a large, white car: disgraced, naked and being dragged along on a leash in public. A man and a woman walked past and Barbara turned to them, appealing silently with her eyes for help but the woman just giggled and the man only stared at her breasts. Barbara wanted to cry out for help and she opened her mouth as if to speak but the Ringmaster yanked the rope around her neck and she choked as it tightened around her throat.

"Please, please let me go ..."

He took no notice, pushed her into the back of the car and it drove away.

Barbara cowered in the deep leather seat, then suddenly she was seized with panic, reached forward to the door handle and frantically tried to open it. The Ringmaster smiled, grabbed her hands and tied them together with the leash so that they were pulled up in front of her neck.

"You're a lively little creature! I think you will be very interesting to train."

She struggled again, pulling at the rope and trying to use her elbows to open the door.

"Sit quietly you fucking idiot!"

His anger only made her more desperate to escape and she threw herself about even more wildly. The Ringmaster pulled the end of the rope through a grab handle above Barbara's door and hauled it up tight. She was pulled off the seat by the tension and her face banged against the top of the window. She hung, gasping and choking with her hands tightly tied in front of her neck and her head at an angle against the top of the window. Her buttocks were raised off the seat and she thought she was going to suffocate but could only fight for breath as she watched the street lights flashing by as the car sped through the city night.

She raised herself higher to ease the tension and managed to get some breath but in the end she sank back under the strain and the flashing lights died away as she fell unconscious.

The next thing she knew she was being pulled out of the back of the car and dragged into a huge, cavernous building. Large metal doors slid back as they entered and when they were inside they clanked together noisily. Barbara looked around and saw that she was in some sort of warehouse. The floor was covered in boxes and crates, some stacked right to the ceiling, and several large cages stood at the end furthest from the door. Further away, in the darkness, she saw some more cages swinging lazily from chains attached to beams in the roof. An articulated lorry stood in the middle of the warehouse and inside she glimpsed more cages but this time containing howling wild animals.

"Welcome to my storehouse!"

The Ringmaster let go of the rope and Barbara fell to the floor.

"Get up, we leave in an hour. Follow me!"

Barbara wanted to run away but she knew there was nowhere to run. She did not want the rope around her throat pulled again and so she got up obediently and, trailing the rope from its noose, she followed him.

"Mercedes!" shouted the Ringmaster. "Mercedes!"

As Barbara walked behind him a surge of embarrassment swept over her. She felt desperately aware of her nakedness and captivity and could hardly believe that only a few hours ago she had been tidying her desk and leaving her office. She folded her arms across her breasts to cover herself but realised it was pointless. She let her hands drop to her sides and looked down in fear.

The Ringmaster stopped and she looked up. There was a large cage in front of them, swinging several feet above the ground. He grabbed a winch control and the cage clanged down to the ground. He swung the door open and it crashed back noisily.

"In there! I've got to sort out a few things and you will wait here."

She stepped forward and walked into the cage, it was completely empty and she stood at its centre, shivering. The Ringmaster closed the door and, after snapping a padlock across the latch, winched it back up. It swung giddily on its chain and Barbara held onto the sides to keep her balance. The Ringmaster walked off between the crates shouting at the top of his voice.

"Mercedes! Mercedes!"

The sound of his voice died away and Barbara stood in the cage feeling hopeless and wretched. After a while she sank to the floor and crouched down, clinging to the bars and wishing it was all a terrible nightmare. She felt so exposed and her feeling of nakedness overwhelmed her as she crouched fearfully inside the swinging cage. The animals started to screech and howl and a wave of panic ran over her. She felt like one of them, like a captive animal locked in a cage: naked, unprotected and vulnerable.

When she heard the Ringmaster's footsteps coming back, she got up and hung onto the bars. She felt like an exhibit, like an animal on display and she shouted out.

"Please, please let me go. This must be a mistake. Please, you must let me go. I can't stand this. You must let me free."

"Bitch! Must! Must! What are you saying? What are you saying to me, the Ringmaster? I must do something? You do not tell me what I must do you fucking bitch."

Angrily, he lowered the cage. It crashed to the floor and she was knocked down by the jolt. The animals started howling wildly in excitement. He undid the padlock, opened the door, reached in and dragged her out by the rope. He was very angry and pulled at her fiercely. She yelled as the rope bit into her neck but her cries only made him angrier and he pulled at her even harder. She struggled to get to her feet and stumbled and tripped as he hauled her through the door.

"Must? Must? I'll teach you who must!"

He pulled the noose from around her neck and undid her wrists. He forced her face-forwards against the bars of the cage. Her face and breasts hit them hard and she cried out in pain. Her nose felt as if it was bleeding.

He wrapped the rope around one of her wrists and pulled it high up on the bars, hauling her onto her tiptoes. He tied the other wrist and pulled it up as well so that her arms were stretched high and wide. She struggled to keep her toes on the floor but the pain in her wrists let her know that they were holding most of her weight. Reaching over to an open packing case the Ringmaster took out some cord and tied it around her ankles. He kicked her legs wide apart and secured the ropes to the bars as well. She was splayed out wide against the cage with her face pressed hard against the bars as she strained with her toes to reach the floor.

"Please, no, please ..."

"Quiet! You need some punishment! Let me see what I can find."

She felt herself shaking and tried to wriggle free but he had tied her so tight she could not move. He walked around looking in some boxes nearby and from one of them drew out a short riding crop. She tried to turn and see what he was doing but it was impossible.

"Perfect! This should be just the right thing to start your training."

He stretched his arm fully back and then brought the crop down hard against her naked buttocks.

Whack!

It landed hard against her taut flesh and she winced in pain.

"You will learn that when you're told to do something you do it!"

Whack!

Another savage blow landed across her bottom. She shrieked and clung onto the bars as the piercing stab of the whip seared through her.

"You will learn that I am the one who gives you your instructions you fucking bitch."

Whack!

Another blow came down stingingly and a burning pain ran through her making her flesh feel on fire and her head reel in torment.

"You will learn only obedience."

Whack!

She screamed as the leather whip struck her again. The pain was terrible, it felt like a flame was licking her buttocks. It scorched her tender flesh then shot like spiky talons throughout her whole body. She screamed again, pleading for him to stop.

"Please, oh please stop, please ..."

Whack! Whack! Whack!

"I am the one that gives the orders bitch! Now be quiet!"

"Please ..."

Whack! Whack! Whack!

Barbara clenched her buttocks tight but it did nothing to stop the pain and she was in agony as the whipping blows rained down on her soft skin. She did not think she could suffer any more and yet she did not dare plead for mercy. She knew she must do what he asked, she knew she must be obedient to him if the pain was to stop. The pain would only stop if she suffered it more and suffered in the way he wanted her to; silently and with obedience. She clenched her teeth together and squeezed her eyes up tightly.

Whack! Whack! Whack!

She felt herself going dizzy and bit down hard onto her lip to stop herself from yelling for him to stop. She knew she must not cry out or the pain would go on forever. She held onto her suffering and pulled in the muscles of her buttocks as tightly as she could. Her hands grasped the bars and she felt dribbles of spit running from her lips as she held on and just hoped he would stop.

Whack! Whack! Whack!

She thought she was going to pass out. She wanted to drift into unconsciousness, it was the only thing that would save her from the pain, if she was unconscious she could take his merciless beating and not cry out.

"Who is your master?"

She could not reply. She did not dare open her mouth in case all she could do was yell and scream. There was so much pain bottled up inside her she thought that opening her mouth would cause it to explode.

Whack! Whack! Whack!

"Who is your master?"

She tried to fight against the pain, she tried to control herself and speak but all that came out was a gurgling, grunting animal sound.

Whack! Whack! Whack!

Each blow took the breath from her but still she tried to speak. She opened her mouth wider and felt the indentations on her lip where she had been biting down. Spit ran freely from her mouth and she felt it dripping onto her breasts. It ran across them and out onto her nipples that were hard and pressed against the cold iron bars. She tried to lick her lips to make them less sore and she tasted the blood than was running from her nose.

"Who is your master?"

"You are," she blubbered at last. "You are my master."

The whipping stopped and she dropped back against her bonds.

"That is all that matters," he said, satisfied. "I am your master. The Ringmaster is your master and you follow only his instructions. Who do you obey bitch?"

"The Ringmaster. Only the Ringmaster."

"Good. You will indeed make a good addition to my little circus of pleasures."

Barbara could hardly hear his words but they filled her with dread. It was as though suddenly she realised that this was not a dream, this was really happening and it was more terrible than anything she could imagine. She had never experienced such pain and such humiliation and her heart went cold at the idea that there was more punishment ahead.

"Mercedes! Mercedes!"

The animals screeched loudly as Barbara hung onto the bars still gasping and dribbling from her beating, then she saw a figure coming towards her from the opposite side of the cage.

"Mercedes, my dear Mercedes. Where have you been?"

Barbara squinted her eyes and peered between the bars as a tall woman slowly approached out of the darkness.

"Mercedes, you look as beautiful as ever."

Mercedes came into full view. She was tall, slim and angular with jet black hair that was cut short and drawn into points that reached just to the hinge of her jaw. Her dark eyes were rimmed with black shadow and her large mouth was edged with immaculately glossed and perfectly outlined red lips. Her long finger nails were painted to match her lips. She wore a loose, silky red blouse that hung slackly across her breasts and was tucked in tightly to the narrow waist of a short, black leather skirt. Her legs were covered to just above the knee by shiny leather boots. Her long arms hung loosely at her sides and in one of her hands she trailed a bamboo cane.

"Ringmaster," she said in a low, soft voice.

She dragged the tip of the cane along the floor and when she reached Barbara she rattled it across the bars of the cage.

"This has got to be a virgin!" she shouted, bending down and rubbing the fronts of her black boots before rising up again with excitement. "This has got to be a virgin!" She bent down again and Barbara saw the glint of a golden ring which pierced Mercedes' left nipple.

"Mercedes, you are amazing. How could you tell?"

Mercedes ignored him and ran the tip of her cane across the bars again. They clattered as the hard tip brushed against Barbara's nipples that protruded between the cold iron rails of the cage.

"Hello little virgin," said Mercedes, flicking Barbara's nipples again with the cane. "What have you been doing?"

"Being beaten, she has to learn who is the master."

"Show me how she takes it, give her some more, I want to see her face and how she takes the pain."

The Ringmaster lifted the whip and brought it down hard across Barbara's reddened buttocks.

Whack!

Barbara screeched, it was harder than before and her bottom was so tender and inflamed that she was seized with a searing pain.

Mercedes looked on and smiled.

"More Ringmaster, I want to see how the virgin responds to pain. More!"

Whack! Whack! Whack!

Barbara clung onto the bars and screeched, spitting and gulping for air as each blow cracked down on the sensitive, aching cheeks of her buttocks.

"Please, oh please ..."

"I like the way she begs, Ringmaster. Let's see some more."

Whack! Whack! Whack!

Barbara's whole body burned with the terrible pain, and her grip on the bars slackened as she began to feel herself losing consciousness.

Through her bleary eyes, Barbara watched Mercedes as she lifted one of her feet onto an open packing case. Her short, black skirt pulled up high into the crease of her thigh and Barbara saw a thick mat of black, pubic hair at her crotch. Mercedes reached out with her cane and poked it against Barbara's cheek and she winced in fear. Mercedes grinned then drew it back and slid the tip between her own thighs. She started to pull it up and down between her pubic hair forcing it to crease and expose the edges of her cunt. Barbara was awakened as she caught sight of Mercedes' swollen pink labia, glistening with wetness as the cane ran between them and tugged them apart.

Whack!

Another hard blow came down across Barbara's buttocks and she was knocked hard against the iron bars of the cage. She gripped them tight and felt her breasts pressing between them and her nipples hardening even more.

Whack!

She gripped harder as the agonizing sting penetrated her body, but all the time she watched the cane prising the edges of Mercedes' cunt wider and wider.

Whack!

The burning pain ran through her in hot flushes but somehow, the pressure of the bars against her breasts and the tightness of her desperate grip made her nipples harder and she felt them yearning for more. She felt them distend-

46

ing and pointing outwards and she sensed their power as they appealed for more pain.

Whack!

They hardened even more and the cane between Mercedes' legs pushed sideways and opened the entrance to her cunt. It pushed the swollen outer labia wide and Barbara could see the pink inner edges and the darkness within. Strands of black pubic hair stuck wetly to the cane as it began to work vigorously to open up the beautiful cunt even more.

Whack!

A terrible blow fell against Barbara's buttocks but this time the pain was welcome, this time the sensation in her burning body was only of desire. Her nipples were aching more than the whip was hurting the flesh of her stinging buttocks. They were so hard that they were pulling at her breasts and she pushed them forwards through the bars as if to try and reach Mercedes.

Whack!

This time the blow was not hard enough. It was too soft and weak, it was not enough to match Barbara's desire for more.

Harder, please, harder,' she cried, hoping that her demands would lead to more punishment, hoping that the Ringmaster would be angered enough to give her more.

Whack!

It was harder but still not enough.

"Please, please, harder, make it harder ..."

Whack!

Barbara crashed against the bars as the whip tore across her buttocks.

"Harder, please, harder ..."

Whack!

Even though the pain was excruciating it was only just

enough as Barbara watched the cane between Mercedes' labia. She was moving it fast and hard and flicking it sideways with every pass across her wet cunt. She opened her legs wide and Barbara gasped. Mercedes' cunt was wide open and the cane whipped hard against it edges, inflaming it to swell more at the sides and open itself even wider. Barbara felt a heat inside her, a deep, penetrating heat. It was like a hot plug that was jammed inside her cunt, and behind it there was a boiling torrent waiting to expel itself and flood her with passion and fulfilment.

Whack!

"Too weak! I said harder! Harder! I need it harder! Whip me, whip me until I bleed, whip me as hard as you can, harder, harder ..."

Whack! Whack! Whack!

The flood broke through and Barbara smashed against the bars as a convulsion of suffering and delight spread through her and drenched her. She screamed so loud the warehouse echoed and she gripped the bars and forced the base of her stomach against them as she pulsated with an uncontrollable paroxysm. She squeezed her eyes tightly shut and her body drew up in an ever-tightening spasm as it claimed her, then she held her breath as it enveloped her. She sensed a vacuum of silence, as if she was floating in space, then a scent and a shiver brought her back. As it subsided she slithered back down and flopped, used and dissipated against the ropes that held her wrists.

Barbara opened her eyes to see Mercedes holding the cane up sideways, offering it for her to bite on. She took it between her teeth and bit down onto it with all her strength. As she felt the tips of her teeth breaking into the hard surface of the bamboo cane she felt another convulsive shiver as a further orgasm washed her into blissful unconsciousness.

Barbara awoke to the frenzied screeching of animals. She lifted her head and opened her eyes. She was still tied to the bars of the cage and the pressure from the ropes had made her wrists swollen and her hands red. She eased herself up to relieve the pain and, as she moved, she felt the flesh of her bottom still burning from her whipping.

"She's awake Mercedes, let's get her dressed, we haven't much time before the train leaves."

Barbara felt herself sag as the ropes around her wrists were undone.

"You're going on a journey my little virgin."

The Ringmaster's words were full of menace and she shrunk back as he grabbed her by the arm and dragged her across to a pile of half-opened boxes.

"Stand there, we need a photograph for your new passport."

There was sudden burst of bright light and Barbara winced and closed her sore eyes. The Ringmaster pulled the photograph from the instant camera, looked at it fleetingly then handed it to Vic.

"Is half an hour enough?"

"It'll be ready when you are," said Vic, taking the photograph into a small office built into the side of the warehouse.

"Now my dear Mercedes, she can go as a prisoner I think, how do you fancy being a prison warder?"

"I think a policewoman would be more to my taste."

"Good, then you shall be a policewoman. Let's see what we can find."

Mercedes bent over the open crates, her short black leather skirt pulling high and exposing the tops of her firm thighs. She drew out some items of clothing and tossed them down on the floor. The Ringmaster picked up a uniform and held it up for Mercedes to see.

"Perfect!"

Barbara watched as Mercedes casually undressed. She undid a small buckle at the waist of her skirt and pulled down a short zip. She pulled her loose, silky red blouse free and let it hang outside her unzipped skirt. Slowly and carefully she unbuttoned the blouse, looking down at her long fingers as they worked the buttons from their tight-sewn holes. As she undid the last button the blouse fell loosely to the sides and exposed her naked breasts; they were full and firm and both her nipples were hard and straining out from the dark surrounding flesh.

Her left nipple had a golden ring through it and it glistened in the harsh lights of the warehouse. She pulled the blouse back off her shoulders and it dropped to the ground. She looked beautiful in her loosened skirt and black leather boots as her long, slender arms hung loosely from her angular shoulders. She twisted her hips and eased her skirt off; it fell down and the supple leather wrinkled up around her ankles. She was not wearing any panties and her pubic hair formed a thick, black triangle at the base of her stomach. She bent down and unzipped her long leather boots then pulled them off one by one.

As Barbara stared at Mercedes' beautiful body she became aware of her own shame; she felt so dirty and used and Mercedes looked so beautiful and elegant. A wave of self-disgust and wretchedness swept over her.

Then Mercedes started to dress in the uniform. She pulled on some black stockings, clipped a black suspender belt around her hips then attached the tops of the stockings to its metal clasps. She pulled on a white blouse and carefully tied a black tie around her neck, tugging at the knot until it lay tightly at the front of the collar. She pushed her arms into the sleeves of a black tunic and pulled it tightly together at the front, then she drew up a black skirt and buttoned it at her waist. Finally, she put on some black shoes and laced them tightly, lifting her feet onto the packing case to get sufficient purchase.

"Here, put these on," the Ringmaster said to Barbara, holding out a blue cotton smock and some scuffed, black shoes.

She took them from him and without questioning his instructions began to get dressed. She was pleased to be covering her body, but when she had the smock on and had laced up the shoes she felt even more ashamed and embarrassed. She felt so dowdy and drab compared to Mercedes and she wanted to hide herself away in shame.

Mercedes took a brown, wooden truncheon, a notebook and some shiny, silver handcuffs from the box. She put the notebook into a breast-pocket of her tunic then slipped the truncheon down a long pocket at the side of her skirt. She held the handcuffs out in front of Barbara.

"Hands out!"

Barbara held her hands forward and Mercedes clamped the handcuffs tightly around her wrists.

Vic came out of the small office and handed a passport to the Ringmaster.

"What do you think?"

"Perfect! Perfect! Bring your prisoner, my dear Mercedes, we must get on our way!"

Within minutes, Barbara was sitting in the back of the white car with Mercedes at her side. She wanted to speak to her but somehow she did not dare. After a while, they arrived at Victoria Station and Mercedes dragged Barbara out.

"Now, no trouble from you, bitch. Remember your last beating? Well, there are worse things I can do to you, so behave yourself and do what you're told."

Barbara nodded obediently; she felt such a prisoner and was so frightened and intimidated by her captor and escort that she had no will of her own. They walked into the huge hall of the station, the Ringmaster bought some tickets and they went to a waiting room. Barbara was made to sit down and Mercedes sat close beside her. Two men sat opposite them, staring at Mercedes and Barbara and smiling at each other and making remarks. One of them leant forward.

"What's she done then? What's her punishment?"

Mercedes leant forward with her elbows on her knees.

"What have you got in mind?"

The man sat back a little surprised, then he turned and sniggered to his companion but did not say any more. A few minutes later, their train was announced and they got up and went.

Mercedes pushed Barbara into the window-seat and sat beside her, trapping her firmly against the side of the carriage. The two men from the waiting room came down the aisle and when they saw two empty seats opposite Barbara and Mercedes they sat in them, smirking at each other as the train pulled out of the station.

"I can think of a punishment," said the man who had spoken before.

"Interesting," said Mercedes, "let's see if it's appropriate. Watch her and I'll be back in a minute."

Mercedes got up and after speaking briefly to the Ringmaster who was sitting further down the carriage she went to the toilet.

"You're a pretty little girl. What have you done to be in this fix?" asked the man.

"Please, can you help me, I've done nothing wrong, I've been kidnapped, please can you help me?"

The two men laughed. Barbara went to get up but the man opposite reached over and forced her back into her seat.

"Please, I'm telling the truth, I've been kidnapped, I'm being treated like a slave! Please ..."

But it was useless. She was pushed back into her seat again and as she fell back her legs stretched out under the table between her and the men. The man opposite reached down and forced his hand between her thighs and she pulled back but he pushed his hand up until it reached her cunt.

"No panties eh? What a tart!"

His fingers probed around her outer labia and she wanted to shriek with fear, then, when Mercedes came back and sat down, he pulled his hand away.

"OK, follow me in five minutes," Mercedes said calmly to the men. "Come on bitch, it seems as if you are in for a little punishment."

Mercedes grabbed Barbara by the wrists and dragged her from her seat. Barbara did not dare struggle, not only because she feared a beating but because of all the people in the train carriage. She was hauled along the aisle of the compartment and hung her head in shame as the passengers stared at her. Mercedes pulled her into the toilet compartment, closed the door behind them and unlocked the handcuffs from one of Barbara's wrists.

"Kneel down and bend over!"

Mercedes pressed her hand against Barbara's back, forced her onto her knees and made her bend forward over the toilet. She lifted the seat, pulled one of Barbara's arms through it and locked the handcuff back onto her wrist.

"Please, please let me go," pleaded Barbara as she struggled uncomfortably on her knees.

53

"Shut your mouth!"

Then there was a knock on the door and Mercedes opened it.

"Right, who's first, but you must not fuck her cunt, she's a virgin and she's going to stay that way, I don't care what you do with her arse but leave her cunt alone."

Mercedes went out and one of the men stepped inside. Mercedes stood at the door with the other man as the latch was pulled from inside.

Barbara craned her neck to see the man; he was middle-aged, blonde and thick-set. He looked down at Barbara menacingly then undid the zip of his trousers and pulled out his already hard cock. The veins on its shaft were thick and pulsating, the glans was red and engorged and, as he squeezed the shaft along its length, the edges of the glans flared out wide.

"Here stick this in your mouth to start with."

He bent forward and opened her mouth wide by squeezing her cheeks together, then he inserted the swollen tip of his cock between her lips and pushed it in until the glans could not be seen. Barbara gasped as it went in and she tried to pull away but the man held her cheeks tightly and forced her to take more. The upper shaft of his cock slid past her lips and she felt the pressure of the glans against the back of her mouth. She started to choke but he did not pull it out.

"Suck it bitch!"

He turned and lifted her smock to expose her buttocks. He looked at them then released his grip on her cheeks and gave her a heavy smack.

Smack!

She was knocked forward roughly. Her breasts were pressed down painfully against the toilet pan, her arms twisted around the seat and her head fell forward.

"Suck it bitch!"

Smack!

She felt the hard cock going even deeper into her mouth and she felt as if she was going to be sick as the glans pressed against the back of her throat.

Smack!

Unable to resist, she tightened her lips around the veiny shaft and started to suck.

"Suck it hard!"

She drew her cheeks around it and sucked hard at the still-swelling tip. She felt the throbbing veins against her cheeks and squeezed her tongue against them. She could feel the blood pulsating inside them and she licked at them like an animal.

"Suck it hard and get it deep you slut!"

Barbara sucked harder and took the engorged glans to the back of her mouth, she swallowed and it entered her throat. She gagged and choked but the man kept it in and she sucked at it furiously, spit running from the corners of her lips as it filled her mouth completely.

"Now, when I say suck deeper that's what I mean, deeper!"

She tried to get it further down but again she gagged and choked.

"Deeper!"

Smack!

A heavy smack sent her forward and the tip of his cock went into the entrance to her throat. It closed around it and a heaving sensation of sickness flooded up from her stomach.

Smack!

Again she was knocked forward and the tip of the cock went further. She could not breathe and she felt a wave of panic spread through her as the hard cock pressed further down.

Smack!

It went deeper and in desperation she swallowed it, drawing it into her throat as if it was food or air and, as it went in, she was gripped by sickness and coughed the cock out.

Smack! Smack! Smack!

"Stay down bitch, let me see your arse."

He bent down and prised open the cheeks of her bottom. He poked her anus with his finger and she gasped and drew away.

Smack!

"Stay still!"

He poked at it again and pressed the tip of his finger inside. Spit dribbled from her mouth and she felt her anus open enough for his finger to go in then close around it as it went inside. More spit drooled from her mouth and she felt like a dirty trapped animal, handcuffed to the toilet seat and staring into the water-covered metal flap at the bottom of the stainless steel pan. Suddenly, as if realising the situation she was in, she was overwhelmed with fear and went into a panic. She threw herself about, yanking her wrists against the handcuffs and yelling and screaming uncontrollably.

"Shut up you fucking bitch! Shut up!"

He took his finger out of her arse and it hurt as her anal muscle snapped closed. This gave her a sense of exposure that made her feel even more desperate and she screamed even louder and pulled her wrists more furiously against the metal of the unforgiving handcuffs.

The man became angrier and suddenly undid his brown, leather belt and tugged it from the waist of his trousers. He held it up high then brought it down across her buttocks.

Whack!

Barbara screeched as it smacked down against her skin.

The edges of the belt fell hard and they stung deeply, the flat surface of the leather scorched her and made her skin feel as if it was on fire.

Whack! Whack! Whack!

She howled desperately and her face sunk deeper into the toilet pan, her cheeks pressing against the metal sides and her mouth resting against the closed plug at the bottom. She did not know what to do, the pain was terrible, she was in agony and then the belt came down again.

Whack! Whack! Whack!

Her face went deeper into the toilet pan, her mouth was now pressed hard against the metal flap at the bottom and her cheeks were squeezed against the sides. She screamed and shouted and she tasted the disinfectant that dripped down the metal sides of the toilet. She did not think she could bear the pain any more and thought she was going to pass out. She screamed into the toilet pan and the echoing screeches filled her ears as more blows rained down. Suddenly, they stopped and she flopped forward in relief, gasping with her mouth wide-open and her tongue hanging into the pool of water in the bottom of the toilet.

Her buttocks felt raw and an involuntary shiver went through her whole body. She lifted her face slightly and licked the edges of her lips, the disinfectant taste burned the tip of her tongue but she licked it again. It tasted harsh and acidic but the burning in her mouth distracted her from the burning across the flesh of her bottom. She licked again then dropped her face forward for more, poking her tongue out as far as she could and tasting the pool of water that lay at the bottom of the pan. The disinfectant stung her and the musky scent of urine pervaded her senses. She licked again, just for the taste, then again and then she started lapping at it thirstily.

The man unlatched the door and squeezed out into the

corridor. The other man came in and looked down at Barbara as she lapped the water in the toilet; he was holding Mercedes' truncheon in his hand.

"It's not finished yet girl!"

Barbara was surprised by his voice and knocked her head on the sides of the toilet pan as she pulled back.

"Stay down there slut, lick the bowl while I give you something up your beautiful arse."

He pressed the end of the long wooden truncheon against her anus. She gasped as she felt the pressure of the wide, smooth end and her eyes widened in fear as he began to push it in. She felt her anus opening and the tip going in then she felt the shaft penetrating her deeply. She gasped again and started licking the bottom of the toilet, slurping at the water and forced her head deeper to get more as the truncheon went in further. She could not believe how full she felt and she lapped at the water like a thirsty dog. The truncheon went deeper and she lifted her bottom to take it. It slid up inside her until the man's fist was pressed against her anus and the truncheon was deeply inside. Barbara drank at the pool of water and began moving her hips higher.

"Please," she murmured, "please, give me more, I'm going to finish, I need more, please, more, more, more ..."

The man thrust the truncheon into her arse as deeply as it would go.

"More, give me more!"

He pushed it harder and she squirmed onto it, desperately trying to get more. He knelt behind her and holding onto the leather strap of the truncheon pushed in the smooth, wooden shaft until her muscular ring closed around the ribbed handle. He leant forward, gripped the flesh of her bottom between his teeth and bit hard into her taut skin.

"More! More! More! I need more!"

Barbara sucked at the water in the toilet; she wanted to

drink it all, she wanted more up her arse, she wanted her cunt filled and she wanted to suck a cock deeply into her throat. She spluttered and drank the water, her tongue burned and her arse ached with the pressure from the huge truncheon and her skin was on fire with the biting that the man was giving it. The pressure in her arse built up and she drank deeply at the water, slapping her face against its surface and poking her tongue out in a frenzy. Her body was flooding with heat and she pressed her hips back, hoping for more in her arse and hoping for the man's teeth to bite deeper. She pressed harder and the pressure caused a surge of heat to run across her breasts, her nipples prickled and tingled as the heat scorched across her stomach, then it flooded inside her as a vast swell of orgasm coursed through her. She gasped loudly and sank her face deeply into the toilet.

The man bit harder and harder into her pink flesh then he reached down onto the floor and pressed the button that flushed the toilet. The disinfected water sprayed out from the rim of the pan, drenching Barbara's hair then running over her face and filling the bowl. She plunged her mouth into it and drank from it as the overpowering orgasm burst through her and sent her into a convulsive spasm. She lifted her buttocks high as the paroxysm gripped her then she threw herself forward as it completely enveloped her. She buried her face into the water and bubbles exploded around her as she sank down into it shivering and jerking in a numbing fit of overwhelming passion.

Barbara was only vaguely aware of being dragged back to her seat and made to sit shamefully in her handcuffs as the other passengers stared at her and made remarks about her wet hair and reddened face.

7

The train pulled into the docks at Folkestone; it was grey and cold and the wind was blowing up a gale. Barbara could taste the moist, salty air on her lips as she was dragged from the train and hauled by her handcuffs down an enclosed ramp to the boat.

The Ringmaster led the way to the lorry drivers' restaurant and Barbara was pushed into a seat next to a dirty spray-covered window. Mercedes went to the serving counter and started talking to some men who were queued up with trays. Men were hauling thick ropes on the dock and the boat was turning out into a rough sea as Barbara stared emptily out of the window. She shivered with cold and pulled her shackled hands across her breasts. She smelled the tangy scent of the disinfectant from the toilet bowl on her fingers and dropped them shamefully to her lap.

She could not believe what was happening to her. She wriggled in her seat and felt the stinging pain on her buttocks where she had been spanked and whipped. She lifted herself up and as she did she also felt the soft edges of her cunt sticking together with moisture. She thought of the orgasms that had overtaken her with such force as she was being beaten and violated and she shivered again as she realised that the terrible punishments she was having were also giving her unbelievable pleasure.

"Sit still girl, save your strength, you're going to need it."

She looked down under the force of the Ringmaster's gaze. After a while she squinted across to see Mercedes pointing her out to the men she was talking to. A wave of fear passed over her and she looked down again, resting her eyes on her handcuffed hands as they rested on the flimsy material of the cotton smock.

Mercedes came over and spoke quietly to the Ringmaster.

"Yes," he said, "as long as you are careful, remember we want the best price for this one so keep them away from that beautiful little cunt."

Mercedes smiled and turned to Barbara.

"Come on""

She grabbed her handcuffs and hauled her across the restaurant to the men.

"It's OK, but, like I said, no cunt, this one is a special prize, so remember, no cunt."

The men nodded in agreement and sniggered at each other as they followed Mercedes down a staircase and through a steel door. The ship turned into the sea and began to wallow in the swell. Barbara fell sideways against one of the men and he grabbed her breasts and fondled them roughly before Mercedes snatched her away. Finally, they came out into the huge open deck where lorries were being chained by the wheels.

Mercedes dragged Barbara towards one of the lorries.

"Let's see how this suits you, slut!"

She unlocked Barbara's handcuffs and pushed them into the hip-pocket of her tunic.

"OK boys, she's all yours, but no cunt!"

Barbara rubbed her reddened wrists, then she realised that she was free and without thinking turned and ran towards one of the lorries. She stumbled on a heavy chain but kept going until she got to the rear of the trailer. She saw a man beside her winching a chain onto the lorry's wheels and he looked in amazement as she grabbed hold of a loose rope and hung onto it panting and gasping for breath.

"Escaped prisoner!" yelled Mercedes. "She's escaped, catch her!"

Barbara stared at the man for a few moments then suddenly he let go of the winch and ran towards her. She let go of the rope and ran around the back of the trailer but as she saw the other men running in her direction she swung around and ran away in panic. They chased her across the deck as she dodged between the lorries and stumbled against chains and ropes. She felt like an animal being chased, she was exhausted and did not know which way to turn, then she ran straight into two of the men and they grabbed her roughly by the arms and knocked her to the floor.

One of the men held her ankles while the other pulled a rope around her neck. They stretched her until she could not move then the others came up and stood around laughing and pointing. Barbara felt trapped and humiliated as the rope tightened around her throat and she began to choke.

Mercedes came up and looked down at Barbara.

"She will have to be punished for trying to run away. Tie her to the side of this lorry to start with, a beating should teach her a lesson."

They dragged her to her feet and pulled her to the side of the lorry trailer. The man with the rope threw the spare end over a tie-hook on the canvas side and pulled it back down again. Barbara thought she was going to be strangled as the man hung his weight on the rope and drew her up tight. Her feet were only just touching the ground and she reached up at the noose to try and slacken it.

She tried to call out but the rope was too tight around her throat and she was unable to make a sound. A man stepped forward and lifted her cotton smock. She pulled her legs together but they were grabbed by two other men and pulled wide. She struggled with the rope around her neck and lifted herself high on her toes until it slackened enough for her to breathe. She gasped deeply but the rope was tightened again and she began to choke as it drew up around her throat.

One of the men leapt up on the side of the trailer and started undoing the strapping of the side-curtain. As he worked his way along, un-clipping the buckles and dropping them down at the sides, shrieks and roars emanated from inside. He pulled a strap and the curtain drew up, the shrieks and howls became frenzied as the caged animals inside were revealed. It was the lorry that Barbara had seen in the warehouse and it was filled to the top with cages all containing wild and exotic animals.

The animals pounced around their cages: monkeys leapt at the bars and flung themselves against the cage doors and a wolf stalked around its iron pen, growling and dribbling from its pointed, yellow teeth. Some smaller cages at the top contained dozens of parrots and, as they flew about in panic, multicoloured feather drifted around them like sparkling rain.

Barbara felt the rope at her neck slacken and she forced her fingers inside the noose to ease the pressure on her throat. She clung to the rope anxiously as two men grabbed her legs and lifted her up onto the side of the trailer. The slack of the rope was taken up as she was turned and pushed forward against the bars of one of the cages. The two men jumped up alongside her and pulled her hands from the noose at her neck. They spread her arms wide and tied her wrists to the bars using the wide webbing straps from the side curtain of the trailer.

Her face pressed in between the bars and she saw the large grey wolf stalking nervously in the back of the cage. She tried to pull back but the strapping at her wrists was too tight. She wriggled her shoulders wildly but only banged herself against the unforgiving bars. She felt her legs being pulled wide apart and for a moment she dropped heavily against the noose and she choked noisily. Then, as her ankles were tied to the bars, the rope was slackened slightly and she could breathe again. The wolf stalked around in the back of the cage, dribbling from his yellow teeth and looking up at her and growling.

Terror spread through her whole body and she started to scream.

"Please, let me go, please, let me go ..."

She pulled her hips back away from the bars but the noose was tightened and she had to squeeze herself as high as she could so that she could breathe.

"Please ..."

The animals started shrieking louder as she cried out in terror and feathers from the parrots fell down around her, sticking to her shoulders and back. The wolf growled and lurched forward and she screamed uncontrollably.

Then she saw two hands grabbing the bars alongside her wrists and felt the pressure of one of the men's bodies against her back. He pushed his hips against her bottom and she felt the bulge of his cock forcing between the crack of her buttocks. She felt its heat and the throbbing of its end as it pressed in further. She tried to wriggle free but knew that it was hopeless, then the wolf lurched forward again and she froze in fear.

She felt the cock sliding between her buttocks then she felt it against her anus. It pressed hard at the muscular ring then it broke in suddenly and plunged inside her without stopping. She shrieked again as it filled her in one quick thrust and the wolf pounced towards her and hung out its tongue which dripped with runny saliva.

The man thrust her arse hard and she was lifted up by the pressure of his fucking. She felt the throbbing end of his cock burying itself deeply and then she felt it swelling as he forced it even further. The thickness of the shaft spread her anus wide and then she felt the semen running up his cock. She tightened herself around it as, in one last deep thrust, he filled her with a pulsating surge of hot spunk. He dropped back and as her anus closed she felt a wet, dribbling heat running down the insides of her thighs.

The wolf ran towards her and flung itself against the bars and she shrieked as she felt its course grey hair against the front of her legs. Then she felt another man behind her. He opened her buttocks and started to push his cock into her arse. The pressure was terrible and even though her anus widened to take it he could not get it in.

"Please, please, no, it's too much, please ..."

He pushed harder and she howled with pain. Her anus dilated more, trying to accommodate the size of his glans but it was too much. She shrieked with fear as he kept pushing the end of his thick cock at her aching anus, then suddenly it went inside and she cried out in pain. Her anus was at its limit as he ran the shaft inside and she felt every hardened vein on it as it squeezed against her stretched, muscular ring. He pulled it back a little then thrust it in again as deep as it would go. She shrieked and cried out and yelled in agony. She thought she would pass out, she could not stand the pain and the feeling of fullness was making her heave with nausea, then suddenly she felt it swelling even more.

She bit down onto her lips and held her breath as the wolf leapt forward and snarled, breathing hotly against the front of her calves. She bit down harder and tensed herself as she felt the cock filling with semen. She could feel every vein on the throbbing shaft as it pressed against the sides of her arse, then it exploded inside her and she let out a terrible shriek. She screamed and howled and the wolf ran towards the bars and leapt at her, crashing against the sides of the cage then dropping to the floor. She felt his hairy coat come against her skin and she howled even louder as the pressure from the cock inside her continued to build. Her arse was on fire as the cock thrust deeply with every spurt of spunk until it was completely finished.

It was still hard and thick when he took it out and her anus was left dilated and stretched. She felt a coolness blow across it as it throbbed and tried painfully to shrink back and she wanted to be sick.   Then the noose around her neck was pulled tighter and she gasped for breath again.

"Give the bitch a beating!"

She felt a heavy blow across her buttocks as one of the webbing straps was brought down hard.

Whack!

"Give the bitch more!"

Whack!

She tightened her buttocks as the painful blows scorched her flesh.

Whack! Whack! Whack!

She tried to scream but the noose was too tight and she felt her eyes going bleary as her head lolled to one side.

Whack! Whack! Whack!

"Let's have her cunt now!"

The beating stopped and another man jumped up behind her and she felt him prising her buttocks back and feeling at the edges of her cunt.

"Not her cunt!" shouted Mercedes.

The man's prising fingers pulled roughly at her swollen labia and she felt them probing inside.

"Not her cunt I said!"

The man's hand fell away. The animals shrieked loudly and the wolf skulked around in circles, looking menacingly at Barbara as she hung hopelessly against the bars of its cage.

Mercedes jumped up onto the side of the trailer.

"Fuck her arse all you want, but not her cunt!"

Mercedes forced her hand between the bars and the front of Barbara's hips and put her palm flatly across Barbara's cunt.

"You will not have this," she laughed and gripped Barbara's labia tightly.

There was a moments silence then Barbara felt another cock pressing into her anus. It went in easily and fucked her hard and deep. All the time Mercedes held her hand tightly across Barbara's cunt and as the man fucked her Barbara felt her cunt opening onto Mercedes' upturned palm.

When the next man fucked her Barbara felt herself moving more keenly against Mercedes' hand and she opened her cunt as much as she could to feel the tips of Mercedes' fingers against the edges of her engorging inner labia.

Then she felt the webbing strap across her buttocks again.

Whack! Whack! Whack!

The pain was intense but with each stroke she pushed her cunt even more firmly onto Mercedes' pressing hand.

Whack! Whack! Whack!

Her cunt was splayed out wide and Barbara rubbed her hard clitoris against the protective hand, then, as another cock came inside her, she felt the heat of orgasm building up in her stomach. Her thighs tightened and she squeezed down onto the warm flesh that cupped her swollen labia. She pressed her clitoris down against it and her orgasm spread through her like a fire. She pressed down even harder and just as the cock spurted its hot semen deeply inside her arse she finished convulsively.

She howled like an animal and dropped her head in exhaustion, not caring about the noose that was pulled tightly around her reddened throat. She felt a warmth against her cunt and pushed down against it for relief. She opened her eyes and saw, instead of Mercedes' upturned hand between her legs, the wolf, licking at her ravenously with its outstretched, salivating tongue.

Barbara did not remember being taken down from the trailer, nor being led back to the restaurant. She remembered looking out of the steamy window and watching the rough waves throwing white spray against the glass, and she remembered feeling sick and giddy as the boat heaved in the heavy swell, but, except for these things, her mind was filled with pain and self-disgust and nothing else.

8

After they got off the boat they got on another train and Barbara went to sleep, twitching occasionally as her dreams mixed with unwelcome memories. She dozed uncomfortably and was only vaguely aware of Mercedes prising her legs apart so that the man opposite could stare longingly at her still-swollen, wet cunt.

She awoke with a start as Mercedes yanked on her handcuffs and dragged her out of the carriage. Barbara stood on the platform of Amsterdam's Central Station, dark-eyed and bemused and looking around anxiously as Mercedes grabbed her handcuffs and pulled her towards the exit.

They emerged into the street and Barbara shrunk back against the glare of sunlight, the noise of trams and the bustle of people. The Ringmaster strode ahead, leading them across tram lines and a broad bridge until they were soon walking alongside a canal. Barbara looked around and saw women sitting in the red-lit windows that lined the street.

Some of them sat, wearing only white thongs with their legs spread wide while others stood and bent forward showing the shape of their bottoms.

Barbara saw one who sat backwards on a chair flicking a short, riding crop against her naked buttocks. As they passed a sex-shop window filled with magazines, vibrators and whips, Barbara's eyes fell on a picture of a woman on all fours being fucked by a large dog from behind. The woman's face rested against the edge of a wooden chair and she was biting onto it hard. Barbara recoiled but could not stop staring at it. She saw another picture of a woman on her hands and knees straining on a leash that was clipped to a collar around her neck. A man held the leash with one hand and with the other wielded a leather whip with split ends. The woman's buttocks and back were covered in thin red lines and she pulled hard against the collar as she sucked a dog's cock and took a savage beating.

Barbara craned her neck, unable to take her eyes from the pictures as Mercedes dragged her along the narrow street. Barbara thought it seemed such a terrible thing to be forced to do, but she could see that the woman was desperate to suck the cock and it was as though she would put up with any amount of punishment to get it. Mercedes yanked the handcuffs hard and Barbara was pulled from the window, still straining for a last glimpse of the frightening images.

They turned down a side alley which was lined with more windows containing women. Some of the girls here lay on couches in pairs and one was working a plastic vibrator around the outer edges of her cunt. She smiled at Barbara as they passed but Barbara looked down in embarrassment.

They arrived at a black door above several steps, the Ringmaster knocked and, when it was opened by a young woman dressed in a silky robe, they went in. The entrance hall led straight onto a staircase, it was dark and narrow and Barbara stumbled twice before they got to the top. The girl in the robe opened a small door at the top of the stairs.

"Is this OK? I cleaned out most of the rubbish."

The Ringmaster looked inside.

"Put her in Mercedes, I've got some business to arrange."

Mercedes thrust Barbara in through the small door and slammed it shut.

It was pitch dark inside and Barbara quaked with fear as she heard the door being bolted from the outside. She reached out to feel the walls and felt panicky as she realised that the room was tiny; hardly bigger than a cupboard. She touched a light switch and pressed it; the light came on and she covered her eyes against the harsh brightness. She leant against the wall and slowly slid herself onto the floor where she sat, still with her hands across her eyes, her legs slightly bent and her feet touching the opposite wall.

Gradually, she got used to the light and looked around. The room was slightly wider than she had thought and she turned so that she could stretch her legs out. She brushed some dirt from her knees and rubbed her neck and thighs. She looked down and saw a magazine lying on the floor and she reached out and turned it towards her.

The picture on the front showed a woman tied on her back to a rack, she was stretched out tightly by her ankles and wrists and two men were beating her with long rods. The blows were falling heavily across her breasts and thighs and red marks laced her pale skin.

Barbara started to think about the pictures in the magazine she had seen the day she had been kidnapped. She remembered how she had felt herself with the magazine laid across her knees as she had sat on the toilet in her office and how she had become so excited as she had drooled over the images of beating and violation. She thought of what had happened to her since and she shivered all over. Her beatings and humiliation had been even worse than the images in the magazine, but even worse than that, she had felt even more excited by her own suffering than by the pictures of the suffering of others. She could not believe how she had been thrashed and punished and how, at the same time, she had convulsed with orgasms that had driven her to demand only more bondage, flogging and degradation.

She ran her fingers across the picture, then picked up the magazine and started flipping slowly through the pages. She felt herself leaning back against the cold wall, then, almost as if they were beyond her control, her hands lifted her cotton smock and exposed her naked cunt. She slipped her fingers down through her pubic hair until their tips made contact with the soft folds at the front of her crack. She pressed lightly against them and they opened willingly against her touch. As they parted her fingers slipped against the silky moisture that ran inside them and she prised them wider and ran her fingers down their full length. Her outer labia swelled and opened as she felt along them and her fingers were wet to the knuckles by the time she reached the back of her cunt. She slipped them forward again and because they were so wet she could not stop them sliding inside. The petals of her inner labia opened and her fingers ran past them into the soft folds of her vagina.

She probed its inner recesses for a while as she turned the pages of the magazine. She parted her legs and her cunt opened wider as she stared deeply into a picture. It was one of the pictures she had seen while being hauled through the streets from the station. Barbara pulled her fingers out of her vagina and slid them up her wet crack until they touched her swollen clitoris. She gasped as a shiver passed across her stomach and down into her thighs and she curled her fingers around the pulsating clitoris and tugged at it eagerly.

She looked closely at the image of the young woman straining against the lead to suck at the dog's cock. The large dog reared up in front of her with its front paws on her shoulders and there were scratch marks where she had been clawed. Its huge, stiff cock was deeply inside her mouth and the collar pulled at her throat as she strained to get more. Barbara saw how savagely the man was beating her and she stared intently at the angry red stripes that laced the woman's back and buttocks.

Barbara pulled down on her engorged clitoris and felt a flooding warmth running inside her cunt. As she stared at the picture she noticed another figure standing behind the woman. It was Mercedes! She was dressed in a black leather basque, black panties and high leather boots and she stood with her legs stiffly apart as she pressed the end of a riding crop against the side of her hip. She seemed to be shouting instructions to the man. Barbara pulled at her clitoris and without warning a convulsive orgasm enveloped her. She reared back and shrieked as it ran through her and the picture fell to the floor as she jerked and pulled at her clitoris in an attempt to make it last longer. But she could not delay it and she flopped back, panting and gasping. She lay back breathing heavily, a dribble of spit running from the corner of her mouth and the insides of the tops of her thighs glistening with wetness.

Suddenly, the door flew open and the Ringmaster came in. He looked down at Barbara, as she lay against the wall, dissipated and exhausted with the magazine crinkled up beside her.

"Ah, you like our little magazines do you? Perhaps you will feature in our next issue, we shall see."

72

Barbara looked up blearily, not hearing what he said.

"For the moment though, we need to get you prepared for the auction."

He reached down and grabbed her arms. She shrunk back and tried to wedge herself against the wall, cowering like a captured animal.

"Why are you doing this to me? Please, you must let me go."

"I told you before, girl, you do what you're told, not what you want!'

He slapped her across the face and she banged her head against the wall as she was knocked back.

"Please ..."

He smacked her again, this time even harder and she felt her cheek scorching with pain.

"Shut up and come with me or I'll thrash you like you can't imagine."

He pulled her arms and, before she could get up, he dragged her out of the little room. She struggled but he was too strong and she was hauled along a corridor on her knees, unable to get up or break free. She tried again to pull away but she was unable to fight against him and allowed herself to be pulled along with her knees painfully scraping along the wooden, boarded floor and her head banging against the narrow, corridor walls.

"Mercedes!" he shouted. "Come and get this bitch ready, I've got a good crowd coming to bid for a our little virgin!"

He pulled Barbara into a large room and when he let go of her arms she fell to the floor in a heap.

The Ringmaster went to a cupboard and removed a razor and some shaving gel.

"Mercedes!"

Mercedes came into the room wearing a long, red dressing gown that trailed to the floor and hung open at the front.

"Mercedes, where the fuck have you been. Get this bitch ready, there's going to be a good crowd and I want the best price."

Mercedes stood above Barbara. She pulled her dressing gown back at the waist and placed her hands on her hips revealing a black, leather basque with loosely trailing suspenders, black silky panties which were pulled up tightly to her crotch and high, black leather boots.

Barbara stared up at her in fear as Mercedes pursed her glossy, red lips and bent forward.

"Oh please let me go, please let me go," said Mercedes mockingly. "Please let me go because I'm a fucking little virgin bitch!"

She grabbed the front of Barbara's cotton smock and yanked her off the ground. She stared into Barbara's face then laughed loudly.

"Come on little virgin bitch, let's get you ready for the auction!"

She pulled Barbara to the centre of the room.

"Give me the razor Ringmaster, I'll show that little cunt off to its best."

She took the razor and shaving gel from the Ringmaster then turned back to Barbara.

"Strip!"

Barbara did not dare do anything else. She raised the cotton smock up over her head and tried to pull it over her arms but she was too slow.

"Strip bitch!"

Barbara struggled to pull the smock off but it got tangled around her wrists and she could not remove it. Mercedes reached up and tugged at it angrily but it got tangled in Barbara's hair and she yelped in pain. She stood with her arms above her head, her face covered by the tangled smock.

"Yes, stay like that, now spread your legs."

Obediently Barbara parted her legs.

Mercedes sprayed some shaving gel around Barbara's pubic hair; it felt cold and she drew her legs together with the shock.

"Keep your legs apart!"

Barbara parted them again and more gel was sprayed on. Mercedes rubbed it into Barbara's pubic hair then between her legs, then she took the razor and drew it slowly across Barbara's flesh. Barbara felt terrified, she could not see what was happening and felt so exposed. She felt the razor gliding across her skin and after it had passed she felt a naked coldness where her pubic hair had been removed. Mercedes bent down and shaved between Barbara's legs, parting her outer labia and shaving carefully around them until Barbara was completely naked.

The Ringmaster inspected Mercedes' work and seemed pleased.

"Now wash her and get her ready."

Mercedes took hold of the smock that was still tangled around Barbara's arms and head and pulled her into a bathroom. She filled the bath and then roughly yanked the smock from Barbara, pulling some of her hair out and making her yell with pain.

"Get in and wash!"

Barbara sank into the bath and felt a surge of relief. She felt so dirty and hurt and the warm water made her skin feel clean and took some of the pains away.

When she had finished Mercedes rubbed her with a towel. She felt Barbara's breasts then ran her fingers between her legs to check that there were no hairs left. Barbara felt warm and comfortable, as if Mercedes was her friend, but when she smiled at Mercedes she received a smack across the face.

"Here - this is what you will wear."

Mercedes held out a wide, black leather belt with a silver ring attached to the back and a strange leather strap with thongs hanging from the side.

"Stand there and I will make sure you wear them right."

Mercedes pulled the thick, black leather belt tightly around Barbara's waist and laced it up at the front, then she took the leather strap and pulled it across Barbara's mouth. Barbara pulled back in fear but Mercedes just pulled it tighter. The strap was thick at the front and Mercedes forced it into Barbara's mouth, tying it tightly behind her neck then lifting her wrists and securing them to its sides with the dangling thongs. Mercedes checked the tightness of everything then stood back to admire her work.

Barbara could hardly breathe. The gag was pulled so tightly across her face that it forced her tongue right down into the back of her mouth. The belt around her waist was also very tight and when Barbara did manage to get a breath through her nostrils she could not hold it in because of the tension from the belt.

Mercedes took a long, leather leash from the cabinet and clipped it to the ring at the back of the belt. She gave it a strong tug and Barbara fell backwards. Mercedes tugged it again and Barbara stumbled and nearly fell over. Mercedes pulled harder and Barbara fell onto the floor.

"Up!"

Mercedes pulled at the leash and Barbara rolled forward on the floor.

"Up! Up!"

The leash was yanked again but Barbara could not get to her feet.

"Up you fucking bitch!"

Mercedes kept pulling at the leash and every time Barbara tried to get up she was knocked off balance. Mercedes started to pull Barbara around on the floor, laughing and shouting at her as Barbara squirmed and struggled and tried to stand. Mercedes took the spare end of the long lead and brought it down on Barbara's buttocks.

Whack!

Barbara struggled desperately to get to her feet but still she could not.

Whack!

The leash stung her bottom and she fell forward gasping for breath and struggling frantically to get to her feet. She felt so humiliated and mocked and wanted Mercedes to let her get up but every time she tried she was pulled over again.

Whack!

She tried again to get to her feet but this time she fell face-forward against a chair. She grabbed hold of it and tried to claw her way up it.

Whack! Whack!

Her bottom stung with pain as the thin leash was brought down harder and harder.

Whack! Whack! Whack!

Barbara clawed at the chair fighting to get to her feet and when Mercedes pulled hard at the leash she gripped onto the chair legs desperately. But Mercedes was too strong and Barbara and the chair were pulled across the floor like toys.

Whack! Whack! Whack!

The blows thrashed down across Barbara's back and she let go of the chair, rolling about on the floor and getting tangled in the leash that trailed from the back of the belt. She wanted to scream out and beg for mercy and as the blows rained down she felt herself slowly giving up the will to struggle. Finally, she lay still on the floor, panting and gasping for breath, while Mercedes beat her unforgivingly.

Then the door burst open and the Ringmaster came in. He looked at Mercedes and she stopped and stood back, sweat running from her forehead and down her flushed cheeks. Barbara lay on the floor, her heart pounding and her back and buttocks burning from the whipping of the leash. The Ringmaster poked her in the stomach with his foot and she rolled over on her side and groaned.

"Is she ready for the auction?"

"Yes, totally ready."

9

Mercedes pulled the leash across her shoulder and, following the Ringmaster, dragged Barbara backwards out of the room. Barbara tried to turn around so that she could walk properly but every time she tried Mercedes yanked the rope and forced her back again. They went down steps and through several doors then out of the back of the building and across a yard containing several empty animal cages to a separate building. The Ringmaster paused outside the door.

"Wait here for a minute."

He buttoned up his black sequined jacket and smoothed down his shirt before opening the door and going in.

There was a roar as he entered and applause as he mounted a small stage and bowed to the room full of men. Some were sitting on chairs but most of them leant against the walls or clustered around the front of the rostrum. The Ringmaster held up his hands for silence and everything went quiet.

"I have a special prize today. A virgin!"

The men shouted and cheered and the ones around the

front of the stage surged forward and pushed each other.

"Yes, a genuine virgin, and a very pretty one at that. She's not been trained but I have given her a bit of punishment myself and I can assure you she is worth a great deal."

The men shouted louder and waved their arms in the air excitedly.

"How can we be sure she's a virgin?"

There was silence.

"You have my word, isn't that enough?"

No one said anything, then there was an uproar of assent.

"Though, I must admit she has been fucked in the arse, but not, I repeat, not in the cunt. She's a virgin alright and I expect a big price. I hope you've got plenty of money with you!"

"What's the deal?" someone shouted.

"The deal is two hours."

The crowd murmured and grumbled.

"Let's see her then!"

The Ringmaster waved to Mercedes and she dragged Barbara backwards onto the stage. The crowd shouted and roared as Barbara stumbled backwards on the end of her leash. Barbara was positioned in the centre then Mercedes opened her long red dressing gown and took a bow. The golden ring through her nipple flashed in the lights and she cupped her breast in her hand to show it off fully. Everyone cheered and clapped as Barbara stood panic-stricken with the gag pulling at her mouth and her hands clasped tightly to the sides of her face.

"I see she has already taken a real beating, look at her back and buttocks! Is that included in the price?"

"Everything is included in the price. You get the virgin's cunt and anything else you care to do to her. Who's going to start me off?"

A clamour of bids were made and several men jostled for position to ensure they caught the Ringmaster's eye.

Barbara watched the men as they waved their hands and shouted out their bids. As she glanced around nervously she saw Ramon sitting with Carlo. She gasped against the gag and looked away before looking back to check that her eyes were not deceiving her. Ramon was nudging Carlo and they were pointing at the Ringmaster and Barbara, then there was some shouting and arguing and she looked down again fearfully. She felt so exposed and humiliated at the idea of being sold and she shivered with fear at the thought of what was happening to her.

The bidding went on frantically until there were only two bidders left, a darkly dressed old man and a swarthy, younger man who seemed to be with a rowdy group. Encouraged by the crowd, the price went higher until the younger man waved his arms and shouted.

"I want a closer inspection before I go further."

The Ringmaster invited him onto the rostrum and the young man climbed up eagerly. He looked up and down Barbara then reached his hand between her legs, feeling the edges of her cunt and running his finger tips along the folds of her outer labia. She pulled back but Mercedes tugged heavily on the leash as an instruction to stand still and Barbara obeyed straight away.

The man walked behind Barbara and felt the red lashes that Mercedes had inflicted across her back and bottom.

"I want to see how she takes a spanking."

"I like a man who tests the goods. Mercedes!"

Mercedes tugged the leash and spun Barbara around so that she faced away from the audience.

"Bend over!"

Barbara bent over slowly but as her head went forward she felt giddy and stopped.

"Bend over you fucking bitch!"

Barbara tried again but stumbled forward as her head bent to the height of her shoulders.

"Mercedes!"

Mercedes threw the end of the leash up to a hook that was fixed to the ceiling above the stage and hauled it tight against Barbara's back. Barbara pitched forward and lost her footing; her feet came off the ground and she swung from the leash like a captured animal. She gasped for breath as the wide belt tightened around her waist to take her full weight. Mercedes held the leash tight then took the end and tied it to a beam at the back of the stage as the crowd cheered and shouted with renewed excitement.

Barbara spun dizzily with her head hanging down almost touching the floor. The belt was pulling agonizingly at her waist and her attempts to breathe through her mouth only resulted in gurgling gulps and she flared her nostrils wide in order to get enough breath to stay conscious. The young man pushed her and the spinning rope began to swing in wide, pendulous arcs across the stage. Barbara felt so sick and fear ran threw her when she thought she might choke on her own vomit.

Mercedes grabbed her by the hair and stopped her spinning, then she pulled Barbara's head in between her own legs and wedged it tight. Barbara gasped through her nostrils as she felt the heat of Mercedes' thighs clamping against her pinioned hands and the sides of her face. She coughed and choked and bit down hard onto the tightly drawn gag.

The young man felt the taut skin of Barbara's upturned bottom.

"This should take a good whipping but," he shouted turning to the crowd, "what shall I use? Any suggestions?"

The crowd shouted and cheered.

"Smack her with your hand!"

"Here, use this riding crop!"

"No, I've got a special leather paddle, try this!"

"A cane, a cane!"

"Try my belt or my shoe!"

"Use this strap and give her a real lashing!"

Barbara could only hear drumming in her ears and a dull roar of noise as Mercedes held her head tight between the tops of her thighs. Barbara looked down with panic-stricken eyes and saw the tops of Mercedes' high leather boots and the contrast they made with her pale skin. For a moment Barbara wanted to have her hands released so that she could plunge them down between the cool, shiny leather and Mercedes' smooth, warm skin, then she was knocked forward as a savage blow came down across her buttocks. A terrifying sting went through her skin and she bit involuntarily into the leather of the gag.

Thwack!

The crowd roared as the flat leather paddle slapped down onto Barbara's taut bottom.

Thwack!

Another hard smack and Barbara felt herself swinging forward under the pressure. She sensed Mercedes' thighs tighten against the sides of her head and she bit harder into the leather gag.

Thwack!

Barbara stared into the tops of Mercedes' long, leather boots and saw a dribble of spit trailing down from her gagged mouth and running into them. It glistened on the shiny leather then ran inside it and against Mercedes' smooth, pale skin. Barbara tightened her hands and stretched her fingers upwards in agony.

Thwack!

She felt the stinging pain fully across her buttocks. It slapped so hard against them and a forceful draft of air blew between the tops of her legs and against the swollen edges of her cunt.

Thwack!

The heavy blow knocked her tighter between Mercedes' legs and she stretched her fingers upwards even more to try and relieve the pain. She watched another dribble of spit running into Mercedes' boots and, as she shivered with pain as the cold air blew across her cunt, she reached up with her straining fingers and touched the tight edges of Mercedes' black, silky panties. She grabbed them and felt the finely-sewn edges between her grappling fingers and she probed them inside to the soft, wide cunt that they covered.

Thwack!

Barbara felt the pain but this time she allowed her buttocks to open more so that the cold air could blow against the flesh of her cunt. She felt her labia opening and squeezing backwards, exposing themselves for the next fierce blow and she reached further inside Mercedes' panties and pushed her fingers inside the wet edges of her swollen crack. She watched the tops of the shiny boots as spit dribbled freely from her mouth and ran in a steady stream down their insides. She pushed her buttocks back as far as she could and felt her engorged labia fully exposed between the crack of her bottom and the tops of her taut thighs. She waited anxiously for the next blow and stretched her fingers higher into Mercedes' cunt.

Thwack!

She pushed her finger tips higher and felt Mercedes' cunt opening eagerly to receive them.

Thwack!

The flat paddle smacked against the edges of her cunt and she raised her buttocks even higher.

Thwack!

This time the paddle smacked fully against her swollen, wet labia and Barbara poked her fingers deeply into Mercedes' cunt. The spit streamed from her mouth and she started to feel the heat of orgasm burning around her hips and flaring down into her cunt.

Thwack!

She knew she could not hold on much longer. She had no control over when she would finish and she fought to get her fingers deeper into Mercedes' cunt before it came. She thrashed about wildly to feel the warm insides of the open vagina and as Mercedes widened her legs, releasing her grip on Barbara's head and opening her cunt for as much as Barbara could get, she was finally overcome.

Thwack!

That was enough and as spit spurted from her mouth and her labia stung with the pain of the flailing she went stiff and reared up against the rope which held her by the waist and went into a convulsion of jerky, and fitful orgasms.

She hung onto the edges of Mercedes' panties and gasped noisily through her wide open nostrils. She could feel the blood pulsing through Mercedes' cunt and felt the wetness that ran from it and dribbled down over her fingers. Her mouth and face were soaking wet and she could see a stream of spit running stickily from her mouth, down the insides of Mercedes' thighs until it disappeared inside the soft leather of the high boots. Finally, completed exhausted and unable to hang on any longer, she let go of the panties and her head dropped down. She hung, suspended by the waist with her hair trailing on the floor of the stage as the young man behind her continued to bring the wide, flat, leather paddle down fiercely on her upturned buttocks.

Thwack! Thwack! Thwack!

The bidding resumed and the man who had thrashed

Barbara so cruelly was the victor. He turned to his friends and shouted gleefully.

"Come on boys, we've got two hours to use the virgin as we want!"

The crowd cheered loudly.

"Do it here, we want to see!"

"Yes, do it here, we want to see the virgin fucked and punished!"

"Yes, yes!"

The Ringmaster nodded to the young man and he shouted to his friends to join him on the stage.

10

Mercedes undid the rope from the beam at the back of the stage and Barbara was lowered to the floor. She crumpled in a heap and a pool of spit settled on the wooden boards beside her face. She still felt the waning heat of her orgasms but that was already being replaced by a fresh sense of fear and humiliation as the young man grabbed her hair and hoisted her to her feet.

"Right boys, let's make the best of our two hours!"

He pulled her to the middle of the stage and yanked her hair back hard. He rubbed his other hand across her breasts, then down across the wide, leather belt to the front of her naked crack. Her eyes widened in fear and she spluttered noisily against the leather gag as she felt his warm hand against her shaved cunt. The man smiled as he fondled the exposed front edges of her labia, slipping his fingers along them and pressing them open at the front.

"What would you like to see?" he shouted to the crowd.

"Fuck her cunt!"

"Beat her!"

"Let's see her suck!"

The young man laughed as his friends gathered around him and he pushed his finger into her cunt and pulled it out and licked it.

"Sweet! I can hardly wait!"

He let go of Barbara's hair and it fell, tousled and greasy with sweat around her neck. She wriggled her hands at the side of the gag but it only made the tight-pulled leather dig into her cheeks even more.

The young man reached behind her head and undid the thongs that held the gag and they fell loosely at the back of her neck. She stood naked and terrified, still clutching the gag in her mouth. Her jaw felt frozen and she held the wet leather between her teeth, unable and unwilling to let it go. She flared her nostrils wide to get a good breath and waited, trembling and exposed.

The man took hold of the side of the gag and tried to prise it from her mouth but she had become so used to it she bit down hard to keep it in place. She felt it was the only thing protecting her and she turned and snarled at the man in the hope he would leave it alone.

"Bitch!"

He grabbed the gag and angrily tore it from between her teeth. It came away wet and soggy and deeply indented with teeth marks. He held it up and looked at it.

"Filthy little bitch!"

He threw it out to the crowd and they cheered and fought over it until someone claimed it and started licking her spit from it.

Barbara felt completely exposed and she looked across to Mercedes but Mercedes just sneered and laughed. Barbara hung her head in shame as the crowd started shouting out more suggestions about what should be done with her.

She tried not to listen but it was impossible and their comments rang in her pounding ears. She began to shake with fear and she wanted to run away and hide.

"Hold her boys, I want to get some value for my money."

Two of the other men grabbed her arms and knocked her backwards. She stumbled, fell out of their grasp and landed heavily on the floor, the ring on the back of the wide belt digging into her back and making her screamed with pain. They reached down and dragged her roughly back to her feet, held onto her arms while two of the others took hold of her ankles, and lifted her off the floor. She sagged in their grip and they swung her from side to side like a toy. She started screaming and wriggling but could not get free and the crowd of men roared loudly as the young man told her captors to open her legs as wide as they would go.

Barbara screeched as they spread her legs wide apart. They turned her and her cunt was exposed to the crowd who cheered and clapped and banged their feet on the floor. She felt completely humiliated as the four men carried her around the stage displaying her naked cunt to everyone in the room. Finally, the young man told them to stop and he stood between her legs, undid his trousers and started pulling out his stiff cock.

"What do you think of that, virgin? This is going to be your first, though not your last today I'm sure!"

The others laughed and lifted her higher so that her cunt was in front of him at waist height. She started struggling again and one of her wrists broke free from the man's grip. She fell down to the floor heavily and knocked her head with a bang. For a second she did not move then suddenly, as if seized with fresh strength, she went into a frenzy of struggling and screaming. The men tried to get a firmer grip on her but she wriggled like a panicked animal and another wrist broke free.

The crowd shouted loudly and the two men who still had a grip on her ankles fought frantically to get her under control. She screamed at the top of her voice and rolled on the floor, twisting her ankles across each other and out of the grip of her captors. She rolled sideways but threw her hands out to stop herself, then she got up onto her knees and crouched at the side of the stage staring at her tormentors.

"Don't want to give it up eh girl?"

The young man dodged towards her but she lunged sideways and avoided him.

"A real fucking animal aren't you? Come on little virgin pussy, puss, puss, puss."

He held his hand out as though he was trying to attract a frightened animal.

"Puss, puss, puss."

She stayed crouching on one knee, looking into his eyes, waiting for his next move; she felt some hope inside her and it was giving her a new strength. Her long hair stuck to the drying spit around her mouth and she licked her lips to take it away.

"Come on little pussy, puss, puss."

She opened her mouth and showed him her teeth. She bared them at him and wanted to snarl and bite and snap at his beckoning hand. She wanted to grab it and sink her teeth into it and savage him and bite him until he bled and died.

"Puss, puss, puss."

She snapped her teeth together and dribbles of spit ran from the corners of her half-open mouth. She felt an animal strength inside her that made her want to pounce on him and rip his throat open and suck his blood and eat him alive, then he grabbed at her and caught her by the shoulders. She snarled and tried to bite him but, as her teeth glanced across the back of his hand, he flung her backwards onto the ground and the others pounced on top of her.

"Fucking bitch, she's bit my fucking hand! Bend her over boys, this little virgin needs a damn good beating before she gets anything else. Bend her over!"

They lifted her up and took her back to the middle of the stage, two of them held onto her legs as another two bent her shoulders forward until her forehead touched the front of her calves. Her feeling of being free disappeared in a surge of panic and when she tried to move she found herself pinned fast.

"Take that belt off her, I think it would be put to better use as a whip!"

The wide leather belt was undone roughly and then torn from around her waist. She was completely naked and bent over so much that the soft pink edges of her cunt were pressed out like swollen lips between the dark wedge of her buttocks. She sank her head lower, not knowing whether the feeling of shame and humiliation or the sense of fear and anxiety were the greatest.

The young man took the belt and swirled it around above his head.

"How many does she deserve?" he shouted to the crowd.

"Six!"

"Ten!"

"Until she drops!"

He held the belt as far back as he could.

"Hold her tight boys, this is going to make her squirm like a snake!"

He brought the belt down onto her buttocks with all his strength and it struck against her upturned bottom with a sickening smack.

Smack!

Her bottom stung as though she had been stabbed and the laces of the belt flailed around the sides of her hips, cutting into her flesh and making her shriek for mercy.

"Please, please, I can't stand it, please, please ..."

Smack!

Another agonizing blow came down. Her bottom burned as the leather belt smacked across her skin and the laces cut her again, this time curling even further around her hips and striking the tender skin of her stomach.

"Please, it's terrible, please ..."

Smack! Smack! Smack!

The men held her firmly as she tightened herself against the ferocious blows; the laces cut her around the front of her stomach and she shrieked and howled in pain.

Smack! Smack! Smack!

She tensed herself like a compressed spring but it did not take away the horrific pain. She felt giddy and her eyes went bleary; she could feel the blood pounding in her head and spit dripped from her mouth in long, sticky strands.

Smack! Smack! Smack!

She felt herself becoming unconscious and began to fall limply against the men's restraining hands. She tried to cry out but she did not have the strength then she toppled forward and fell to the ground.

"Ready for more eh? Lift her up boys, let's see if she's ready for a fucking up that tight, little virgin cunt."

Four men lifted her and held her spread-eagled in front of the young man. He stood between her legs again, pulled his hard cock out of his already undone trousers and grasped it firmly in both hands. It was long and thick and the glans was purple and swollen as he squeezed its veiny shaft.

Barbara looked down over her breasts and saw him coming closer. She knew there was no point in struggling, she had tried to escape and failed and she felt too weak from the terrible beating to try again. She looked at the pulsating cock in his hands and felt the men at her legs widening them to expose her cunt as fully as possible. The cock looked so thick and long and although she had often probed her cunt with her fingers she did not know what it would be like to be filled by such a huge, throbbing cock. She realised again how she was being violated and in desperation she wrenched herself against the firm pressure of the hands on her legs; but the men held them even tighter and she cried out in pain as their nails dug into the skin of her calves.

The young man pushed closer to her cunt and she felt the material of his trousers rubbing against the soft skin on the insides of her thighs. She felt the heat from his body and, as he brought the pulsating cock within reach of her cunt, she felt the heat radiating from the swollen glans. It touched her distended outer labia and a burning sensation spread across her breasts and her face.

She shrunk back as the hot glans pressed against the tender folds of skin that edged her cunt but she could not resists it and they opened easily under its touch. As it began to penetrate her, she felt their inner wetness spreading across the still-swelling tip of the young man's cock. It felt so hot, so hard and so forceful and she lifted herself away in fear at the thought of being filled by it. He pushed it in further and it went in until the flanges of the glans pressed past the soft petals of her inner labia and they folded back over it, sealing it tight into the entrance to her vagina.

A terrible realisation of being fucked for the first time swept through her. She did not want any more, she could not stand any more, it felt too much to take and she felt desperately frightened of the idea of having something like that inside her.

"Please don't," she pleaded. "Please don't take me like

that, I have never been taken like that, please don't ..."

Her begging went unheard and the young man pressed in further. She opened her eyes wide as it went deeper and she gasped as she felt the coarse texture of the blood-filled veins on the hard shaft. The heat from his glans radiated deeply inside her and she felt as if she was on fire. It burned and stung her tender flesh and sent her body into a panic of terror, but as she squirmed against the cock she also sensed the burning of an increasing desire.

She wanted to plead with him to stop, she wanted to thrust him away and deny herself to him, but she also wanted to open her legs more and suck his throbbing cock so deeply into her vagina that she could feel his balls against the swollen edges of her distended labia.

"Take that!"

He thrust his cock in up to the hilt. His balls pressed against her wet, stretched labia and she shrieked with a mixture of terror and dismay. She was horrified by its size and the pressure it caused inside her yet, at the same time, she was disappointed that it had not gone deeper. She was filled and her cunt was sucking so hard against the veiny shaft but she wanted to feel it more and she wanted to feel it deeper and suddenly she burst out in a shrill howl that set the crowd into an uproar.

She yelled at the top of her voice and struggled against the men holding her arms. The cock went in a little further and she realised there was more to have. She struggled frantically, squirming her hips down onto the massive cock until she broke free. She tossed herself forward and threw her arms around the young man's neck. She shook herself from the grip of the men holding her ankles and she wrapped them around the young man's hips, entwining them together and digging her heels into his muscular buttocks. She tightened her grip still more and fastened herself onto him like a parasite, pushing her breasts against his face and thrusting her cunt down onto his cock with all her weight.

Barbara screeched as she felt the whole shaft deeply inside her cunt. She could feel the tip pressing against the top of her vagina and the broad base of the shaft stretching her already distended labia as wide as they would go. She pulled up and felt her labia tugging at the veins on his pulsating cock then drew herself further up the shaft until she felt the flanges of his glans pressing against the insides of her swollen labia. She held herself high for a moment, feeling the tightness and the stretching of her soft flesh, then she dropped down heavily and let the throbbing tip penetrate her to the limit.

She felt a wave of abandonment sweeping all her reserve away and she threw her head back, turned her hips forward and fucked at his cock like an animal. She grabbed his hair and pulled at it hard, watching his face contort as the pain seized him and feeling his cock lengthening and thickening in response. She pulled harder and fucked down even more, throwing her weight onto his cock and drawing it in as deeply as it would go. Then she felt him falling backwards and she dragged herself up the shaft and pressed forward, leaning across him and making him fall over.

They crashed to the floor with Barbara lying above him still fucking him and clawing at his hair. The young man shouted in pain as Barbara's heels dug into the small of his back and he lifted his hips against her weight to relieve the pressure. Barbara's body shook with the impact as they hit the floor and she gasped for breath but she did not stop her frantic fucking. The shock sent a sudden, swelling jolt through the young man's cock and it stiffened and grew as his buttocks squeezed together under the impact. Barbara screamed as she fucked down on the swollen cock and she tore at his hair as she pounded her whole body down upon him in a frenzy.

She bent her face towards his and licked out her tongue towards his mouth. She ran its tip around his lips then forced it inside, driving it to the back of his throat and pushing at the tightening hole until she felt him choking. Finally, she drew back, her tongue aching from the strain, and dripped spit across his reddened face before bending forward and slurping it up like a thirsty cat.

She could no longer hear the shouting of the crowd which was now in an uproar. They pounded the floor with their feet and clapped and whistled and several jumped up onto the stage to get a closer view.

Barbara did not feel her buttocks being parted as one of the young man's friends stretched them wide, and to begin with, she did not feel the throbbing tip of another cock forcing against her anus. Even when it began to enter she could hardly feel it but, as it slipped inside and began to penetrate her, she felt its size and pushed back onto it at the same time as she drove herself down onto the young man. She sensed the balls of the man behind her lying against the young man's shaft whenever she had them both as deep as they would go. She felt their cocks squeezing together as they forced hard against the lining of her arse and her cunt. She screeched as she felt the swollen tips at their limit at the same time and she held onto the young man's hair and banged his head against the floor every time she got their full length.

When the first cock was presented to her mouth she did not wait to look at it, she just opened her wet lips and sucked it as deeply as she could. Immediately it went to the back of her throat and she could not breathe. She knew she should draw back and take in some air but she swallowed onto it and as her lungs stretched and pulled against her diaphragm it seemed like breathing. She swallowed again and the action in her chest was the same. She thought she did not need to breathe and sucked the cock right down, as if swallowing food and breathing at the same time. The tip went into her throat and she did not choke or gag. She allowed it deeper and when she was forced to take another strange, strangled breath the swallowing action took it down until the base of it pressed hard against her tight lips. She could stand it no more, the pressure in her chest was too great, and she exploded and choked the cock out. She felt its length pulling up her burning throat and thought she was going to be sick the instant it ran across her squashed and aching tongue.

She took the next one easily and sucked it until its semen erupted in a flood down her throat. She lapped at the spunk that it left around her lips as the next one slipped in over her tongue. She fucked at the young man as she felt the cock in her arse swelling as its semen flowed up in heavy pulses towards the hot tip. She grasped the young man's head and banged it hard against the floor. His face contorted in pain and, as she looked down at his agony, a wave of uncontrollable desire flooded through her. She felt her orgasm beginning to fill her, it flowed across her flesh then drove her hips together as finally, in the grip of a massive paroxysm she banged the young man's head against the floor for a last time and finished, howling and yelling and spraying semen and spit from her wide open mouth.

She flopped forward, gasping and dizzy, her hips still fucking uncontrollably as spit and semen ran from her mouth in a flood. Her eyes rolled as she jerked out the last pulse of her orgasm then she threw herself back in ecstasy as she felt the twin surges of hot spunk splattering high up in her vagina and deeply inside her arse. The cocks pulsated and forced their semen out in huge waves, filling her to overflowing then flowing back down between her flesh and the throbbing shafts and finally running down her already soaked legs. Her face was saturated with sweat as another cock was forced into her arse and she kept fucking the young man even though his cock had softened slightly until it finished again.

She hardly felt conscious as she was rolled onto her back and fucked repeatedly by all those who were on the stage. Some of them finished in her cunt, others sprayed their semen over her breasts, some came into her mouth or over her face and others finished in her hair, under her armpits and across her thighs, legs and feet.

After they had finished with her she lay on her back, her legs wet and wide and her cunt distended and swollen. She rubbed her hands across her breasts and felt the sticky mess of semen running over her skin and when she swallowed she tasted its salty tang inside her mouth and down her still-burning throat.

She moaned as she felt her hands being tied tightly behind her back and called out weakly in pain as she was dragged roughly across the wooden floor of the stage, but she remembered nothing else.

11

Barbara awoke suddenly and jumped up, gasping as if released from an unbearable nightmare. Her eyelids pulled against the sticky film that glued them together and when they finally opened her dark pupils stared out in fear. She twisted her shoulders and immediately felt the tension of the rope around her wrists. She pulled at her bonds but they were so tight they cut into her wrists and she had to stop. Then she heard the screech of animals and the door opened into the tiny room into which she had been locked.

"I hope you've got your strength back!"

The Ringmaster stood above her as she cowered, with her head down to shield her eyes from the light.

"You were a good prize at the auction but now there is some serious training ahead for you. You were a good fuck, that was obvious, but you were undisciplined and you let your own desires get the better of you. That will not do, but I can soon knock that out of you!"

He reached down, grabbed her hair and pulled her to her feet. She whimpered as she got up painfully, bending her head and squeezing her shoulders together in an effort to relieve the tension of his grasp.

"Please, Ringmaster, I can't stand any more, please let me go, I feel so afraid, please, let me go, please ..."

"Quiet! Forget being free. You are mine now and you will be trained to serve my purposes."

He pulled her hair and she screamed in pain as he dragged her from the room. He hauled her along a corridor, occasionally tightening his grip on her hair, until they arrived at a large, bolted door. He pushed her against the wall and held her there with his shoulder while he undid the heavy padlock. As the door swung open a tremendous din of howling and screeching flooded out and as Barbara glanced inside she shrunk back in terror.

The Ringmaster pushed her inside and slammed the door behind him. The room was very large and high, there were animal cages everywhere, some on the floor and some hanging from the ceiling by heavy chains. There was a wolf walking around in circles in one, a baboon in another and some of the higher cages were filled with multi-coloured parrots and exotic birds. Monkeys swarmed inside the bars of several cages and they screeched and bared their teeth at Barbara and the Ringmaster. In the centre was a sawdust ring surrounded by a high-barred, circular cage. There were several rostrums inside, one was on the floor and the others stood at different heights on metal stools. The cage was empty but the sawdust was scuffed up in piles as though a large creature had been running around inside it.

"Get in bitch! This is where your training starts!"

He pushed her forward and she stumbled against the iron bars of the circular cage, hitting her face heavily and drawing back with shock and pain. The monkeys screeched loudly and she pulled back more as they shook and rattled their bars noisily.

The Ringmaster opened the door of the cage, punched Barbara in the back and thrust her inside. She fell face-forwards onto the sawdust floor and coughed as the sawdust went into her mouth. It tasted musty and dry and, as she struggled to get up with her hands tied behind her, she felt it sticking to her face like a mask.

"Get up there!" shouted the Ringmaster, pointing to the platform that stood on the floor. "Get up there you fucking little animal!"

Barbara looked around in fear as the monkeys screamed excitedly. She managed to get up and went towards the platform uncertainly, looking back to the Ringmaster before doing anything else, fearful that she might have misunderstood him.

"Get on there you fucking little animal!"

With difficulty, she climbed up and stood unsteadily on the circular platform. It was only then that she realised she was completely naked and, as she looked down in shame, she saw her shaved cunt and felt even more humiliated.

"Stand upright!"

She tried to stand more upright but she felt feeble and exhausted and she could not get her legs straight because they were so stiff.

"Stand up animal!"

She lifted her head slowly, pulled her aching shoulders back as much as she could and stood shivering on the platform struggling to stand up.

The Ringmaster ignored her efforts, went over to the side of the cage and picked up a long bull-whip. He flicked his wrist and it weaved behind him in a long curve then cracked as the end sprang back. He cracked it again then in the other hand he picked up a long, thin cane and walked over to Barbara.

She was unable to contain her fear. She felt hopelessly alone and exposed and a swell of panic flooded up inside her. She wanted to jump down from the rostrum and throw herself at the Ringmaster's feet; she wanted to beg him for mercy, she wanted to plead to be freed from this terrible captivity and if he would let her go she would promise to do anything he asked.

"Please ..."

"Silence animal! Silence or you will have an early taste of the bull-whip. Silence!"

Barbara shrunk back in terror as he came towards her, flicking the bull-whip and making it crack noisily.

He reached behind her but she squirmed away fearful of what he was gong to do. He stood back angrily and cracked the whip, sending a plume of dry sawdust into the air and she dropped her head in fear and he reached behind her again. This time she did not try to avoid his touch, then suddenly she felt her wrists fall free from their bonds. Her arms dropped loosely to her sides and she felt relieved; she thought he was setting her free and a wave of excitement filled her stomach at the thought of escaping at last from this terrible nightmare.

"You are free of your bonds my little animal, but don't

think you are free of my control. Now you must learn how to be obedient."

Her heart sank as he stood back, cracked the whip and smacked the splintered end of the long cane down on the edge of the platform.

"Sit!"

She did not know what to do. She knew what he was saying but she did not understand exactly what he wanted of her. She bent her legs hesitantly and reached her hand down to the platform, looking at him all the time to see if she was doing the right thing.

"Sit you fucking animal!"

She crouched lower but still she was unsure. The Ringmaster pulled the whip back and as it curled and cracked loudly a puff of smoke come from its ragged tip. He grinned then smacked the cane down hard on the edge of the platform and its splintered tip grazed the top of her foot. She flinched and drew her leg up behind her.

"Pull you legs up and sit on your bottom!"

Shaking with fear, she sat down uncertainly, pulling her legs up in front of her, wrapping her arms around them and looking back at him hoping she had done what he had ordered.

"Good! At last! Now crouch on your knees!"

Barbara unwrapped her arms and got up, then she bent down, curled her knees beneath her buttocks and rested herself down on them.

"Now stay there until I tell you to move."

She sat on her legs, staring ahead into the circus ring. The monkeys clung to the bars of their cages and screeched loudly as the wolf stalked in circles around his cage, licking his tongue out and dribbling onto the floor. The parrots shrieked and flew noisily above her and occasionally a red or yellow feather fell softly onto the sawdust that was spread around the circular, iron pen. She wanted to hide away but she realised she must do only what she was told and she stayed kneeling and perfectly still and waiting for her next instruction.

The Ringmaster strutted around the cage, cracking the whip and tapping the tops or edges of the other rostrums with the long cane.

"Enough, up here animal!"

He rapped the end of the cane on a podium at the other side of the cage which stood several feet off the ground on a tubular steel frame.

"Quickly or you'll taste the whip!"

He cracked the whip loudly. She got up and climbed down from her rostrum. Her calves tingled from lack of blood and she found it difficult to walk and, as she stumbled nervously across the sawdust ring towards the platform, she realised she was too slow.

"Quickly I said. Stop where you are and bend over!"

Barbara stopped and stood still. She knew she had been too slow but her legs felt so shaky and she just could not go any faster.

"Please, I'm sorry, but ..."

"Bend over animal! Let's see if this makes you think twice about being lazy!"

She bent over slightly and rested her hands above her knees, squeezing out the naked edges of her shaved cunt and feeling them pulling against the soft skin at the tops of her thighs.

Crack!

The bull-whip cracked across her bent bottom. She shrieked and the monkeys jumped around their cages in a frenzy. She had never felt anything so painful. The cracking whip burnt scorchingly as it touched the soft skin of her buttocks and sent a lacerating sting deep inside her.

She threw herself back in shock and agony, reaching around and gripping her bottom with her hands.

"Bend over animal! And keep your hands away!"

She tried to bend over but she was too frightened. She did not think she could suffer another agonizing crack from the whip and froze.

"Please ..."

"Bend over!"

She started to bend but she was too frightened to take any more then, without warning, the whip cracked again across her back.

Crack!

She shrieked in distress as the cutting pain burned through her again and she spun around, panting and gasping for breath. Her chest heaved as she slowly got control of herself but as she breathed again the sensation of pain grew even stronger.

"Obedience, that's what you will learn in the cage! Obedience!"

He pulled the whip back and she ran to the side of the cage in panic. She clung to the bars and shook them frantically as the monkeys jumped around inside their own cages, screeching and howling. The wolf looked at her and growled menacingly, then the whip came down across her breasts.

Crack!

She curled over and fell on the floor as he whipped her across the back until she was reeling in agony around the sawdust covered floor.

Crack! Crack! Crack!

"Now, animal, I said bend over!"

She struggled to her feet and bent over shakily, trying to rub her breasts to ease the pain that was still shooting through them.

"Further!"

She bent over more until her bottom was taut and fully exposed.

"Hold your ankles animal!"

She reached down and held onto her ankles waiting for her punishment. She felt the edges of her cunt stretched tight and she felt a wetness on them as they were squeezed together by the strain of bending over so far.

Crack!

A single crack of the whip lacerated her buttocks and she fell forward screaming in a fresh convulsion of pain.

"Now, up here and quickly!"

The Ringmaster fiercely smacked the end of the cane onto the high rostrum and cracked the whip loudly. Barbara got to her feet and, still smarting from the lashes of the whip, she scuttled across the sawdust ring and started to climb onto the rostrum. She clambered up the side, frantically hoping that she was quick enough to please the Ringmaster, and when she got to the top she crouched on the podium nervously like a frightened animal.

"Now this one!" he shouted, smacking the cane down on a still higher rostrum on the other side of the cage. And quicker! You're still too slow!"

In a panic, she climbed down the side of the rostrum and dashed across the ring to the next. She climbed up its side but because she was so frantic she lost her grip and fell back to the sawdust floor. As she scrambled to get up she got sawdust in her eyes and immediately fought to clean them with her hands. She could not see and she fell over again when she tried to get up. She felt terrified and desperate and fought to get the burning dust from her eyes but, as she fell back again, she felt another searing crack fall across the back of her legs.

Crack!

She shrieked and pulled herself away but she did not

know where it was coming from because she could not see; she felt panicked and cornered. Another crack burned her back and she jumped up, still half-blinded and ran towards the rostrum but it was the wrong one. The Ringmaster cracked the whip down again.

Crack!

She crumpled over, wiping her eyes and fighting to see. She saw a rostrum in front of her and climbed up the sides, clawing at the steel framework and scuffing her knees against its sides. She managed to get to the top and clung to it as it swayed beneath her shaking body.

"Now this one, animal!"

The Ringmaster smacked his cane against another one, the highest of all. She climbed down and ran towards it desperately. As she climbed up its sides it wobbled and shook and when she got to the top she did not dare stand because it was rocking around too much. She felt dizzy and sick and she felt overwhelmed with shame and humiliation. Her face was wet with sweat and sawdust stuck to her cheeks and lips where she had dribbled and rubbed her face. As she glanced down giddily she saw angry red marks across her breasts and legs and then she felt faint and toppled from the podium crashing to the floor heavily.

She lay with her face in the sawdust, gasping and panting, hardly able to breathe from panic and fear. Her heart was pounding and she could feel her veins sticking out on both sides of her neck. Her face felt as of it was on fire and she had searing pains all over her body. She wanted to pass out, she craved to be unconscious, but the Ringmaster's whip lashed at her again.

Crack!

"Here!" he shouted, smacking his cane at the base of the first podium. Here!"

She crawled to her feet and slowly went over to where

he stood.

"Now bend over the podium. I am going to cane you. You are not tied and I want to you do it only because I order you. Bend! Do you understand?"

"Yes, I understand."

Barbara laid herself across the top of the podium. She stretched herself out obediently, laying her hands flat against the sawdust-covered floor and pressing her stomach down against the smooth, cold surface of the metal top. She extended her legs backwards and pressed her toes against the floor to stretch her calves as tightly as she could. Now she realised that she only wanted to do what he ordered. She knew she was going to be punished and she realised it would hurt but she only wanted to do what he said; she did not want to run away or escape, she only wanted to obey. But even worse, she saw inside herself an even darker desire for punishment and pain.

"Please," she said quietly, stretching herself out even more, "please make it hurt."

12

Barbara lay awake in the tiny room trying to make some sense of what had happened to her. She felt so desperate and alone and she hung her head and started weeping. She knew she had to believe what had happened to her but, at the same time, it seemed too incredible to imagine.

She lifted herself up slightly and felt the sore skin of her bottom. The Ringmaster had beaten her so hard and she knew she had not been tied or restrained, and she knew she had been consumed by orgasms as the pain had increased, but now she felt only remorse. She felt as if she was an animal, corrupted by her carnal lust and punished for her obscene desires and shamelessness.

She ran her hands down between her legs and felt the front of her shaved crack; it was still wet and her labia were swollen and distended. She poked her fingers inside them and felt the warm wetness of the entrance to her vagina. She opened her legs wider and pushed her fingers deeply inside and wetness ran down them and smeared itself silkily over the palms of her hands.

The door opened and Barbara squinted her eyes together against the glare. Mercedes stood against the light, her tall, angular body resting against the door frame and her long, red robe flowing down towards the floor. Barbara could just make out the line of Mercedes' panties that were pulled tightly against the folds of her cunt and high up onto her hips.

"Ready for more training, girl?"

Barbara pulled her fingers away from her cunt and sat up against the wall; Mercedes sounded angry and Barbara did not want to displease her.

"I wish I could be released," she pleaded.

"Ha! You can forget that little animal!"

Mercedes kicked at Barbara and she pulled herself up. "Please don't ..."

"Stop bleating you fucking little bitch!"

Mercedes kicked at her again and caught the front of Barbara's calf with the pointed toe of her long, leather boots. Barbara lifted her leg to get it out of the way but that made Mercedes even more angry and she kicked at Barbara again and this time punched the toe of her boot heavily against Barbara's thigh. Barbara winced and bent down to protect herself as the heavy blow dug into her skin.

"Please don't ..."

"Stop fucking whining!"

Mercedes lashed out again with her boot and stabbed the side of Barbara's bent shoulder. Barbara cried out in pain and turned towards the wall, holding one hand across her shoulder and the other across her naked breasts.

Mercedes lifted her boot high and started kicking Barbara's buttocks. Barbara shook with fear as the leather boot dug into her and she crouched against the wall, but Mercedes kept kicking her until Barbara fell to the floor.

"Get up!"

Mercedes kicked at her again and the toe of her boot stabbed into Barbara's stomach. She gasped as the heavy blow knocked the breath from her. She tried to curl up and protect herself but Mercedes kept kicking at her, aiming her boot wherever she saw that Barbara was exposed, and laughing as Barbara twisted her body and tried to defend herself.

"Bitch!"

Mercedes reached down, grabbed Barbara's sticky, wet hair but dropped it again as soon as she felt how dirty it was.

"Filthy little bitch!"

She thrust her hand down, pushed it between Barbara's thighs and grabbed Barbara's outer labia between her fingers. She squeezed hard and Barbara cried out as a burning pain shot through her. Mercedes squeezed harder and Barbara shrieked, gasping and shocked but unable to move. She froze as Mercedes pinched her labia tightly between her fingers then twisted the soft flesh and pulled on it fiercely. Barbara's eyes widened in fear as she dropped back, unable to ease the pain and unable to escape the agonizing pinching.

Finally, Mercedes released her grip and stood back.

"Up and follow me."

Barbara struggled to her feet and followed shakily behind Mercedes as she strode out of the tiny room and down the long corridor. Mercedes turned occasionally and glared triumphantly at Barbara and every time she did Barbara dropped her head. Barbara felt so humiliated by the way Mercedes was treating her and she felt so ashamed of herself for following so obediently like a dog trailing after its cruel master.

Mercedes led the way into the huge room with the sawdust covered training ring and as Barbara entered she shuddered with fear as the monkeys leapt around their cages, screaming and pulling at the bars.

"The Ringmaster says I must train you to please his clients. I think I will enjoy it. You are now part of the Ringmaster's circus, his 'Little Circus of Pleasures' he calls it, and you will be expected to perform anything our clients want. And believe me they want everything they can think of. That's the whole idea, they come here to act out their fantasies and the Ringmaster provides them with the goods."

Barbara tried to say something but her heart was pounding so loudly and she was so short of breath that she could make no sound come out.

"You know that the Ringmaster will not tolerate disobedience, and he won't put up with any failure, he expects every client to go away pleased. Bend over!"

Barbara did not respond quickly enough.

"Bend over bitch! When you are told to do something you do it!"

Barbara bent over obediently.

"When a client tells you to do something you do it! Now lie on your back and open your legs, I want to see your cunt!"

Barbara lay down on the floor and opened her legs.

"Wider!"

She felt the soft edges of her cunt peeling apart as she stretched her legs as wide as they would go.

"Now show me how you would fuck. Show me how you would writhe if you were being fucked by the biggest cock you had ever seen."

Barbara did not know what to do.

"I said show me how you would fuck the biggest, stiffest, widest cock you can imagine. Open up wide and show me how you would put it in."

Barbara pushed her hands down towards her stomach. She dropped her fingers against the front of her open crack and felt how wide the outer labia were as she stretched her legs apart. The soft smoothness of her skin inflamed her finger tips and she probed them around the base of her clitoris.

"Go on, let me see how you would put it in."

Barbara tried to imagine the cock and she took her fingers from her cunt and stretched them out as if to take hold of it.

"It's so big," she said nervously.

"Yes, but you've got to take it, you must take it."

Barbara cupped her hands together as if to encircle the huge cock and she imagined its thickness and squeezed at it to feel its weight.

"It's so big, I can hardly hold it, I cannot get my hands around it, it's huge."

"Yes, but you've got to take it, you must do what you are told."

Barbara drew her hands around the cock and slowly pulled it until she felt the wide, engorged glans; she felt its heat and her fingers throbbed as it pulsated against her fingers.

"Take it in!"

She placed the hot, throbbing end against her open labia and felt it sting her stretched flesh, but she pushed it hard until she felt the tip of it squeeze past her distended labia.

"It's too big, much too big, its stretching me terribly, I can't take it in, my cunt is too small."

"Stick it in, stick that huge dick in and feel it filling you and stretching you."

Barbara pressed her hands harder against her cunt and felt the tip opening her labia even more, she felt them peel back painfully then suddenly she felt them close around the flared edges of the throbbing glans.

"It's in, the end of it is in!"

"Take it all you bitch!"

Barbara folded her hands tightly on the cock and drew it further inside. She felt its enormous veins pulling at the sides of her vagina and stretching her painfully but still she kept pulling it inside. She gasped as she felt its full width and she felt sick as the end of it touched the top of her vagina. Still she pulled it in until she felt it pressing so hard against her innards that she thought she was gong to burst.

"What's it feel like bitch? What does it feel like to have that enormous cock deeply inside?"

"Marvellous. Marvellous. I'm so full, so marvellously full."

Barbara lifted her hips to take more and grasped her hands together eagerly. Suddenly, she felt her hips going higher, she could not stop them, she felt the pressure from the huge cock and lifted herself onto it. Then she felt a surge of heat inside her whole body and she dropped herself onto the thick cock and started to finish. The orgasm ran through her in waves, prising out every corner of her flesh and stinging her so that she shivered and jerked. She opened her mouth, she wanted that filled as well but she knew there was nothing to put in it and she just hung her tongue out as far as she could and gurgled noisily as spit ran back down her throat. She choked and she felt the pressure of her cunt tighten up on the massive cock and she felt herself finishing even more. She rose in repeated spasms as more heat prickled across her skin and her eyes blazed with every convulsion as she gulped at the air from her wide-open mouth.

As the heat finally subsided, she fell back and dropped her hands to her sides, still convulsing as spasms of orgasm ran through her limbs like electric shocks.

Mercedes stared down at her then kicked her viciously in the side.

"Up! That's not all the fucking you've got to do."

Barbara struggled to her feet. She still felt the sensation of being fucked and she was still shaking and twitching with the remnants of her orgasms as she stood in front of Mercedes. She reached up to wipe a dribble of spit from her mouth but Mercedes smacked it down. Barbara felt shocked and suddenly hurt, then a wave of embarrassment swept over her as she realised how easily she had imagined being fucked and her face flushed red as she thought how she had finished so readily under Mercedes' instructions and prying gaze.

"Put this on! I need a fuck!"

Mercedes held up a wide, black leather belt with a huge erect cock attached by braiding to the front panel. The cock was black and covered in rough veins and the long shaft rose stiffly to a broad glans with hard, flaring edges.

"Put it on, I said I need a fuck!"

Barbara took the belt and pulled it around her waist. The soft leather felt cool as she eased it against her skin and she pulled up the straps as tightly as she could. The black cock stood out in front of her, pulling the belt at her back with its weight. She felt the tension of the strap around her hips and a fresh wetness in her cunt as she looked down and imagined the large, black cock was hers. As she bent to stare at it the muscles tightened across her stomach and the cock lifted against the strain. She reached down and held it in her hands and the throbbing feeling she had felt before returned and swept through her body in heavy pulses.

"Stand against that cage." ordered Mercedes, indicating the large cage containing the wolf.

Barbara looked startled and hung back.

"Now!"

She edged back towards the cage. The wolf looked under his eyes at her and slunk to the back, still pacing in circles and hanging his tongue out loosely from between his salivating jaws.

"Against the cage, bitch!"

Barbara moved back until her back rested against the bars. The wolf jumped forward then turned and banged himself against the bars on the opposite side. Barbara flinched with fear and pulled away.

"Against the cage I said!"

She edged back to the bars and rested her back against them uneasily as she felt the coldness of the iron against her shoulder blades and imagined the pacing wolf licking at her heels.

Mercedes dropped her long, red robe off her shoulders and it fell to the floor in a silky pile. She stood in front of Barbara, her short, black hair brought to points on her temples and the ring in her left nipple glistening in the flickering light. Barbara looked into the gap at the top of Mercedes' long leather boots and stared down into the opening where her slender thighs disappeared into a beckoning darkness. Mercedes' panties were pulled tightly around her cunt and Barbara could see the shape of her outer labia as they pressed against the flimsy material.

Mercedes looked down at the long black cock that stood out from Barbara's groin then turned and bent over in front of her. She reached back and slowly pulled the edges of her panties from her hips; they came down slowly, pulling at her firm flesh as the elastic was stretched. Barbara stared at Mercedes' buttocks as her panties were peeled down; they were tight and firm and very pale. Mercedes pulled the panties lower until the waistband was drawn tightly across her cunt. She held them there for a moment, then she pulled them further and the soft material tugged at the crease of her crack until it was finally released and came down onto her thighs.

Mercedes let go of the black panties which were now wound up in a tight twist just above the loose tops of her black, leather boots. She reached between her legs and prised open the edges of her cunt with her fingers, peeling them apart and revealing the soft inner folds, already wet and glistening.

"Fuck that bitch!"

Barbara held the shaft of the cock and pressed it towards Mercedes' cunt. The tip touched the exposed outer labia as Mercedes held them back and they were so wet that the leather cock slid past them and Barbara felt the pressure of the tighter inner labia. She pushed harder and felt the tip of the cock push the soft, pink folds slowly aside. The cock slid in further and Barbara watched the shaft disappearing past Mercedes' labia which she was still holding apart with her fingers.

"More bitch!"

Barbara pressed the cock in further and now she could feel Mercedes' vagina drawing it in. She could feel the soft sides sucking at the cock and she pushed her hips forward and slid it in until its base was pressed against the distended edges of Mercedes' cunt.

"Fuck it I said!"

Barbara pulled the cock back and when it came out it was glistening with wetness. She pushed it straight back in and this time it went in more easily, running in on the silky moisture that was dripping from Mercedes' cunt.

"More!"

Barbara pulled it back again then pushed it in, this time harder. She drew back then forced it in again and felt the strength of her hips controlling the cock as she began fucking Mercedes rhythmically. Every time Barbara drove the cock in Mercedes pushed back more to feel the pressure and Barbara grabbed hold of Mercedes' hips so that she could fuck her even harder. She gripped them tightly and squeezed them hard, pulling them back against her thrusting cock and digging her nails into Mercedes' firm flesh.

"Hold my tits!"

Barbara reached forward and grabbed Mercedes' breasts. They were full and firm and she took them in her hands and squeezed them hard and every time she thrust the cock in she squeezed harder.

"Pull the ring in my nipple bitch!"

Barbara felt the small ring in Mercedes' left nipple and clutched it between her finger and thumb. She pinched her finger into the ring and pulled at it hard. She fucked Mercedes frantically, watching the wetness on the black cock as it drove in and out of the open cunt and pulling at the ring in Mercedes' nipple until she could feel Mercedes tensing with the pain. She wanted to smack Mercedes' bottom, she wanted to bring her hand down hard and smack her until she yelled but she was too afraid.

"Now smack me, I want to finish, smack me as hard as you can!"

Barbara did not hesitate and smacked her hand down hard against Mercedes' buttocks. She watched her hand coming down and she saw Mercedes tense her bottom as it smacked across her pale skin.

Smack!

Barbara felt a surge of heat in her cunt. She could feel its wetness dribbling against its open edges and the more she thrust the cock inside Mercedes' cunt the more she felt the wetness. It was running down the insides of her thighs and she pulled her bottom back, squeezing her buttocks together to feel it more while she watched her smacking hand and the glistening wet cock.

Smack!

Mercedes tensed again.

More!"

Smack!

"More you fucking bitch. More! More!"

Smack! Smack! Smack!

"Harder! Harder!"

Smack! Smack! Smack!

Barbara smacked her as hard as she could. She held the cock back and pressed her bottom against the bars of the cage. She smacked Mercedes with all her strength and every time she smacked down her cunt felt warmer and wetter. She watched Mercedes' bottom getting redder and then suddenly Mercedes cried out, dropped forward and fell onto her knees at Barbara's feet.

"More! More! More!"

Barbara got down and, still pressing her bottom against the bars of the cage, smacked Mercedes until she finally dropped face-down into the sawdust on the floor, twitching and jerking and writhing her reddened buttocks.

Barbara dropped her head exhausted but still pressed her bottom against the bars of the cage, exposing her open cunt to the licking tongue of the ravenous wolf.

Mercedes rolled over and gasped. She was flushed and her buttocks were stingingly red. She went and picked up an electric winch control and it hummed loudly as one of the cages swung down to the floor. Mercedes opened the cage door.

"Get in bitch!"

Barbara picked herself up off the floor, her eyes filled with fear.

"Take that belt off and get in!"

Barbara unstrapped the belt from her waist. Her hips were red from the pressure of the leather edges and the cock was dripping wet. She handed it to Mercedes then stepped forward cautiously into the cage. The floor was made from the same iron bars as the sides and top and she tried to stand between them as she entered. Mercedes slammed the door-grill shut, locked padlock through a bolt, the stepped back and winched the cage up from the floor. It swung upwards and Barbara's feet slipped down between the bars. She lifted them and tried to stand across the steel rails but the cage swung so giddily she could not get her balance and her feet fell back down. The cage went higher, swinging wildly, as Barbara struggled clumsily to get her feet back between the bars.

Mercedes laughed as she watched Barbara's frantic efforts and when she stopped the winch the cage swung abruptly and Barbara fell over awkwardly, her legs still dangling down between the iron rails of the floor. The monkeys screeched in a clamour of noise as Barbara tried to hold onto the bars but the cage swung wildly on the end of the rope and everything Barbara did seemed to make things worse. Finally, she managed to pull her feet out between the bars and clung to the side of the cage feeling giddy and sick. She stared down into the room as the monkeys continued screeching and Mercedes strutted out and bolted the door behind her.

13

Barbara was kept in the cage every day. She was fucked by Mercedes using the leather cock and sometimes Mercedes ordered Barbara to fuck her. One day Mercedes bound Barbara's legs to her wrists with ropes and the tight bonds were pulled from a noose around her neck, across her breasts and around her waist. She worked carefully with the knots and pulled them all so tight that it cut off Barbara's circulation.

Then Mercedes gagged her and tied her down on her back to a small table and left her there, the ropes pulling tightly between the crack of her cunt and the gag stifling her breathing and causing her to suck air in through her flared nostrils. After she had been there for a while, Mercedes brought in a man who wanked over her. Barbara strained against the ropes but could not move at all as he directed his semen over her face, stomach and into her eyes.

Sometimes the Ringmaster brought someone to see Barbara as she clung to the bars of her cage. As they walked around the Ringmaster prodded her with the long cane to make her twist and turn and show herself. Once, a man asked if he could spank her and the Ringmaster held her over his knee while the man smacked her bottom until she screamed for mercy.

Every morning the Ringmaster trained her with the whip and cane, tormenting her and caning her across the buttocks as she was forced to clamber from one rostrum to the next. At night a young girl, dressed only in flimsy, white bra and panties, brought a small plate of food and pushed it through the bars before Mercedes came in and Barbara was winched back up to dangle all night in the swinging cage.

Before Mercedes came in to winch the cage off the floor, Barbara tried to talk to the young girl but she seemed too frightened to answer and always shrunk away into the darkness without speaking. One night, the young girl came with the food and Barbara noticed red weals across her back. She asked her if she was alright and the girl nodded shakily. When Barbara asked her where she was the girl suddenly blurted out 'Langestraat, 15 Langestraat' before turning fearfully and running off into the darkness of the room.

Barbara repeated the address to herself all the time, imagining how it was spelt and going through every letter so that she would not forget it. Even when she was having to fuck Mercedes or when she was being beaten by the Ringmaster, she still repeated it. Then one night, as Mercedes tied her to the bars of the cage by the ankles and wrists and fucked her arse with the leather cock, Barbara saw a nail on the floor. When Mercedes finally released her and Barbara slumped to the floor exhausted, she picked up the nail and hid it in her mouth. That night she scratched the address along the insides of the bars then each night she looked at it and repeated it to herself, hoping that one day she would somehow be able to let someone know where she was.

One morning Mercedes winched the cage down and as Barbara rubbed her bleary eyes Mercedes tossed some items of clothing in through the bars.

"Get dressed, we've got an important client this morning and he has chosen you."

Barbara knew what was expected of her and picked up a shirt and tie from the pile and started to get dressed. She enjoyed pulling the white shirt over her shoulders, it was ages since she had worn anything and the material felt soft and comforting. She buttoned it up and smoothed the front down over her breasts as Mercedes watched her closely.

"Now the tie."

Barbara turned up the collar and pulled the red and white striped tie around the back of her neck. She had worn a shirt and tie like this when she been at school and she wove the tie into a knot at her throat and pulled it up against the top button without a second thought. She folded the collar down, straightened the tie and buttoned up the cuffs of the shirt.

The bottom edge of the white shirt just stopped short of her naked cunt and she felt exposed without any panties. She bent and picked up the pair from the pile; they were white satin and very thin and flimsy and quickly she pulled them over her ankles and drew them up over her thighs. As she pulled them up against her cunt she felt the soft edges of her labia settling into the silky material and she pulled them up high so that it parted them and squeezed deeply into her crack.

"Put a skirt on, you little bitch! Cover yourself up!"

Barbara suddenly felt embarrassed and hurriedly pulled a short grey skirt around her waist; it was pleated and fanned out as she twisted it to find the button at the side. She did the button up, then pulled up the small zip below it and carefully smoothed down the pleats against the fronts of her thighs. The hem finished several inches above her knees and when she bent to pick up the white socks it rose up at the back and exposed her silky, white panties that were pulled tight across her bottom. She pulled on the white ankle-socks on then tightened the buckles of the black, leather shoes.

Mercedes opened the cage door.

"Come on girl, you have been very naughty and the Headmaster is going to have to punish you."

Barbara hung her head and felt her face redden with embarrassment at the thought of what she might have done. She stepped out meekly and Mercedes pushed her through the door and into the dimly-lit corridor.

They stopped at a closed door at the side of which was a small wooden chair.

"Sit there my girl, you will be called in when he is ready."

Barbara sat down on the chair. Her short skirt folded up at the back and she felt the coldness of the wooden seat coming through the filmy panties. She squirmed her bottom against the seat and the panties pulled tightly at the crack of her cunt. She put her hands onto her uncovered knees and hung her head, feeling a wave of anxiety spreading through her stomach as she wondered what was going to happen to her.

"Now wait there until you are called."

Mercedes strutted down the corridor and disappeared into the gloom. Barbara sat on the wooden chair alone and worried, fidgeting with her fingers and twirling them around the hem of her pleated skirt.

"Come!" commanded a voice from behind the door.

Barbara looked up in surprise.

"Come!"

The voice sounded angry and nervousness filled Barbara's stomach.

"Come in!"

She got up off the chair and turned towards the door. She hesitated for a moment, then gripped the brass handle nervously and began to turn it.

"Knock!"

Barbara released the handle and stood back.

"Knock before you enter!"

She clenched her fist weakly and knocked timidly at the heavy door.

"Enter!"

She felt so fearful she knocked again before taking hold of the handle with her sweaty hand and turning it fully. She pushed the door open slowly and entered the room. Behind a desk on the opposite side of the room sat a dark-haired man in a large leather chair. The desk was covered with papers and books and a black briefcase was open in front of him.

"Do you want me to come in?"

"Sir!"

Barbara hesitated and worriedly clasped her hands together at the front of her skirt.

"Do you want me to come in Sir?"

"Close the door behind you girl!"

Barbara closed the door then put her hands together in front of her skirt again and waited.

"Come here girl!"

She walked towards the man and stood in front of the large desk.

"You have been very naughty, very naughty indeed. I am going to have to punish you."

Barbara felt her face reddening again and a sweat broke out under her arms and between her legs. She felt very nervous and worried about her naughtiness and what her punishment might be.

"You have been to me before haven't you girl?"

"Yes, yes Sir."

"And I told you then that if you came again I would not give you another chance."

"Yes, yes Sir."

"And here you are!"

"I'm so sorry Sir, I didn't mean to be naughty, honestly

121

I didn't mean it ..."

"Quiet, you have had you last chance and now you are going to have to be punished."

"But please sir ..."

"Quiet girl, no more excuses!"

Barbara felt a terrifying sense of dread as the Headmaster stood up and glared at her.

"Now, let me think, what shall it be?"

He walked over to a hat stand in the bottom of which were arranged some bamboo canes of various lengths and thicknesses. He drew one out and bent the end against his thigh. It sprung back sharply as he released it and when he pointed it towards Barbara she clasped her hand together more tightly and shrunk away in terror. He placed the cane back and selected another one. He bent it across his knee then turned and smacked it down hard across the edge of his desk. It cut through some of the papers that were strewn on the desk and a book flew off the edge and landed on the floor. Barbara's eyes widened with fear as she gripped her fingers together and grasped the pleats of her skirt and pulled at them anxiously.

"No, I think you need a spanking to start with."

He threw the cane back amongst the others and came over to Barbara.

"Please, please, I won't do it again, I promise I won't be naughty again ..."

"Quiet girl! And stop fiddling with your hands. Put them down at your sides!"

She unclasped her hands and pushed them against the sides of her thighs then hung her head as he walked behind her. He took hold of the hem of her skirt and lifted it to her waist.

"You are wearing those panties again! I have told you before that they are not school uniform!"

"I'm sorry Sir, I won't do it again."

He rubbed his hand across her bottom, feeling the smoothness of her silky panties and the tight edges that pulled into her firm skin. He pressed his fingers into the crack between her buttocks and ran them down to the gusset that was pulled tightly against her naked cunt. He dropped the skirt and went over to his large, leather chair and sat down.

"Come here and be punished."

She walked behind the desk and stood beside him.

"Bend over my knees."

Barbara bent across his knees.

"Bend over completely! Put your hands on the floor! I want to see those panties drawn tight across your young bottom."

Barbara bent across his knees and stretched her hands down to the floor. Her satiny panties pulled tightly into the crack of her cunt and she felt its swollen edges pressed hard against the soft material. She stretched down as far as she could and he lifted her pleated skirt and started rubbing his hands across her bottom again.

"This is going to hurt, girl. Your little bottom is going to be red and sore by the time I have finished with you. I hope you will learn your lesson from it."

She stretched further and felt his fingers playing between the crack of her buttocks, pressing the silky material towards her anus and feeling its tension against the softness of her cunt. Then she felt him slowly peeling them down. He held the thin material at the waist and, as he pulled it slowly across her buttocks, she felt the cool air spread across her tender skin as it was exposed to his gaze. He pulled them down to the tops of her thighs but they were so tight around her cunt that the gusset remained deeply stuck into her crack. He grabbed the material that was pulled in between her labia and peeled it away, opening her cunt and exposing its glistening wetness. She felt her bottom lifting higher as he drew the material down and as she tightened her muscles in readiness she felt the moist edges of her cunt pressing softly against the insides of her thighs. She also felt the warmth coming from his groin and the hardness of his cock inside his trousers as it pressed against the front of her stomach.

"You shall have six to start with!"

As he raised his hand high, she stretched her hands forward against the floor until she could hardly breathe, then he brought it down hard on her naked bottom with a dreadful, heavy smack.

Smack!

She stretched out further and bit onto her lips as she felt the sting across her bottom.

Smack!

She gasped as the smarting pain covered the whole of her bottom and she bit down harder on her lips to stop herself screaming. She knew there was only four to go and she tightened all her muscles to take them.

Smack!

She gasped again as the searing pain went through her body. She bit down hard again, panting through her nostrils and tensing her muscles. The pain was still flooding through her as the next one came down.

Smack!

Only two more to go and she gulped another breath before biting down onto her sore lips. She thought she could stand two more without screaming and she tensed up and waited.

Smack!

This one was so hard it knocked her forward. Her hands slipped on the floor and she folded over his knees heavily as she tried to get herself balanced again. But he did not give her chance to recover.

Smack!

She squirmed around still trying to get her hands back flat on the floor, but then she started to relax as she realised it was all over.

"Stop squirming!"

Smack!

She was thrown forward again and she screeched out in pain and surprise.

Smack!

Another heavy smack came down and she screamed loudly.

"Please, no more, please ..."

Smack! Smack! Smack! Smack!

He smacked her relentlessly across the bottom as she screamed and cried out for mercy. He took no notice, but finally it stopped and she fell forward panting and dribbling.

"Get up and bend over the desk, I have not finished with you yet!"

He pushed her off his knees and pressed her face-down onto the desk. She lay there gasping for breath as he went to the hat-stand and selected a cane. When he came back he yanked her panties further down and she cried out as they pulled against her skin.

"Please, I can't stand any more, please ..."

Thwack!

The cane lashed down against her bottom and she jumped back in agony. He pressed her back down against the desk and brought the cane down again.

Thwack!

A lacerating blow fell fully across her buttocks and she screamed wildly.

Thwack!

She felt the cane cutting into her bottom and she reeled backwards, gulping and shrieking in agony.

Thwack!

"Please, please ..."

Thwack!

He leant his arm heavily across her back and no matter how much she struggled she could not get free.

Thwack!

The stinging pain was unbearable and she thrashed about like a tortured animal, dribbling across the papers in the briefcase and throwing her head about in panic.

Thwack!

She buried her face amongst the contents of the briefcase then she felt the lid snapping shut across the back of her neck. Her head was trapped inside and she flailed about in terror as the papers stuck to her face in the half-darkness and the edge of the lid was forced down against her neck.

Thwack!

This time she could not move her head at all and she began to choke as he pressed the lid down even harder. The edge of the briefcase bit into her throat and the lid pinioned her neck. She thought she was going to suffocate and reached back with her hands to try and get free but he grabbed them and knocked them down onto the top of the desk.

Thwack! Thwack! Thwack!

She felt her eyes turning upwards as she gulped hopelessly for breath and she felt the pain moving out across her body as she began to drift into unconsciousness. She could not see anything clearly and her head sagged loosely into the contents of the briefcase. She felt the wet papers around her face and she tasted them in her mouth as the cane lashed down unforgivingly.

Then the beating stopped and she felt his cock against her anus. It pressed hard against the tight, muscular ring then went in fully. She wanted to screech out but she did not have enough energy but as he fucked at her arse she felt the wetness in her cunt and she began to match the rhythm of his thrusting cock.

Barbara bit into the papers around her mouth and sucked his cock into her arse as deeply as it would go. As the cock pressed against her innards, she felt herself wanting more spanking and she fucked back onto his cock even harder. As she felt the surge of spunk running up his throbbing shaft, she wanted to call out for him to cane her even more; she wanted to be thrashed harder until she passed out, she wanted him to beat her into senselessness with the cane and then spank her while she lay there unconscious. Suddenly his spunk shot deeply inside her, running hotly against the insides of her arse and setting her on fire and she sucked it in ravenously. Her mouth lay wide open and spit ran from her gaping mouth as the fiery passion of her own orgasm spread across her like heat from a furnace. She squeezed her buttocks together and tightened her anus around his cock as it spurted semen deeply inside her and she jerked with powerful convulsion as if in a fit. Her seizure continued as she sucked every drop from his cock and did not stop even when he pulled it out and left.

She lay with her face still trapped in the briefcase, panting and throbbing all over, then she realised she was alone and slowly released herself. Her anus gurgled with his semen as she stood up and she pulled her panties up to cover herself. She looked down at the desk and noticed some postcards, ready-stamped and unwritten. She grabbed one and thrust it inside her shirt with a pencil just as Mercedes came in to take her back to her cage.

Mercedes made her strip off but Barbara managed to

keep the postcard and pencil hidden away from her. When Mercedes had winched the cage up on its rope Barbara crouched in the cage and wrote to Mr Simms, 'Please, save me. I am at this address. Please, please, save me'. Later that night when the young girl came to feed her she asked her to post the card. At first the young girl was unsure but in the end she agreed.

The next day Barbara was sent for by the Headmaster again. This time he spanked her even harder and then he made her suck him while he held her across the desk and thrashed her with a cane. He did not fuck her but when he had beaten her senseless, he wanked over her face and made her suck all his spunk and swallow it down. All the time she was suffering her punishment she thought about her letter to Mr Simms and the thought of rescue helped her stand the pain of the terrible beating.

14

Barbara was woken by the humming sound of the winch and the rattling of the rope through the pulley as her cage swung down to the floor. She clung to the iron bars as it banged onto the ground with a jolt.

"Out!"

Mercedes pulled the door open and grabbed Barbara by the hair.

"There are some clients who want serving! Get dressed!"

Barbara bent down to a pile of clothes lying on the floor. She lifted them up and held them in front of Barbara's naked body.

"Your customers are waiting!"

Mercedes pushed Barbara hard against the shoulder and

she fell back clutching the clothes against her breasts.

"Put them on, you lazy bitch!"

Barbara lifted up a blue waitress's dress and a white apron. She pulled the tight-fitting dress over her head and wriggled it over her hips. She pulled the neck of the apron around her neck, wrapped its strings around the back of her waist and tied them in a bow.

Mercedes grabbed her hair and pulled her out into the corridor. She dragged her out into a back alley then in through a door with a red and yellow neon sign hanging over it. Mercedes pulled Barbara's head back and drew her mouth close to Barbara's ear.

"This time bitch it's only service, these fuckers have not paid for anything else so they don't get anything else. Understand? I hope so if you want to avoid another beating."

Mercedes pushed her into a dimly lit room full of men.

"About time!" shouted one, putting down a pool cue and walking over to a small bar. "Come on girl! We need serving!"

Mercedes pushed Barbara behind the bar as some of the other men gathered around and ordered beer.

"Get on with it! These men need serving!"

Nervously, Barbara found some bottles in a crate, opened them and poured the frothy beer into some glasses. The men took them and went back to the pool table as Barbara leant on the bar and Mercedes sat down by herself near to the pool table.

There were seven men altogether, four were playing pool and the others watched, shouting encouragement, cheering when balls went into the pockets and laughing and poking fun when they were missed. The bar was short and surrounded by a low canopy from which hung glasses and coloured trinkets. When one of the men came back for more, he demanded draft and Barbara pulled it from a large beer pull that stood in the centre of the deeply stained, shiny wooden bar top. The beer foamed over the tops of the glasses and the man complained but he did not seem particularly worried and went back to the pool game laughing and joking.

Barbara hung her hands casually onto the white, enamelled beer pull, pushing her fingers up towards its shiny brass cap and running them around its tip. She looked over at Mercedes who was leaning back on a chrome-plated chair, smoothing the front of her short, black leather skirt. She noticed Barbara's stare, looked up and smiled, pulling her thin, red lips wide and exposing her shiny, white teeth. Barbara thought of smiling back but there was something ominous in the way Mercedes looked at her and she bent down behind the bar and began moving some bottles from a crate.

Barbara served more beer and the men became increasingly rowdy. She laughed as one of them tripped over his pool cue and fell on the floor but immediately regretted it when he turned and shouted at her.

"Get on with your work girl, or it will be the worse for you."

After that she tried to busy herself, tidying the top of the bar and washing glasses, but the man she had laughed at would not stop glaring at her. Even when she turned her back to him, she was aware of his eyes as he stared at her and grumbled about the service and the frothiness of the beer, then he came over and leant on the bar.

"I bet you'd make a good fuck."

He turned to his friends.

"What do you think boys? I bet she'd make a good fuck."

Barbara looked across to Mercedes and saw the ominous smile turn into a broad and menacing grin.

The man reached across, grabbed the front of Barbara's

white apron and pulled her against the back of the bar.

"Would you make a good fuck bitch?"

"Please, let me go ..."

He grabbed her by the throat and squeezed it hard.

"Boys, I think she'd make a really good fuck. Let's see!"

He released her throat and she gasped for breath but she had not recovered from the shock as he took hold of her hair and started shaking her furiously. Her head was tossed from side to side as she reached up to his hands and tried to pull them away. He knocked her hands away then pulled her over, face-forward onto the bar, banging her head down heavily and making her cry out as a sickening pain went through her nose.

"Please, you mustn't, please ..."

Barbara glanced across to Mercedes for help, but two of the men were holding Mercedes against the wall by the pool table. Barbara suddenly felt terrified; everything seemed out of control.

"Stop! This is not allowed!" shouted Mercedes, but one of the men holding her smacked her across the face. She tried to punch him but he grabbed her wrist and twisted it behind her back. The same man stuffed a handkerchief into her mouth, plugging it completely and making her gasp for breath through her flaring nostrils. He pulled a black, leather belt across her mouth and drew it tight into the buckle at the back of her head. When she tried to punch him again with her other hand, he pulled both her arms behind her and secured her wrists with another belt that he then tied to a coat hook on the wall. He pulled it tightly through the buckle and she hung forward, struggling, gasping and enraged by her captivity.

The man holding Barbara's hair dragged her over the top of the bar and she crashed to the floor, shouting and screaming. She struggled frantically as he hauled her across

131

the floor towards the pool table. He threw her against its side then the four other men lifted her and forced her down, face-forward across the green, velvet cloth. They held her arms and legs outstretched then tied her wrists and ankles tightly to the netting ball bags at each corner. They wrapped belts around her knees and pulled them tightly to the middle ball holes, stretching her thighs wide apart and exposing the pink edges of her splayed-out cunt. She could only move her head and she threw it about wildly, begging for them to stop.

Then one of the men pushed his fingers across her bottom teeth and forced her mouth wide open. Spit shot from her mouth as her cries were stifled and she fought for breath. He prised her mouth as far open as it would go and tried to force a pool ball into it but she locked her jaw and he could not get the ball inside. He poked his fingers into her spit-filled mouth and pulled at her savagely but still she kept him from getting the ball past her teeth.

"Give her one with that cue!"

Whack!

The pool cue came down hard onto her taut buttocks.

She yelled and spit spurted out of her gaping mouth, running over the man's fingers and soaking his hands. He tried to force the ball in again but she clamped her mouth down hard onto his fingers, biting them hard and forcing him to pull them out.

"Fucking bitch! Give her another one, but make it harder!"

Whack!

The cue came down across her buttocks again. She shrieked as it stung her tightly-pulled flesh and she gaped her mouth wide-open. The man pushed the ball in, stifling her cries as it went in past her teeth and filled her mouth completely. She was consumed with panic as she gagged and a wave of sickness spread burningly up her throat. She choked but could not move her tongue and her throat tightened and she could not breathe. She gulped heavily and heaved repeatedly against the shiny, cold ball that was plugging her mouth. She did not know what to do; she thought she would not breathe again and gulped frantically, lifting her bottom up and convulsing in an uncontrollable seizure.

Whack!

Another hard blow sent a piercing pain through her outstretched buttocks and she threw her head back in an effort to open her throat.

Whack!

She tightened her hands into fists and pulled at her bonds, craning back as far as she could, then suddenly she felt air in the back of her throat and she knew she was breathing again.

Whack!

She clenched her buttocks together as it struck and she shook all over in a fit of agony as another man took a cue and started to beat her as well. The two of them rained alternate blows down on her bottom, bruising it and reddening it as she continued to fight for breath. Every time a cue smacked down she bent backwards in an involuntary spasm as the pain tore deeply though her fear-racked body.

Whack! Whack! Whack!

Whack! Whack! Whack!

When they stopped, her buttocks were covered in deep red stripes and her face was lying in a pool of foamy dribble that poured profusely from her ball-filled mouth.

"Get her over boys, now let's see how she fucks!"

As they untied her and turned her over, she glimpsed Mercedes still struggling with her shoulders pulled back as she hung forward on the coat hook. Barbara felt terrified, as though Mercedes being tied up left her unprotected and vulnerable. Suddenly, she thought the ball might not come out of her mouth and she was thrown into a desperate panic. She thrashed about wildly as the men struggled to tie her down again and spit ran down across her face, smearing her chin and cheeks and running back up her nose. With her eyes wide and feeling completely terror-stricken, she gulped and heaved and sucked in air through her spit-filled nostrils.

The men pulled her down firmly against the table, stretching the belts at her knees as tightly as they could and forcing the outsides of her legs flat against the green, velvet cloth. The soft edges of her cunt were spread wide and revealed her glistening inner labia as they lay in two, wet folds around the dark-pink opening to her vagina.

The man who had dragged her over the bar by her hair, grabbed a pool cue, jumped onto the table and stood astride her. He crouched down across her, facing her feet, and laid the thick end of the cue against her moist cunt. She felt the coldness of the smooth wood and tried to pull back but she was tied too tightly to move. Spit started running down the back of her tongue and into her throat and she started choking again, biting down involuntarily around the ball as it pressed against the roof of her mouth and forced her tongue down painfully.

The man moved the thick end of the cue around her outer labia, parting them and folding them back. They peeled apart then closed back against the sides of the cue as it entered. He pushed it further and it slid between her inner labia easily as it found the entrance to her vagina. He pushed it in and she breathed heavily through the spit in her throat as she felt the thick end of the cue probing deeply into her tender flesh.

He pushed it until it would go no further, then he drew it back and she felt her flesh tugging at the smooth wooden surface. When he pushed it back in again she felt herself welcoming it and sucking it in and as he drew it back out again she squirmed herself around it and tightened her vagina onto it. He thrust it back and she drew it in eagerly, then as he pulled it back she followed it, encouraging him to plunge it again deeply inside.

He started to move the cue faster and Barbara lifted her hips and matched the rhythm. She closed her mouth tightly around the pool ball and forced her cunt onto the cue, each time trying to get it further in. She moved her cunt around it, squeezing herself onto it, sucking at it and using all her strength to pull it in and when its end came close to the entrance to her vagina she forced herself at it desperately, anxious that it should not come out.

He bent between her wide-stretched legs and fucked her harder and faster with the but-end of the pool cue. She panted hard and could not swallow, but her dry throat was slaked by a steady stream of dribble and spit that ran copiously from the back of her squashed down tongue. Spit also ran from her mouth, saturating her swollen lips and soaking her tight-drawn cheeks. As the cue went faster, its hard surface rubbed against her clitoris, pulling against it and making it swell and stand proud of the front of her distended crack.

As her engorged clitoris pulled and tingled a heat began to spread from deep inside her vagina, out across her labia and through her hips and legs. She bit down over the pool ball as the heat ran back up across her breasts, into her throat and across her face, reddening it and causing her head to spin and pound with the pressure of blood and the tightening of her muscles. She felt it burning her from inside, sending scorching thrills of heat throughout her whole body as if she was on fire. It was overcoming her and she wanted to call out for more but her mouth was so plugged by the ball she could barely breathe. She felt the heat burning into her cunt and she tightened as a flood of orgasm ran through her in a vast, hot wave. She lifted herself onto the cue as much as she could and drew it in as deeply as it would go then she fell back, jerking with spasms of pleasure and fulfilment and sucking the ball painfully into the back of her mouth.

The man kept fucking her with the cue for some time after she finished but she did not stop responding to its pounding and she finished again before he finally took it out. Her cunt stayed open after it was withdrawn and she tightened the insides of her thighs as she felt a cold draft of air passing across the distended flesh at the entrance to her vagina.

Then one of the men wanked over her and, as he pulled hard against the throbbing shaft of his cock, she felt a hot surge of spunk splashing across her face. Another finished against her stretched mouth and she felt his sticky semen running inside the splayed edges of her lips. She tried to lick it but could not move her tongue against the plugging ball that filled her mouth. She widened her jaws and coughed in the hope of choking it out but it remained firmly stuck and the spunk ran down her chin and onto her throat.

The men undid her bonds and lifted her from the table. As they held her upright, the spunk on her face and around her mouth ran down her neck and she felt it sticking the inside of the top of her dress to her heaving chest. They carried her, still with the belts trailing from her ankles, wrists and knees and took her to the bar.

"Lift her up boys, let's see how much she can take!"

Two of them held her legs apart and another two lifted her under her armpits until they held her above the large, white beer pull. They pulled the belts at her knees up tightly around her neck, forcing her head down so that she stared into her splayed out cunt. They forced her legs wide and lowered her until the edges of her distended cunt touched the shiny, brass top. She felt a shock of coldness as it pressed against her warm flesh, then she felt it forcing her labia apart as they lowered her down onto it.

She stared across the room at Mercedes, tied and gagged and hanging forward on the leather belts from the coat hook. Mercedes shook angrily on her bonds as she watched Barbara being lowered further and further onto the huge beer pull.

At first the tip splayed her cunt apart and slid in easily, then as the widening shaft of the huge handle went in further her cunt would not expand to take it. She wanted to scream for them to stop but she only choked and felt sick as the ball pressed down hard against the back of her tongue. They pushed her down and slowly she felt the wide handle splaying her cunt wider and wider. She could not feel the tip inside her vagina because the pressure of the wide shaft was spreading her flesh so wide. She held her breath and bent her head down even further in the hope of widening her legs and making her cunt big enough to take the huge white, handle. Suddenly, it sank in, gigantic and hard, its widest point breaking past the restricting confines of her entrance and thrusting inside her until the brass tip pushed against the top of her aching vagina.

They held her on it and, as she tried to breathe again, she was overcome with panic. Her cunt felt completely filled and she could not imagine how it would come out again. They lifted her up and she felt it slowly slipping out, pulling at her flesh and stretching her again at the entrance to her vagina as its massive girth drew down her stretched flesh. They lowered again and this time she felt more of it as her cunt folded around it. The tip reached the end of her vagina again and she gasped, petrified but already eager to feel it again even before she was drawn off it.

They lifted her up again and her flesh tugged at its shiny surface and as the brass cap reached the outside edges of her vagina she pushed herself down, not wanting to even run the risk of letting it go. She bent her head lower and down she went again and this time they let her go further. The tip pressed against the top of her vagina and then it probed hard against the muscular ring that lay at its top. She threw her head back as it touched and she felt it prising into her and shocking her with fear, dread and desire. She wanted more and dropped herself onto it, squeezing her hips down and forcing the beer pull in until its hard, brass base touched the distended edges of her dripping cunt.

As she looked at the base of the beer pull pressed against the splayed edges of her cunt, she felt a heat flooding up inside her. She did not need any more movement to finish and as they lifted her again and her flesh pulled eagerly against the huge, white handle a deep coursing orgasm seized her and threw her into a long, jerking convulsion. She lifted her head, then threw it back and let them bring her up and down the beer pull faster and faster.

Then she felt a coldness against her anus as one of the men forced the neck of a beer bottle deeply into the muscular ring. Its sent an uncontrollable spasm through her body and she wanted them to let her go so that she could fuck them all. She imagined their cocks inside her one after another, fucking her arse, then her cunt then finishing in her mouth, in her hair and under her armpits. She wanted them to squeeze out their spunk into her eyes and ears and up her flared nostrils and she wanted to be rubbed all over with it and then rolled in it and made to lick it up from the floor. She wanted them to wank again in her mouth so that she could swallow all their semen and lick their cocks and pull the ends of them into her throat and swallow them as well.

Then one of the men undid the strings of her apron and pulled it up over her face. It wrapped around her neck and covered her face closely as he tied the strings to a hook above the bar. He yanked the ends down against the hook and she felt her neck being pulled up savagely against the thin strings. She could hardly breathe and she could not see but she kept fucking the beer pull and drawing the neck of the bottle deeper into her arse. She felt the ring of her anus spreading wider as the neck of the bottle went in deeper but she did not stop bearing down on it.

She felt her dress being lifted at the front and then a spurt of semen drenching her breasts. She felt hands rubbing it across her chest and stomach and then she felt a cock pressed against the front of her distended crack. When that finished the beer pull ran up and down her even more easily and she pounded herself onto it frantically and without stopping.

She could not control her orgasms and she absorbed each one, building on it with the next as they ran through her in waves of exhausting heat. Slowly they blended into one unbearable stream and she felt herself losing consciousness. She stared blankly into the tightly-pulled material across her face, and she gulped to get air through her gagging, strangled throat but, in the end, she could not take any more and faded away into senselessness.

After they had finished with her they threw her onto the floor, still with the ball jammed tightly in her mouth and the apron pulled over her face. Mercedes bent over her semen-drenched body and drew the apron down over her face. Barbara's eyes widened slightly as Mercedes reached her fingers inside Barbara's mouth and pulled the pool ball free. Spit dribbled from her mouth and ran freely in bubbly streams as it mixed with the sticky spunk that covered her

139

chin and neck. Suddenly, Barbara came to, gasping loudly and coughing as she tried vainly to try and swallow again.

"I warned you bitch! You shouldn't have let them fuck you like that."

Before Barbara really knew what was happening, Mercedes pulled her to her feet, dragged her out of the bar and into the alley. Mercedes pushed her against a wall, pulled Barbara's arms up and handcuffed her wrists around the wall-fitting of a gutter downpipe. She picked up a broken piece of wooden crating that lay on the ground and beat Barbara until she flopped unconscious onto her bonds.

After it was over, Mercedes pushed Barbara back into the cage and she hung to the iron bars weakly as it was hauled up by the humming winch. After a while, she recovered enough to remember most of what had happened to her and she reddened with shame. She was overcome with a feeling of desperation and began to think again of her card to Mr Simms; it was her only hope of escape. She waited patiently for the young girl to come with her food and when she arrived, holding a plate in her hands, Barbara shouted down to her.

"Did you post my letter?"

The young girl looked up nervously, her eyes were darkened and heavy-lidded, her tousled blonde hair fell in knotty strands around her neck and her thin, white bra and panties were pulled tightly around her slender frame.

"My letter! Did you post my letter?"

The young girl reached up and pushed the plate between the bars. Barbara grabbed it and, as the girl still clutched it in her thin fingers, Barbara tugged at it as if trying to wake her up.

"Please, please say you posted my letter!"

The young girl looked so tired and confused, she started to speak but gave up then just nodded, looked down anxiously and left.

Barbara held the plate underneath her chin and stuffed the food into her mouth ravenously, dreaming of the post card and her eventual rescue.

15

"Wake up bitch!" yelled Mercedes as she winched Barbara's cage down to the floor.

Barbara rubbed her blackened eyes and squinted nervously from between the heavy, iron bars.

"Come on!"

Mercedes poked a stick at Barbara and stuck it into one of her thighs.

"Wake up! You have a client waiting!"

She poked her again and Barbara jumped back anxious and alarmed.

Mercedes opened the cage door and pulled Barbara out by the arm; Barbara stumbled forward and felt dizzy as Mercedes hauled her out into the corridor. When Barbara stumbled Mercedes jabbed her with the stick and Barbara yelped like a dog as the pointed end of the stick cut into her skin. Mercedes pushed Barbara ahead down some dark, stone steps and when Barbara tripped Mercedes punched her in the back. Barbara was thrown forward and only just managed to save herself by gripping onto a thin, iron handrail.

"Fucking bitch!" shouted Mercedes, as she poked the stick between Barbara's shoulder blades.

The steps opened out into a huge stone dungeon. Barbara shrunk back as she looked around the candle-lit walls but Mercedes punched her in the back again and she was thrown forward onto the ground.

She stared up from the floor and felt panic-stricken. On the dungeon walls hung whips, chains, leather thongs and ropes. There were several iron rings attached to the walls and from some of them heavy chains dangled loosely but two of them were pulled down tightly by the full weight of the young girl who came to feed Barbara. She hung limply in her flimsy white bra and panties, her head on one side, with her wrists held tightly inside two iron rings and her feet dangling loosely.

Barbara looked away shocked and saw a coke brazier with long, hot-tipped irons resting in the white heat at its centre; a galvanised bucket filled with water stood at its side. She turned away from this as well, unable to believe what she was seeing, then, on the far side, she saw a set of stocks with metal clasps and on the other a long wooden rack bolted to the floor with heavy iron staples.

"Here she is Master."

A figure came out of the shadows and walked towards them; it was a tall dark man with large muscular arms. He wore a leather mask which covered his eyes and nose and had a heavy, leather apron pulled tightly around his waist. Except for leather sandals on his feet and some thin, leather thongs hanging loosely around his neck, he was naked and his sweat-covered muscular thighs and buttocks glistened in the light of the brazier as he walked towards them.

His eyes glinted in the light as he nodded to Mercedes. "Leave us."

Mercedes turned and went. Barbara heard her footsteps clipping up the stone stairs and disappearing into the distance. She shivered with fear as she realised she was alone with the masked man and moved back as he stepped towards her but he laughed and grabbed her by the arms. She struggled but he was enormously strong and, as his thick

142

fingers dug painfully into her flesh, she bent over in pain and allowed herself to be held. She cried out as he spun her around and looked at her naked body, then he grabbed her cheeks and squeezed them hard together, pushing her lips out and making her eyes bulge under the pressure.

"Lick your tongue out,"' he ordered.

She tried to poke her tongue out but he was squeezing her cheeks too hard and she could not force its tip past her squashed lips.

"Lick your tongue out!"

She tried again and just managed to get the tip of her tongue to poke out, but it was not enough and he dragged her angrily across to one of the walls. As soon as he released his grip on her cheeks she poked her tongue out as far as she could but he took no notice and threw her roughly against the stone wall. She turned to him and opened her mouth wide forcing her tongue out painfully as far as it would go.

"Too slow!"

He pulled her arms up high and, one by one, clamped her wrists into two manacles that dangled on heavy chains from the wall. Her body was stretched up painfully and her breasts were pulled tight across her heaving chest. She pulled her tongue in as she gasped for breath and bit the end of it as he jerked at the chains to make them tighter.

"A few lashes should make you more responsive!"

He picked up several long chains that were held together at one end with a rope binding. He held them up and dangled them in front of Barbara who was gasping for breath under the strain from the tightly pulled-up manacles. She pulled back in terror as he shook the chains and they fell heavily against her breasts and her hard nipples. The Master grinned, then, in one movement, he lifted the chains behind his shoulder and brought them down hard across her tight-pulled breasts.

Lash!

Barbara gasped in pain and shock. The pain was intense as the links of the chains scoured across the tender flesh of her breasts. The separate chains pulled together as they smacked across her, pinching her nipples and pulling and burning her skin. But almost worse than the stinging pain and pinching of her soft skin was the heavy shock as the weight of the chains knocked the breath from her completely.

For a moment she could not breathe at all. She went rigid with fear and was panic-stricken. Her mouth gaped wide open and her chest heaved heavily but her throat felt gagged and she was unable to suck in any air. She thought she was going to faint, then suddenly, in an explosive gasp, she managed to draw in a lung full of air. She panted loudly as she took another breath and then the pain started again.

Lash!

The shock arrested her breathing again and she fought to stay conscious. The pain was terrible and the chains tore at her nipples, pinching them viciously and pulling and stretching them out like tortured fingers.

Lash!

Again she fought for breath and again her nipples were dragged out by the pinching chains.

Lash!

Again the blow lacerated her skin and she felt the stinging pain running through her like fiery ribbons.

Lash!

She could not take any more; it was unbearable. She wanted to plead for him to stop, she wanted to promise to do anything, she wanted to beg to serve him in any way he chose, but she could not stand any more and she wanted him to stop.

Lash!

She gagged completely and although her chest rose and fell in frantic heaving pulses she could get no air. She held her mouth open in the hope of breathing and flung her head back to try and open her throat but it did not work. The pain ran through her like fire and her body shuddered and convulsed in a paroxysm of suffering and distress. Then at last, just as her bleary eyes filled with redness, her throat opened and she gulped in air, dropping forward, exhausted, terrified and drowning in distress.

The Master stood back and smiled.

"Lick your tongue out bitch!"

Barbara could hardly hear his words but she heard enough to do what he said. She poked her tongue out of her mouth until its base was strained and painful and she held it there, shivering with fear and racked with pain.

The Master took one of the thin leather thongs that hung from his neck and bent its centre into a loop. He reached it towards her tongue, dropped the loop around it and pulled the loose ends around the back of her head where he tied them tightly. She gasped and tried to swallow but the tension from the looped thong held her tongue forward and made it impossible. She tried to pull it back but it was too tightly tied and she started to breathe out in convulsive gasps. Her throat went dry with terror and, as she gagged and choked, sweat broke out across her forehead and her face started stinging with redness.

After a while she found that even though her throat still burned she could breathe without choking but, because she could not swallow, spit dribbled over her wide-stretched lips and ran down her face in sticky streams. With terror-stricken eyes she watched the Master as he bent down and tied her ankles together with a rope; he pulled it tight and a gasp gurgled from her dribbling mouth. He took the other end of the rope and threw it over a hook that was fixed to the ceiling. He tugged at it and pulled her off her feet so that she hung between the rope at her ankles and the manacles that were clamped painfully around her wrists.

The Master pulled hard on the rope and slowly hoisted Barbara's feet high into the air. The pressure on her wrists was immense and she gasped in pain as her full weight fell against them. As her feet were hauled higher, and she began to turn upside down, the strain went onto her ankles and the rope dug into them deeply. He hauled the rope up through the hook until she was hanging fully upside down by the ankles with her arms stretched back down to the manacles on the wall. The manacles cut into her wrists and the rope pulled agonizingly at her ankles as she was stretched between them. When the Master had pulled the rope as tight as he could, he tied it off to a cleat on the wall and went to the brazier in the centre of the room.

Barbara hung stretched out, dizzy and disorientated. Her head was spinning and she felt the blood pounding through her veins and flushing her face hot and red. She started to feel sick and a surge of panic ran through her at the idea of vomiting past the gag on her tongue. Still she could not breathe properly and she gasped in short bursts drawing hot air across her prickly, dry and burning throat then tightening her ribs to force it out again. Gradually, she brought her breathing under the control and the feeling of sickness passed over. As her dizziness faded, she looked across at the young girl and thought she was smiling at her.

The Master pushed the hot irons about in the coke brazier and sparks flew up and drifted into the air on the rising heat. He pulled one of the irons out, turned to see if Barbara was watching, then plunged its glowing tip into the bucket the water. There was an explosion of steam and bubbles as he sank the red hot iron into the water. It crack-

146

led as the heat-filled bubbles broke frantically to the surface and a plume of hot, steamy air wafted across the room and hit Barbara across the breasts and stomach. The steamy heat burned her skin, drying the tip of her tongue and parching her throat even more, but as she tried to turn away she found it impossible to move at all.

"Hot enough for you?"

The Master laughed and pushed the iron back into the brazier and the water that now clung to it sent smoke and sparks flying up in a curl of heat and flame that rose to the ceiling of the dungeon.

"You'll have to wait a while before it's ready again. Perhaps I should give you a little entertainment until then?"

He walked over to the young girl.

"Pretty little thing isn't she?"

He grabbed hold of the waist of her flimsy, white panties and pulled them down to expose her blonde pubic hair.

"Very pretty, I think I need a lick."

He pulled her panties down, entwining them into a braid until they reached her knees. He forced her legs apart, tearing and shredding the panties, and pushed his head between her thighs, reaching his tongue up and running its quivering tip along the soft edges of her outer labia. The girl did not seem to have the strength to resist and just hung on her chains limply with her lips slightly parted and her eyes hardly open.

The Master licked the young girl's cunt, exposing the flat, wet surface of his tongue and drawing it across her wide open crack. Her labia glistened as he slurped his tongue across them and moisture dripped from her tousled pubic hair. He reached down, lifted her limp legs and draped them around his shoulders. He licked her ravenously and as Barbara watched she saw the girl's legs slowly tightening their grip around his muscular neck. The more he licked

147

the more her muscles tightened and the firmer her grip became and when Barbara looked at the young girl's face she saw that her mouth was opening and closing and she was screwing up her eyes.

The Master licked deeply into the fleshy folds, pulling the young girl's bottom higher and running his tongue eagerly up between her wide-stretched buttocks and around her anus. The young girl's face tightened more and Barbara saw her twisting her feet together and pulling herself against the Master's dripping tongue. She reared higher and bore down heavily against his masked face, pushing rhythmically against his tongue and opening herself wider with every thrust. The young girl strained her arms against the shackles around her wrists and twisted and turned as she fought for more licking. She threw her head back and it banged against the hard, stone wall and she threw it back again, banging her head forcibly and gaping her mouth as wide as she could as the pain increased. Barbara listened to the young girl's heavy breaths foaming from her spit-covered mouth and watched her writhing body as it fought painfully for more of the slurping tongue.

The Master drew back and turned to Barbara, his face was dripping with spit and the wetness that was running from the young girl's open cunt. The young girl twisted and turned violently on her chains, thrashing her legs about to try and get a grip of the Master's head and draw him back against her distended cunt.

"Want to see more?"

Barbara stared down at him, unable to respond as she hung upside down, stretched between the tight rope at her ankles and the chains that pulled her manacled wrists down to the wall.

The Master reached up and unlocked the young girl's manacles. She dropped to the floor, still writhing with her legs wide open and her wet pink cunt shining with spit in the flickering light of the dungeon. He grabbed her by the hair and she screeched as he pulled her, with her legs training on the floor, towards the wooden stocks.

Barbara choked as she tried to swallow and again felt a wave of sickness building up inside her. She bit against her protruding tongue to fight it back and as she breathed more easily it passed.

The Master lifted the top of the stocks and bent the young girl down in front of them. She lifted her bottom up high to expose her cunt, still trying to open it for more licking as he forced her neck down into the middle cup of the stocks, then laid her wrists on either side. He dropped the top bar and it crashed down heavily, trapping her wrists and neck and causing her to stretch her legs backwards in fear and shock. He locked the iron clasp at the side and stood back as the young girl struggled frantically to get free.

Barbara started choking again and this time felt a burning wave of sickness running into her throat. She started to panic and tried to pull her tongue free of the leather loop that held it out tightly from her mouth. She held her breath and again managed to fight the sickness back but, as she breathed again, she immediately choked as the cold air gushed in against her dry throat.

Barbara's attention was diverted as the young girl started to scream. She was in a panic as she fought to free herself from the stocks; she twisted her wrists violently and wrenched her arms wildly as she tried to pull her hands through the small carved holes. She threw her head from side to side, forcing her knees against the floor and pulling back against the leverage they provided to try and release herself.

"She has been in the stocks before," said the Master,

leering at Barbara. "She knows what to expect."

The Master grabbed the torn and tangled panties that stretched in thin tatters against the young girl's straining legs and pulled them down over her ankles. She kicked out at him as he tugged them away and he laughed as he went around to the front of the stocks

"Shut up bitch!"

She screamed and spat and he pushed the white panties into her mouth. She spat them out and continued screaming and thrashing her legs. He pushed them back in and with his fingers forced them deep inside. She tried to spit them out again but this time they were too deep, nearly plugging her throat and she could not choke them out. He took one of the leather thongs from his neck and bound it across her mouth and around the back of her head. She choked and coughed to start with but as he bound the thong around again it became too tight for her to do anything but submit.

The Master went over to a selection of whips, chains and canes that stood against the wall and selected a leather flail with a bound leather handle. He lifted it up and its tangle of separate leather thongs dropped out loosely. They were thin and split at the ends and together formed a thick mass but, when he lifted it behind his shoulder and twisted it forward, the separate leather thongs spread out wide. He smacked it down against the side of his black, leather apron and the separate thongs curled around his muscular leg.

The young girl's eyes widened in terror as he approached, still whacking the flail against his shiny, leather apron. He stood behind her and paused for a moment as she tried in vain to turn and see what he was doing, then he lifted the flail behind his shoulder and brought it down fully across her upturned buttocks.

Whack!

The flails smacked down across her bottom and curled around the sides of her hips. Her eyes widened even more and her scream was muffled by the panties stuffed in her mouth as she was knocked forward painfully in the stocks.

Whack!

Another muffled scream burst from her mouth as she bit deeply into the leather thongs. Barbara saw lacerating red stripes already appearing on the young girl's bottom and winced as the Master drew the flail back again.

Whack!

The young girl bit down harder into the leather thong and this time a deep gurgling screech spat from her tight-pulled mouth. Barbara tightened herself against her bonds as the flail was drawn back again but she could not look away.

Whack!

The young girl's bottom was reddened all over, her pale skin hardly visible beneath the red weals that were appearing like angry tears across her flesh.

Whack!

The young girl bit deeply into the thong between her teeth and it broke. She coughed and choked and as the panties burst from the back of her mouth her screech broke through as a frightening howl.

Whack!

She howled again and spit flew from her mouth as she was thrown forward by the pressure of the stinging blow of the flail. It wrapped itself around her hips and cut into the tender skin leaving her reddened and convulsing with pain.

Whack!

She howled continuously, tightening her body in spasms and fighting against the restraining grasp of the heavy stocks. She pulled and wrestled to escape but it was hopeless and the Master brought the flail down repeatedly until finally she went quiet.

The Master left her and came over to Barbara. He looked up at her red, swollen face and laughed, then he undid the manacles at her wrists and she swung forward sickeningly on the ropes at her ankles. The room spun around her and the images of the girl, the Master and the roaring brazier dashed giddily before her eyes. She started to spin and the room flew around her as her hanging body whirled around uncontrollably. Suddenly, the Master grabbed her and the sickening spinning was halted. He went over to the cleat on the wall, released the rope from it and slowly lowered her towards the floor.

Barbara's head was still spinning as she felt her trailing hands touch the cold, stone floor. She pressed her palms against it and took some of the weight from her ankles. She felt relieved as the pressure was eased and a wave of nervousness passed through the side of her stomach as she thought that at last she was gong to be released. The Master lowered her more and her back bent as she curled up against the floor. She reached forward automatically to grasp her ankles and rub them but as she touched them she felt the Master grab them. He lifted her legs and spun her over onto her front then pulled her hands behind her and lashed them to the rope that was holding her ankles. Before she could move or recover he was pulling her back up on the rope, this time she was bent backwards, her legs and wrists pulled together at the rope and her body arched back and hanging fully on the taut rope.

He pulled her up high towards the ceiling then tied the rope into the cleat. She swung giddily, her body arched painfully and stretched forward in a taut bow high above the young girl who was now pulling her head and wrists slowly and hopelessly against the weight of the heavy stocks.

152

16

Barbara's body was stretched so tight she could hardly breathe. Her breasts were pulled taut against her chest and her hips were forced forward as her pulled-back arms and legs took the full weight of her body on the tight-bound ropes that hung from the hook in the ceiling. Again she felt the surge of nausea and her throat burned as she heaved with sickness. She breathed in as deeply as she could and held it in her lungs waiting for the sickness to pass.

The Master reached up as high as he could and drew his hand across her taut stomach, pressing his fingers against her tight flesh and running them around the front of her naked crack. It was pulled so tightly by the curve of her body that her outer labia were forced open at the front and her clitoris stood out red and hard against the tightly-pulled pink edges of her stretched cunt.

"Now you can see what's waiting for you!"

He went over to the brazier and pulled one of the irons from its red hot centre. Sparks flew from its end and curled upwards on the heat and Barbara flinched as she felt the scolding waft pass across her agonized face. Her tongue was still fastened by the loop of leather but it was working loose and she probed it around frantically in the hope of getting it free.

"Watch how your little friend enjoys the feel of the hot iron."

Barbara could not take her eyes away as she dangled above the young girl in the stocks. The Master took the red hot iron and stood behind the young girl, holding it close to her skin and grinning up at Barbara. When she felt the heat, the young girl tried to pull away but she did not seem to have any strength left.

"See how she shrinks back from its scorching tip."

He held it closer and the young girl bent her hips as much as she could to keep herself clear of the searing iron.

"Ah! I think she wants it closer."

He pushed it towards her buttocks and she screamed like a wild animal.

Barbara looked away for a second as the young girl's screeching filled her ears but she could not resist it and had to look back. There was something about the young girl's taut bottom and the imminent pain from the scorching iron that made Barbara want to see it. She felt ashamed of herself but the desire to watch every detail of the girl's torture overwhelmed everything else and she stared down intently. The Master held the hot iron close to the young girl's already reddened flesh and she shrieked in horror as she felt the scorching heat. She threw herself around in jerky spasms, pulling at her neck and wrists in a frantic effort to escape.

Barbara squinted her eyes but kept watching; she wanted to see the red hot iron against the young girl's skin, she wanted to see the Master branding her like an animal and she wanted to hear the young girl's pain as she howled and shrieked and filled the cavernous dungeon with the sound of her suffering.

Barbara hung her head down and pushed her tongue forward and backward in the loop of the thong. It was wet and slippy with her spit and she felt the end of her stretched tongue loosening against the saturated leather. Then it slipped free and let her aching tongue spring back into her mouth, relieving the pain at its base and causing her to dribble spit in long, sticky threads that dangled down to the ground.

"Closer," she implored. "Closer."

The Master looked around, surprised to hear her voice.

"Closer Master, please, closer."

He took the iron back to the brazier and poked it deeply into the red hot coke; a plume of sparks and flame burst up and a wave of heat spread out across the dark ceiling of the dungeon. He went to the cleat in the wall and released the rope, letting it down slowly until Barbara hung closer to the captive young girl.

"Closer Master, please, closer."

He dropped it some more until Barbara's face was hanging against the young girl's bottom. She could smell the sweat that covered the young girl's thighs and she looked closely at it glistening on her skin in small droplets then running down her legs in tiny streams onto the floor.

The Master tied off the cleat then went to get the red hot iron again. He brought it back and held it against the young girl's taut buttocks.

"Watch all you want bitch, it's your turn next!"

The young girl screamed again and Barbara could hear spit gurgling in her throat as she gasped desperately for breath. Barbara stopped straining against the pressure on her arms and legs and let her full weight hang loosely on the rope. She felt her hips drop forward even more as she released some of the tension and she felt the warm air from the hot iron wafting around her skin as it rose in a curling haze from the red hot tip. The angle she hung at increased and forced her cunt forward even more and the shaved mound at the base of her stomach stood out prominently. Her labia were splayed open and her hard, engorged clitoris poked out, throbbing and stiffened at the front of her open crack.

The Master stood behind the screaming young girl and pressed the end of the red hot iron against her left buttock.

155

The young girl stiffened in terror and pain as her skin sizzled beneath the searing branding iron. Barbara felt her cunt tighten and her labia pull back against the entrance to her vagina as she watched the young girl's flesh burn against the pressure of the fiery brand.

Then the Master walked around to the front of the stocks and stood in front of the screaming young girl. He lifted his leather apron and draped it across the back of her head and her screams were stifled as he forced his hard cock into her mouth. She choked to start with as she continued to try and scream but he pushed his cock in hard and deep and in the end her mouth closed around it and she began to suck.

Barbara dropped her head down as far as she could and her face slid between the young girl's wet buttocks. Barbara could smell the young girl's cunt as it glistened and ran with moisture and she could feel the heat coming from her branded flesh. Barbara strained as hard as she could and pushed her nose in between the young girl's silky, soft labia. The wet petals folded around Barbara's nostrils and she breathed in deeply, inhaling the scent and feeling the wetness drawing into her nostrils. Barbara's face was reddened by the strain and her blood pulsed through her veins as she licked her tongue out and lapped the back edge of the young girl's crack. She breathed in deeply, filling her nostrils with the sweet scent and feeling her own stretched cunt flooding with wetness.

Then she felt the heat of the iron as the Master stretched his hand across the top of the stocks and held it above the young girl's right buttock. Its heat scorched the side of Barbara's face and she felt her hair singing. She pushed down further and licked the young girl's cunt, lapping her tongue flatly against its edges and dribbling spit across the open flesh. She licked along its length and ran her tongue against the young girl's tight anus. Barbara felt her own cunt dribbling as she tasted the edges of the dark, muscular ring and she pushed her tongue forward to insert it into the young girl's arse. She forced it into the hard ring of muscle and it tightened around the tip of her tongue like the leather noose. She pushed it further and her tongue went in, probing forward painfully and seeking out the depths of the young girl's innards.

"Suck my cock bitch! I want to finish in your sucking mouth while I brand you again. Suck it hard and deep and when you feel it coming you will know that the hot iron will be against you tender skin. Feel the heat again bitch! Suck it hard."

Barbara felt the young girl's body tense as a sense of fear spread through her but she also felt her sucking harder at the Master's cock in an effort to bring the pain on even quicker. Barbara pushed her tongue deeply inside the young girl's arse and felt the edges of her innards squeezing tightly against her straining tongue. She could feel the young girl's efforts to suck the Master to a finish and she probed deeper to accelerate the pace. She imagined the Master's cock pressing against the back of the young girl's throat and she imagined the dreadful desire to be filled with spunk and branded at the same time.

Then she felt the red hot iron coming closer and she pushed her tongue in as deeply as she could. She held it there and felt the young girl's body tightening as she felt the flow of semen coming into her mouth. Barbara strained her tongue in even more and the tip was squeezed by the young girl's convulsing innards as the hot branding iron smacked down onto her right buttock. The young girl went completely stiff as she sucked the Master's semen down her throat and pushed up against the scorching pain of the hot iron. Barbara's tongue was squeezed tightly and she felt her own body pulling back against its bonds as a scorching orgasm flowed through her painful limbs. It started in her tongue and spread down her throat, it heated her stomach and stung her exposed cunt then it ran out all over the surface of her body and tightened her fingers and toes as if she had been electrocuted.

Then the young girl started to scream again as she choked the Master's still throbbing cock from her mouth and tightened her body again in an anguished paroxysm. Barbara pulled her tongue out and swung aside on the rope, her face covered in wetness and her tongue hanging out of her mouth and dribbling a stream of spit down to the floor. She watched as the young girl slowly relaxed and finally lay in the stocks, exhausted by her efforts and depleted by her pain and suffering.

The Master pulled the apron away from her head and the young girl's hair fell in wet curls and trailed against the floor. The Master pulled his hand along the stiff shaft of his cock and Barbara watched as a final spurt of spunk shot from its throbbing and engorged tip.

"Please Master, me as well," she murmured.

The Master released the young girl from the stocks. She collapsed on her side then, panting and choking, she crawled to a wall and curled up with her arms around her shins. He let Barbara down and she rolled on her side to make it easier for him untie the knots from her wrists and ankles. To start with, she could not move at all and lay with her arms and legs pulled back and her shaved mound sticking forward as before but slowly she stretched forward and pushed out her fingers and toes to help her muscles relax. The Master grabbed Barbara by the hair and lifted her up. He pulled her, turned her forward roughly then bent her down across the stocks, dropping the upper bar across her neck and wrists and trapping her tightly.

As he branded her for the first time she felt herself going unconscious and by the time the second one came, and she was sucking his cock deeply into her throat, she passed out. She was only vaguely aware of his spunk spurting down her throat and could barely sense the paralysing orgasm that flooded though her at the same time as the pain from the hot iron scorched across her skin.

She looked up at him, semen dripping from her lips as she was released from the stocks and dragged over to the rack. He tied her on her back, stretching her arms out and tying her wrists to the two ropes that led from the drum at the one end and her ankles to the ropes that were fixed at the other. He turned the drum and pulled the ropes as tight as they would go. She opened her wet mouth wide but could not say anything; she could no longer scream or howl, she did not have the strength, but even if she had she would have kept silent. She felt the pain running through her in waves and it filled her thoughts; it was as though there was nothing else in the world to think about. Suddenly, as if overcome by an uncontrollable panic, she started to screech, then the scorching of the hot iron came back and the pain on her buttocks burned through her like a knife, cutting her from inside and searing through her veins.

She kept screaming as the Master thrashed her with the heavy, leather flail. He brought it down brutally across her breasts and stomach and the lacerating thongs cut across her nipples and stung the swollen edges of her labia. He beat her until her skin was covered in red weals and when he threw the flail down and left her she was still screaming and jerking uncontrollably in repeated seizures of agony.

Barbara convulsed and twitched as spasms flowed through her like electric shocks then slowly she relaxed and dropped back. She managed to twist herself slightly as she lay stretched out on the rack trying to take her mind off the pain. She thought of her card to Mr Simms and how she had imagined he would come and rescue her, but somehow it seemed a vague hope now. It had been ages since the poor young girl had taken the card away and Barbara could only think it must have got lost or Mr Simms had ignored her plea for help. Her feeling of hopelessness allowed the pain back and she moaned loudly as she lay stretched out in the dark, cold dungeon.

17

Barbara did not remember being taken from the rack - the next thing she knew she was lying on the floor of her cage as it swung giddily from the ceiling of the large room. She lay there all day and in the evening, when the young girl usually arrived with some food, no one came.

That night, she slept lightly but kept waking with a start and gasping for breath as she remembered where she was and what was happening to her. Every time she awoke she felt the pains in her wrists and ankles where she had hung from the rope in the ceiling of the dungeon, and the aches in her arms and legs where she had been stretched on the rack. But when she stretched to try and ease the pain she was stung by the searing burn of the brand across her buttocks that she had begged so eagerly for the Master to inflict. As she turned and stretched in the cage she looked down and watched the wolf padding around his cage, dribbling from his hungry mouth and howling into the night.

As the night went on, she slept fitfully and dreamed of being fucked and whipped and as she rolled over anxiously the pain of the brands on her buttocks woke her again and she listened to the rhythmic prowling of the dribbling wolf.

She jumped up startled as Mercedes came in and

winched the cage down to the floor.

"You look a mess, girl! Get out!"

Barbara dragged herself out of the cage and stood with her head hung in front of Mercedes.

"Bend over, right over, hold your ankles tight. I think you need a beating to wake you up!"

Barbara slowly turned and bent over. Her buttocks were still painful and as they tightened the pain of the branding stung her deeply. She winced and stopped bending but Mercedes punched her in the back and she bent fully, clasped her hands around her ankles and held onto them obediently.

Then there was a noise at the door and two men burst in. Mercedes swung around as Carlo ran over while Ramon stood at the door looking back up the dark corridor.

"Who the fuck are you?" shouted Mercedes.

"Old friends of your little slave! She's caused us a lot of trouble and now we're going to get some value out of her!"

Barbara turned around shocked. Her first thought was that she was being rescued and she felt a wave of relief, but when she saw the look of menace in Carlo's eyes she was overtaken by a flood of fear and apprehension.

Carlo reached forward and made a grab for Barbara but Mercedes stood in front of her and spread out her arms to stop him. Carlo punched her in the face and she fell backwards clasping her hands across her nose.

"Ringmaster! Ringmaster!"

Carlo kicked Mercedes in the side and she rolled over in agony as blood streamed from her nose and ran between her fingers.

"Grab the bitch!" shouted Ramon from the doorway. "Quick, let's get out of here!"

Ramon pulled Barbara against him, pushed her hands behind her back and tied them with a short rope. She hardly realised what was going on and her eyes blinked anxiously as he pulled a wide band of sticky tape across her mouth. He looked around for something to put around her and found the cotton smock she had been made to wear when she was first kidnapped by the Ringmaster. He pulled it over her head and it bound her already tied arms tightly against her back.

"Come on!"

Ramon grabbed Barbara's arms through the thin material of the smock and pulled her out into the corridor. Carlo led the way out into the street where they pushed her roughly into the back of a waiting car and drove away along the side of a broad canal.

Ramon forced Barbara onto the floor of the car and pressed his feet against her back to keep her from getting up. She could not see anything and stared fearfully into the dirty carpet as he pushed his feet down harder and wedged her painfully against the runners of the front seats.

When the car stopped they dragged her down a narrow alley and in through the door of a gaudy sex-shop. She glimpsed some pictures of women being spanked and whipped as she was thrown into back room and locked inside.

Barbara lay face-down on the floor of the small room breathing heavily through her nostrils. She pulled at her arms but her wrists were too tightly bound to get free and the cotton smock pulled her elbows so tightly against her back that she could hardly move them at all. She struggled onto her side and looked around; the room was filled with a huge variety of black leather clothing most of it studded with silver rivets or held together with silver-buckled belts. There was a stack of whips of different sizes and lengths in the one corner and gags with leather balls and a pile of studded, leather masks laid out on a small table.

Then the door opened and Ramon came in.

"Like your new home? Now you're going to repay us for our lost jobs. I hope you're up to it!"

He dragged her to her feet and pulled the cotton smock roughly over her head. Her hair fell in tangled strands around her taped-up mouth and she shrunk back against the stack of whips.

"I've been waiting to give you your punishment for some time!"

He grabbed the side of the tape over her mouth and ripped it away, leaving a broad, red mark across her cheeks and chin.

"Please, I didn't mean you to lose your job. Please let me go, I can't take any more. Please ..."

"Shut up or I'll stuff your mouth with this!"

He held up a wide leather gag with a leather ball covered in shiny, silver studs attached at its centre. The idea of having her mouth plugged again filled her with fear and she pushed herself back against the wall, banging into the stack of whips and knocking them sideways onto the floor.

"Clumsy little bitch aren't you? That's going to mean a few extra strokes!"

"Please, please ..."

"Shut your mouth and bend over!"

Barbara turned and bent down obediently.

"Hold onto your ankles. This is going to hurt but every time you scream I will give you more. Do you hear?"

"Yes, yes, I hear."

"Now, what shall I use?"

He picked through the stack of whips that had fallen onto the floor and selected a short leather strap. It had a thick, braided handle and the other end broadened out and finished in a flat spread of thin strips. He smacked it against the side of his leg and Barbara flinched as a surge of air blew from it and wafted against her tight-stretched thighs.

"Are you ready bitch?"

Barbara tensed her muscles and clasped her hands as tightly as she could around her ankles.

"I said are you ready?"

"Yes," she said quietly.

"Good, this is the first and I want to know what it feels like!"

Whack!

The whip came down hard against the taut skin of her upturned bottom. She was thrown forward and threw her hands out to stop herself falling over.

"Hold your ankles, no one told you to let them go!"

She gripped her ankles again and another blow of the whip smacked across her bottom.

Whack!

She was knocked forward again and she felt her legs bending under the force, but this time she kept hold of her ankles as the pain scorched across her skin and she tightened her buttocks as much as she could.

"Now, what did that feel like?"

Barbara did not know what to say. She opened her mouth to speak but before she could say anything another stinging blow smacked down.

Whack!

"I said what did it feel like bitch!"

"It hurts, it hurts terribly! Please ..."

"Good!"

Whack!

Barbara grabbed her ankles tightly and felt her nails digging into the skin at the base of her calves.

"What did that one feel like?"

"Terrible, oh terrible, it hurts so much."

Whack!

"The pain is awful, I can't stand it any more, please stop, please ..."

Whack! Whack! Whack!

"Please, it's too much to stand, please ..."

Whack! Whack! Whack!

He continued the beating until her words became fainter and fainter. She clung onto her ankles until in the end she could hold on no longer and fell forward against the wall.

"Up!"

Barbara tried to get up but she fell again, rolling sideways and lying on her back with one of her legs up against the wall.

Ramon threw the whip down and grabbed some ropes from the table. He pushed Barbara's legs up high until her knees pressed hard against her breasts. While she struggled, he wound the ropes around the tops of her calves and pulled them as tight as he could. He pulled them around her upper arms, drawing her legs up high until her knees pressed against her flattened breasts and her hands hung outside her wide-stretched thighs. Finally, he wound ropes around her wrists and bound them tightly to her thighs.

Barbara lay on her back gasping for breath. Her cunt was splayed out wide and its soft edges were stretched by the tension of her buttocks.

"Perhaps you will like it better like this!"

Ramon pulled a broad leather paddle from the stack of whips and laid it against Barbara's exposed cunt; the leather flattened against her soft flesh and she felt a chilling thrill of coldness spreading across her distended outer labia.

Ramon drew the paddle back, held it for a moment while he looked closely at Barbara's cunt then brought it down hard.

Smack!

Barbara gasped as the leather paddle smacked across

her naked cunt. It stung her labia and the skin of her stretched buttocks and the pain shot up through her body in a massive, shocking surge.

"How do you like that bitch?"

"It hurts, please ..."

Smack!

Another hard blow smacked down across her naked flesh and she tried to tighten her muscles but it was impossible; she was tied so tightly that she could not move or do anything to reduce the pain.

"It hurts! It hurts!"

Smack!

This time she felt the leather paddle fully against her outer labia and knew that they were swelling. She could feel them opening involuntarily and presenting themselves to the painful smack of the smooth leather.

"It hurts!"

Smack!

The heavy contact was even fuller now. She felt a wetness as the leather stuck momentarily to the peeled back edges of her cunt and, as the pain went across her flesh, she drew it in and it flooded up her vagina. Her clitoris stuck out hard and engorged and its tip was caught by the flat surface but it only served to make it swell more.

Smack!

The flat leather adhered to her swollen labia for longer this time; it smacked against them and stuck wetly as they folded back more to receive it. Barbara felt her cunt opening and welcoming the pain in her soft flesh and the stinging pain in her clitoris turned immediately into an intense wave of desire. As the leather peeled away she felt her inner labia pulled as well and the flesh of her vagina tightened as the soft edges of her cunt lifted and clung to the smooth surface of the paddle.

Smack!

Her cunt was fully open now and the paddle smacked noisily against the wetness of her distended flesh. Her clitoris was fully stretched and met the smacking leather with its hardness, absorbing the shock and converting it into overwhelming sensations of heat and wantonness. She felt the impact run up inside her vagina as the leather stuck to her dribbling wetness and she wanted it filled. She tried to speak but another smack landed against her naked, open cunt before she could say anything.

Smack!

She wanted him to ask her how it felt; she wanted him to force her to tell him what she was feeling.

"How does it feel bitch?"

"More!"

Smack!

She pulled her arms back to expose herself even more and, as the ropes eased against her wrists and calves, a sudden disappointment spread through her as she felt them relax.

"More! More! And tie me tighter. Tighter!"

Ramon bent down and pulled the ropes tighter. Barbara gasped as he bent the fronts of her thighs tight against her sides and pulled the ropes at her wrists as tight as he could. She pulled against them and they did not give at all and when she tried to pull her legs higher they would not move. She felt wetness dribbling down the crack of her buttocks and running into the dilating ring of her anus.

"More, harder, harder!"

Smack!

The paddle came down again and smacked wetly against her fully open cunt. She felt the pressure of air forcing up into her vagina and she opened herself more as it ran along the insides of her flesh like a fierce gust of wind.

"More! More! More!"

Smack! Smack! Snack!

Every time the paddle smacked against her open cunt it forced a hard draft of air inside her and her vagina stretched under the pressure; it was like a strange cock, forcing at her innards and pulling at her reddened flesh.

"More! I need more! Smack me harder!"

Smack! Smack! Smack!

The surges of air were causing her to writhe and strain as she lay on her back, open and exposed and absorbing every scorching pang of the terrible beating. Then she sensed the heat of orgasm radiating from her hard clitoris, spreading across her open cunt and flooding into her vagina.

"I need fucking! I need fucking! Quick! Quick!"

Smack! Smack! Smack!

The leather paddle thrashed her remorselessly and the heat in her vagina was suddenly released in a rushing flow of fire as it spread throughout her whole body. She stretched her legs open as much as she could and her neck went red as the heat travelled through her. She held her breath and bit down onto her lips as her face reddened and her eyes widened in desperation for it to end, then it exploded inside her and she threw herself back in a taut convulsion as the orgasm broke like a mighty wave. She screamed until it passed and then lay, dribbling from her open crack as Ramon continued to beat her as hard as he could across her reddened buttocks and distended, swollen cunt.

When he finished beating her he fucked her where she was. He pushed his large, stiff cock deeply inside her and thrust her roughly as she lay gasping on the floor. When he was ready to finish he pulled his throbbing cock out and pulled his hands hard along the shaft, spurting his spunk all over her cunt, her breasts and into her face. She felt it dribbling around the edges of her mouth and licked her tongue out to taste it, probing the tip of her tongue around until she found enough to lick up then swallowing it greedily.

"More," she said quietly. "More!"

He lowered his cock into her mouth and she drew it down until his balls hung against her chin and the still-pulsating glans was deeply into her throat. She gagged but stopped herself from choking and, as her throat closed tightly around his cock, he finished again and she let it spurt down into her throat without breathing or swallowing onto it.

18

The next thing Barbara knew she was being dragged along a corridor by Carlo and Ramon; she was naked and her knees scuffed along the ground as they pulled her roughly between the narrow walls.

"You're going to work for us now bitch! And remember, do what you're told or we'll beat you and toss you out into the street to starve!"

They pulled her out into a narrow alley then in through a door and down some steep steps into a large, brightly lit basement gymnasium. In the centre was a boxing ring built onto a wooden rostrum; it had a grey canvas floor encircled with heavy, red ropes and thick leather bolsters at its corners. Two muscular black men sparred with each other at its centre, their padded, leather sparring helmets dodging and diving in the bright lights that shone from above. One of them was wearing silky blue shorts with a white line down the sides and the other wore soft, grey tracksuit trousers that were darkened with sweat at the crotch and between his muscular buttocks.

Ramon shouted to them and they stopped and came to the side of the ring. The one in red shorts hung his huge arms lazily over the top red rope.

"How much and how long?"

Ramon let go of Barbara's arm and went up to the black boxer. He climbed up on the side of the ring, exchanged a few words then shouted down to Carlo.

"Let the bitch go Carlo, she's here for the day."

He turned back to the boxer, shook hands then jumped down and went over to Barbara.

"Listen up, girl! We get our money when we come and collect you. You do a bad job and we get nothing. You'd better not let us down or it'll be the worse for you. Understand?"

Carlo squeezed her arm tightly then let it go and they both left.

The boxer with the grey tracksuit trousers climbed out of the ring, pulled his gloves off, then with his massive taped-up hands picked up a rope and started skipping rapidly. Barbara looked at his muscular chest and watched the sweat running down its centre as he breathed noisily through his widely flaring nostrils. The boxer in the red shorts ducked lazily between the red ropes and came over to Barbara. His muscles rippled as he walked towards her, pulling at the ties to his gloves with his teeth then throwing them down on the ground.

Sweat dripped from his nose as he reached forward and grabbed her arm. She cried out as his huge fingers circled it completely and when he pulled her she fell forward as though she weighed nothing at all. She could not believe how strong he was as he lifted her up the side of the ring and tossed her over the ropes onto the grey, canvas floor.

She rolled over several times and hit one of the leather covered corner posts. She dragged herself up and shrunk back against it as he stepped towards her and lifted her up again. She felt like a toy as he bent her over one of the top red ropes with no effort at all and she thought she was going to tip straight over the side. She gasped in fear as she saw the ground coming closer but he grabbed the back of her cotton smock and held her fast, preventing her from falling but keeping her dangling dizzily over the side. Her head hung down towards the outside edge of the ring and her feet were off the ground as all her weight hung painfully across the hard rope which dug deeply into the front of her hips.

"Please, please let me go, please ..."

The boxer laughed as he started to wind sticky binding tape around one of her ankles. She struggled but he was much too strong, and she feared falling headfirst out of the ring as she bounced sickeningly on top of the rope, so she stopped. He wound the tape many times around her ankle until she could feel her foot tingling as the circulation was cut off. He pulled her legs wide and placed the taped-up ankle against the bottom rope. She tipped forward slightly and gulped with fear as he bound the tape around the rope, pinioning her ankle tightly against it. He did the same with her other ankle, binding it first then stretching it out wide and taping it tightly to the rope.

She felt so terribly exposed as she lay tied out against the rope and tried to pull herself back but the rope swung underneath her and she felt herself tipping giddily forward again. The boxer reached down and grabbed one of her wrists, pulling it hard and sending a sharp pain through the point of her shoulder. He taped this as well and pulled it down to the bottom rope, winding more tape around it to secure it at the centre of her wide-stretched ankles, then he grabbed the other wrist and did the same. The pain on her hips was almost unbearable and she breathed heavily as the blood ran to her head and pounded in her throbbing temples.

The boxer who was skipping stopped and jogged towards the ring, picking up another rope as he approached. He pulled against the ropes that Barbara was taped to and they sprung back violently. She felt as if she was being catapulted out of the ring as the ropes strained against the leather-covered corner posts, springing back and forth and sending agonizing pains through her hips. Then he jumped up into the ring and sprung onto the heavy, canvas floor and Barbara felt the shock of the heavy crash as his muscular frame landed on the taut material.

"Nice arse."

He dropped one of the ropes to the ground then folded the other one in half and stretched it tightly across her buttocks, pressing it against her flesh and making two long creases across her pale skin.

"Yeh, well branded too, but it needs a few red stripes before anything else."

He pressed it harder against the tight hollows between the tops of her thighs and her buttocks. The rope squeezed against her exposed cunt and, as the two halves twisted together, they pinched the tender skin of her outer labia. Barbara cried out but both the boxers ignored her and the one with the rope pressed it harder, twisting it eagerly and causing her to scream again.

She felt the folded rope binding tightly and pinching the flesh of her outer labia between its braided surface and as he twisted it more she felt her flesh stretching and her inner folds being exposed. Finally, he let it go and she sensed her pulled flesh relaxing but still lying slightly open and swollen around the edges of her cunt.

He dropped the loop of the rope down around her neck and pulled it back tightly. She gasped as it tugged against her throat and pulled her pounding head backwards sharply. He took the two halves across her back and pulled them into the crease of her buttocks and she strained back in an effort to breathe as he parted the ropes either side of her swollen cunt and drew them down as far as he could.

Barbara gasped loudly as she struggled to breathe and reached her head back until her shoulders stiffened in cramping pain. The edges of her cunt were outlined by the tightly pulled ropes and, as he drew them down even tighter, they squeezed her labia wide and exposed the dark pink entrance of her moist vagina. She managed to get a breath, holding it then allowing her head to drop against the strain from her shoulders, before she reared up again and gasped for another. She rose and fell rhythmically, gaping her mouth as she took in air then closing it firmly and holding it in while she fell forward against the strain from her shoulders.

The boxer knelt down and knotted the two ends of the rope together, then, as Barbara stared between her legs, holding her breath until she could find the energy to reach back for another, he offered the knot to her mouth. She shook her head and reared back, gasping heavily before dropping forward again. He offered the large knot again but still she shook her head and pulled back frantically for more air.

He reached forward, grabbed her hair and held her head between her legs. Her pounding head started to spin and she struggled vainly to get back up for another breath. He offered the knot again and she shook her head in an anguished and desperate frenzy; she needed to breathe and pulled unsuccessfully against his grasp. The pain in her chest was overwhelming her as he offered the knot again. There was nothing else she could do, he was so strong, and this time she took it between her teeth. He let go of her hair and she threw her head back and gasped, still gripping the large knot between her clenched teeth.

As she reared back with the knot in her mouth she felt a cutting tension of the ropes around her cunt. They dug into her flesh deeply and her swollen labia were squeezed out until their inside edges were rolled back against the pulling ropes. She dropped back down and bit hard onto the knot then, when she pulled herself back again, the tension against her cunt was even greater. She did not dare let go of the knot, she did not want to, and she drew in a deep breath and dropped her head, this time reliving the feeling of the tension of the ropes until the next time she had to rear back for air.

The boxer with the red shorts picked up the other rope, hung it across his massive hand and found the centre. The two ends dropped down to the floor and, snapping his wrist, he pulled them back, curling them and making them crack.

"Ready bitch?"

Barbara threw herself back again, gasping for breath and squeezing her buttocks together against the tightening strain of the ropes that splayed her cunt out wide.

Thwack!

The folded rope came down across her bottom with enormous force. She shrieked and the knot in her mouth burst out and fell loosely between her legs. The other man grabbed her hair and held her head down until finally, exhausted and out of breath, she stopped screaming and opened her mouth to take the knot.

Thwack!

She reared backwards with the knot in her mouth as the heavy blow cut into her taut buttocks. She gasped for breath and when she felt the air rushing into her lungs she also felt the searing pain of the rope between her upturned buttocks and the squeezed-out flesh of her swollen cunt. She bit hard into the knot, dropped forward and tensed herself.

Thwack!

As soon as it landed she threw herself backwards, gasping for air and screaming with pain at the same time. She gripped the knot tightly between her teeth and spit ran over her stretched lips as she dropped back down against the tension.

The boxer with the rope turned sideways to Barbara and brought the ropes down between her legs.

Thwack!

It cut across her exposed cunt and its flailing ends curled forward against her stomach and breasts.

Thwack!

She tried to scream but she was biting too hard against the knot and she could not think of anything else but getting another breath. She reared back and gulped for air and as soon as her lungs were filled she felt the searing pain across the soft flesh of her cunt and the stinging across her stomach and breasts.

Thwack!

This time the ropes came down even harder and their ends reached almost to Barbara's throat. Unable to suppress her agony she spit the knot from her mouth and screamed like an animal until she ran out of breath again and tried to throw her head backwards for more air. But the other boxer was holding her hair and he would not release her until she took the knot again. She bit onto it in panic and drew back, gasping and panting and shaking with fear.

The boxer with the rope kept flailing her across her cunt as, every time she pulled herself back frantically for air, it was squeezed increasingly between the ropes that were pulled so tightly against its edges.

Thwack! Thwack! Thwack!

Finally, the beating stopped and she dropped the knot

from her aching mouth; it swung freely between her legs and its tension around her cunt was eased. She strained back and gasped for breath then slowly let herself down and breathed freely.

The boxer with the shorts undid the tape from around her right ankle and then from her right wrist. She lunged forward as a sense of freedom flooded through her but straight away he grabbed her and twisted her around, pulling her back against the leather cover on the corner post. He pulled her legs and arms as wide as they would go and bound her back tightly to the red ropes on the opposite side. The tapes that he had left done up were twisted around her wrists and ankle and she felt the blood pounding in them painfully as she hung limply on the ropes, exhausted and filled with fear.

The boxer with the red shorts grabbed the front of her cotton smock and ripped it apart from the neck down to the hem. It hung in tatters from her outstretched shoulders and fell in loose folds over the tops of her outstretched thighs. He grabbed the material at the shoulders and tore it until the smock fell to the floor in a heap.

Barbara hung, completely naked and stretched out wide on the red ropes. She looked down and saw the red stripes that the rope had made across her stomach and breasts and she saw the swollen edges of her cunt that had been pulled so wide by the tightening rope that had led from her straining neck.

The boxer with the shorts stood between her legs and slowly pulled his shorts down, stepping out of them with his glistening, muscular legs and exposing his huge black cock as it strained out from his groin, hard and stiff and pulsating along its veiny length. He clasped his large hands around it and drew them up the massive shaft, pulling the skin along it until it folded up against the wide flanges of his throbbing glans. He held it there for a moment, then he pulled back down towards his balls and the throbbing tip expanded even more.

He stepped towards Barbara and placed the hot end of his cock against her widespread cunt. The heat from it was intense and she tried to pull back as she felt a scorching shock penetrate to entrance to her vagina. He pressed it harder and the swollen outer labia folded around the throbbing black tip. She bent her head down and watched it slowly going inside, feeling her inner labia parting and the entrance to her vagina opening to take it as the glans slid in. She felt the wide flanges at its back edge and the tight-drawn skin which was below it before she felt the hard veins that pulsated along its full length. She saw it disappearing until she felt his heavy balls fall against her arse. Her eyes widened as she felt the throbbing glans expanding as it pushed as far as it could and she opened her mouth and dribbled over her bottom lip as she felt his weighty balls resting against her dilating anus.

He drew back and she felt the veins tugging at the soft flesh of her vagina and throbbing against her clitoris as it engorged and hardened and reached out for contact with his huge cock. As the glans came to the outside edges of her vagina she squirmed her hips forward to keep it in and when it pushed back she pushed against it in the hope of getting more.

Again it drew back and again it went in, slowly at first but each time quickening. Barbara stared into his black, sweating face and licked her tongue out, hoping her would drip some of his spit onto it or hold it between his teeth and pull it and bite it. He quickened the pace even more and soon he was fucking her in fast, muscular thrusts. With each heavy thrust he pushed it deeper and then she felt the coursing of semen running along the pulsating underside of his mighty cock. It ran up until the end expanded for one last time as it released a long, hot stream of spunk into the depths of her eager cunt.

He kept it up there while his cock throbbed and shot his hot spunk as deeply inside her as it would go and as she felt the hot liquid spurting inside her she felt it igniting her own scorching fire. The heat from his spunk kept splashing against her flesh and set off burning flames of desire raging through her body. Every time his cock throbbed to eject some more her own body drew it in and took its heat. She felt her scalding passion spreading up inside her until it reached her throat, then it exploded and surged along her arms to her throbbing hands and along her outstretched legs to her tight-bound feet. She tightened all over as yet another surge of spunk shot into her and the heat consumed her and she pulled up on her bonds and felt the surging rush of orgasm coursing through every part of her body. She screamed and howled as it ran through her in waves, burning her and setting fire to her flesh and choking her with its intensity.

She did not feel him pull it out but she felt the next one going in. It slid into her vagina on the dribbling spunk that filled her and its hot shaft thrust straight up to its base. Still she held herself out tightly against her bonds but she pushed her hips against the veiny cock and sucked it in frenziedly. Her orgasm was still running through her and the thrusting cock kept it going as she grunted and growled with the strain of sucking it inside.

When she felt its end expanding and his spunk running up the thickening shaft, she was still finishing. Her face burned hotly and she tensed her neck as a final convulsive wave of orgasm spread over her. It built to a peak just as his semen burst from the end of his throbbing cock and she yelled and howled as she dropped forward in complete exhaustion.

They left her there for a while, but before Ramon came back for his money they had untied her and fucked her again, this time both at the same time with one in her arse and the other deeply inside her eager cunt. Ramon could not get her to stand up to start with and he threw a bucket of cold water over her to wake her up. She opened her eyes but could not move and just lay against the leather covered corner post of the ring with her legs outstretched, water running from her straggly hair and dripping across her face and down onto her breasts and stomach.

19

Barbara was only vaguely aware of being taken out and hauled through a back alley by Ramon and Carlo.

They dragged her into a large room with black drapes around the walls and a glass cubicle in the centre containing a shiny, metal chair. They pushed her inside the cubicle and she stood by the chair, naked and looking worn-out and fearful. They went and she sat on the chair; it was cold and she wriggled her bare bottom against the metal-strapped top. She did not know what to expect and sat back nervously, occasionally biting her nails or pulling at strands of her hair. A wave of fear streamed through her as she began to think about what was happening to her. She thought of the things that had been done to her and she flushed with shame as images of her humiliations came flooding into her mind.

A man came in and stood by the cubicle and she looked away as he stared at her, then another man pushed his way past the black drapes and he was followed by two more.

They all gathered around, pointing at her and glaring at her naked body.

Barbara felt desperately humiliated and shamed as they stared at her as she sat, trapped and terrified in the glass cubicle. When she looked to the side to avoid their gaze she saw Ramon holding back the drapes.

"Do what's asked of you or you know what to expect. And open your legs, give them something to look at!"

She turned back towards the men and slowly opened her legs.

"Feel your cunt, bitch!" one shouted through the thin glass.

"Yes, let's have a look at that lovely cunt!"

Barbara widened her legs and stretched them forward, then, obediently, she moved her hands down to the base of her stomach and settled her finger tips against the soft edges of her outer labia.

"Come on, let's see what you can do!"

She prised the soft petals of her cunt apart and exposed the moisture-covered inner leaves. They parted under only slight pressure and her clitoris stood out, engorged and red at the front of her beautiful crack. She pressed the tips of her fingers against its base and felt a surge of tingling pleasure surging through her cunt. She pressed it again and felt it swelling and hardening even more as her head filled with images of punishment and perversion.

She stared back at the men as they looked at her cunt but she was not thinking of them or the humiliation of sitting in the booth; she was thinking only of the ways she had been whipped and fucked and how she had been made to scream in agony until it had turned into screeches of overwhelming pleasure. She thought of her orgasms and the way she had stretched out against her bonds and she remembered how she had fought for breath with her mouth plugged and her throat strangled.

"What are you thinking of bitch! Tell us!"

Barbara pressed harder at the base of her clitoris and squeezed it until it tingled in delightful pain. It rose up between her fingers and she felt it throbbing as it continued to swell and stiffen. She opened the soft edges of her cunt even more and showed the men the wet inner leaves. She felt their stares penetrating her and she tugged at the soft folds of flesh until she exposed the dark entrance to her vagina; she wanted them to get closer and stare right up inside her and she wanted them to press their eyes against her cunt and look closely at the droplets of moisture that stuck to her wet flesh.

She dropped her mouth open and stiffened her arms, taking her fingers from her cunt and pressing the insides of her thighs as far apart as she could. She tensed her legs to return the pressure from her hands and felt the muscles of her buttocks pressing her hips forward and exposing her open cunt even more.

"Come on bitch, what are you thinking about?"

She dropped her jaw more and pressed it down towards her chest. She strained her neck to feel the tension in her shoulders and she licked her tongue out as if trying to reach the wetness of her crack. She felt her body heating all over and she put her fingers back against the base of her hotly throbbing clitoris.

"Spanking," she said quietly.

"Tell us more."

"Spanking, that's what I'm thinking about."

"What about spanking? Do you want spanking?"

"Yes, terribly."

"How hard?"

"As hard as you can do it."

"Why do you need spanking so hard?"

"Because I have done so many awful things, so many terrible things."

She pulled at her clitoris and pushed her legs stiffly out in front of her, lifting her bottom off the metal seat of the chair and straining painfully against its sharp back.

"What have you done?"

"Will you spank me if I tell you? Please will you spank me if I tell you?"

"If it's that naughty yes."

"It is, it is, please you must spank me, you must."

"Tell us what you've done."

"I have fucked two men at the same time, one in my cunt and one in my arse. I have been tied down and raped and I enjoyed it, I have been whipped and flailed and I finished while I was being beaten. I have been fucked by a woman using a leather cock and I have fucked her as well and I have sucked a ... Please, is that enough? Will you spank me for that?"

One of the men opened the door to the glass cubicle and went inside.

"Bend over then!"

Barbara stood up and, still with her fingers clawing at her throbbing clitoris, she bent over the back of the steel chair. The hard frame pressed against the backs of her wrists as she leaned down on them, still stretching her hands between her legs and pressing around her clitoris. Her forehead touched the seat of the chair and her dark hair fell across its metal seat as she lifted her bottom as high as she could.

"Spank me as hard as you can."

He lifted his hand and brought it down onto her bare bottom.

Spank!

She gripped her fingers onto her still-swelling clitoris

182

and pulled at it eagerly.

"Harder!"

Spank!

The flat of his hand smacked across her taut flesh but she did not cry out or scream, she just pressed harder at her clitoris and felt its hot, throbbing stiffness pushing between her fingers.

"Harder! Harder!"

Smack!

Her hips were pressed against the back of the chair and it swayed under the force of his smacking hand but still she did not cry out.

"Harder! Harder! Harder!"

Smack! Smack! Smack!

She wanted to feel the pain across her buttocks so much that it made her finish, she wanted to feel the stinging smack igniting her orgasm and sending it burning through her body, she wanted to feel the intensity of punishment and pain and what she was getting was not enough.

"I need it harder, I need my bottom spanking so hard it will make me finish. Harder!"

Smack! Smack! Smack!

Still, it was not enough and she let go of her clitoris and turned around and faced the man.

"Please spank me harder, I will do anything for you if you will just spank me harder. Please, I need it so much."

The man reached down to her tousled hair and pulled it aside; her lips were wet and her dark eyes were wide with expectation and desire.

"Stick your tongue out. I want to wank and finish onto it, then I want to watch you swallow it."

"How many times will you spank me for that?"

"Twice."

Barbara sat on the chair then opened her mouth wide

and hung her tongue forward over her bottom lip. She curled up the end slightly so that the flat, pink surface cupped slightly in the middle and bubbly spit drained into it and settled in a small, frothy pool. She held it there as he undid his zip, pulled the front of his underpants down and drew out his stiff cock. He held its end over her tongue and she sat there expectantly as he pulled his fingers up and down the veiny shaft.

As he pulled his fingers along its length he squeezed it hard and the reddened glans swelled up, its flanges engorging and spreading back and the pressure from his encircling hand pulling wide the hole at its centre. She kept her tongue beneath it as he pulled it faster and she watched his heavy balls as they swung and struck the back of his hand every time he pulled it down to his cock's base. His glans became redder and fuller and its engorged flanges looked purple as they spread back against the taut skin of the throbbing shaft. He pushed the fingers of his other hand behind his balls and pressed the hidden base of the straining shaft as he squeezed it hard with his tightening fingers.

She watched the hole at its centre dilate and she looked into the darkness of its pulsating channel as his spunk began to surge up the wide rib on the underside of his heavy cock. She saw it surge from the end and it sprayed across her nose before he directed it down onto her tongue. His spunk shot out in pulses and settled in the cupped centre of her waiting tongue. He squeezed it every time a fresh surge ran to the end and he held it there until no more would come. He stood back and looked at her as she sat on the chair with her tongue out, holding the full measure of his spunk in the soft hollow made by its upturned sides.

"Now swallow it, bitch."

She looked up at him still with her tongue forced out of her gaping mouth and began tipping her head back slightly.

As her tongue tipped the pool of spunk started to run stick-ily towards its back. She stared into his watching eyes as she slid the hot liquid further back, lifting herself slightly off the chair and moving herself towards him so that he could see more closely. The semen ran further back until she felt its heat touch the base of her tongue then run down to the back of her throat. She did not swallow or gulp but let it run down in a long sticky stream until, except for some drips that still stuck to the side of her nose, there was none to be seen. She licked her tongue across her lips, then drew it back into her mouth, breathed in deeply and took one long swallow, taking all his spunk down fully in one go.

Then she stood up and bent over the back of the metal chair.

"Spank me now."

Spank! Spank!

She was knocked forward with the force and struggled to stop herself falling.

"What else do you want to do to me?"

"Fuck you."

He pushed her down hard between the shoulder blades and thrust his spunk-smeared cock inside her arse. She gulped as it went in up to its base and she gripped the thin legs of the metal chair as he fucked her frantically.

"Spank me, please spank me."

Spank!

He smacked his hand against her bottom, leaving a wide, red mark across her branded buttocks.

"Harder!"

Smack! Smack! Smack!

Suddenly, he finished deeply in her arse and although he continued to spank her the punishment was not enough. She wanted more and, as his cock slid out of the tight muscular ring of her anus, she rolled over on her back and opened her legs.

"Punish me however you want, I will do anything."

The other men came into the glass cubicle.

"I will beat you across the cunt with my belt if you will fuck two dicks at the same time."

"Please, please, I will do anything."

Two of the men pulled their trousers off and stood facing each other; they pushed their hips forward and pressed their stiff cocks together.

"Get on these, bitch!"

Barbara scrambled to her feet and clawed up onto the men, grabbing their shoulders to raise her open legs above the two thick cocks. She squeezed her breasts against the face of one of the men and lowered herself down onto the throbbing tips that pulsated beneath her naked cunt. She felt them touch its soft folds and a hot thrill ran through her. The tip of one pressed hard against her engorged clitoris and the throbbing end of the other pressed against the rear of her swollen crack. She dropped herself onto them and she felt them squeezing together as they forced themselves into her gaping cunt.

She grabbed hold of the man's head and opened her legs as wide as she could, all the time driving her hips downwards and trying to get the stiff cocks in. She felt the tips squashing together and squeezing past the engorged folds of her outer labia and she shrieked with pain as they stretched her wide. She felt them going further and she felt the entrance to her vagina stretching to accommodate them, then suddenly they were in and she howled with pain and horror as she was filled completely with the two cocks.

She tried to pull herself back up but they were too tightly inside; she could not move and she felt as if she was going to be rent apart. They lifted her up a little and she felt the veiny shafts pulling against the squashed flesh of her vagina, then they thrust inside again and she shrieked as she felt the tips swelling and hardening and going even deeper.

She wanted to scream that it was too much for her but she could not form any words and she howled like an animal as they pulled her up and down the throbbing shafts, stretching her cunt to the limit and filling her vagina completely. They turned her sideways and the pressure against the sides of her cunt was overwhelming. She thought she was going to pass out as her legs were lifted and she was twisted until they stood at her sides, thrusting her even more deeply and holding her legs up high in front of her.

Then they bent her forward and she felt as if she was going to explode as her head was folded down between her outstretched knees. She yelled for them to stop but all that came out was a blubbering howl as spit ran in frothy streams from her gasping mouth. Suddenly, she felt a pressure against her anus as one of the other men pushed his throbbing cock against it. She was already spread so wide by the two cocks in her cunt that she could do nothing to resist and his cock pressed inside her arse until it was buried up to its base. She shrieked and felt a wave of nausea sweeping over her and she gaped and threw her tongue forward expecting to be sick but, as she heaved, she felt her face grabbed and another cock sinking into her open mouth. It went deeply inside, past the base of her tongue and into the back of her throat.

Her head spun as they fucked her remorselessly, filling her cunt and arse and penetrating her throat with savage thrusts from their stiff and throbbing cocks. When the first one finished in her arse she tried to rise up and suck out the spunk but she could not move; she was pinioned by the two cocks in her cunt and her face was being thrust down against the cock in her throat so hard that she could not even squeeze her buttocks together. She knew she was finishing because her body was throbbing with heat but she could not tell whether she was convulsing in a terrible muscular spasm because of her orgasm or whether she was seized with stiffness because they were holding her so tight and filling her so full.

Then the one in her mouth started to spurt its spunk onto the back of her tongue and she choked as the hot stream burst against her gagging throat. She heaved again but her spasms only served to draw a more intense burst of semen from his cock and it filled her breathless throat, plugging her up and making her giddy. She felt her self being lifted up as the two cocks in her cunt expanded against her vagina and finished together in a huge burst of spunk. She had never felt so much spunk as they spread it deeply inside her stretched and aching cunt. They pulled her up and down on the cocks until they were emptied and then they lifted her off and dropped her to the floor.

She lay on her back, gasping and dissipated, spunk running freely from her widely stretched and still open cunt. It ran down her distended crack until it mingled with the frothy semen that was bubbling from her anus. It dripped from her gasping mouth and her face and hair was smeared with its stickiness. She reached up and held her throat, trying to relax it and get some breath. She coughed and choked as more spunk ran from her mouth then slowly she began to breathe more normally. She opened her eyes and looked down between her legs.

"Now beat me," she said quietly. "Beat me hard."

20

Barbara had been senseless when Ramon and Carlo had dragged her out of the glass cubicle but she started to come to as they pulled her roughly into the alley. They hauled her in through a narrow door and up a few steps then thrust her into a tiny room with a large window onto the narrow street.

"That's your workplace from now on and we don't want to hear any clients complaining."

There was a chair in front of the window above which was attached a heavy, brass rail with curtain rings and hooks. At the back of the chair was a red curtain hung from another heavy, brass rail and behind that was a narrow bed by the side of which was a small, wash basin and a toilet.

"Get the picture? You sit there and get some clients. We'll deal with them at the door and when they come up you do whatever they want. Do you hear bitch? Whatever they want!"

Barbara nodded, hardly aware of what was expected of her.

"Here, put this on and tidy yourself up a bit, you're a fucking mess."

Ramon handed her a silky, white thong then they both went back down the stairs to the door leaving her standing aimlessly in front of the window.

She sat back onto the small wooden chair and twirled the soft thong absently between her fingers. A man tapped on the window and she looked up surprised, as if she had been woken from a dream. Suddenly, she was aware of her exposure to the street and quickly pulled the thong up over her legs, tugging it tightly between her buttocks and pulling the filmy gusset against the soft edges of her shaved cunt. The man mouthed at her, as if he was asking something. She did not know what to do, then the man's attention was caught by Ramon standing just inside the door alongside the window and the man moved towards him and out of Barbara's sight. A few minutes later, another man came and stared at her and the same thing happened, then she heard someone coming into the small room and Ramon shouted up from the doorway.

"He's paid for anything he wants so make sure he gets good value, eh?"

A tall, dark man dressed in a long, black overcoat came in and stood at the door. He carried a large, black canvas bag which he dropped heavily to the floor. He looked around, ignoring Barbara, then he pulled back the red curtain and peered into the small back room, pressing the bed with his large hands and running his fingers across the taps of the wash basin. He took his coat off and hung it up, then took his trousers, shirt, underpants, shoes and socks off and laid them down neatly on the bed. He turned, bent down to his bag and unzipped the top, it fell apart as the contents pushed the sides apart. He took out a pair of red leather stiletto-healed shoes.

"Put these on, whore."

She stretched her trembling hands forward and took the shiny leather shoes; she ran her fingers across the smooth leather uppers then along the unmarked sole and down the long, narrow heel.

"I said put them on, whore!"

Still sitting on the chair, she turned slightly, lifted her right foot and slipped the shoe on; it was tight and pinched her toes. She pulled the left one on and stood up unsteadily in front of the man. She looked down in embarrassment as he walked around her.

He bent down and ran the palms of his hands along the insides of her legs, starting at the tops of her thighs just below the thin gusset of the white thong and running them against the soft curves of her calves until he reached the red shoes. He stopped just above them, then bent further and put his face against the smooth red leather. He licked out his tongue and ran it wetly across the top of the shoes, licking each one slowly and methodically and leaving spit glistening on the soft, pliable leather. He pulled away and lay on his back with his head between her feet and stared up at the tight-pulled thong that barely covered her cunt.

Barbara felt the intensity of his gaze as she stared down at his hardening cock; watching it filling and stiffening then rising up until it throbbed massively from his hairy groin. She gaped at its weighty length and she felt a tingling wetness on the inner edges of her soft labia. She opened her legs a little to relieve the pressure of the thong against her cunt but he grabbed her feet and pulled the shoes tightly against the sides of his face.

"Suck it, whore!"

Still with her feet clasped at the side of his head she bent forward and spread her knees at the side of his broad chest. She sank down until she felt the pointed heels of the stiletto shoes against the taut skin of her outstretched buttocks. She lowered her head towards the throbbing cock and encircled her wet lips around the massive, engorged glans, pressing her tongue around the raised, blue veins that pulsated beneath the smooth, stretched skin.

Barbara pushed her mouth further down the shaft of the cock and felt the pointed heels of the shoes digging deeply into her buttocks. She drew back to ease the pain but the man thrust his hand against her back, pushing her head forward and squeezing her bottom hard against the sharp tips. His cock forced to the back of her throat and she gagged and pulled back, fighting against the pressure from his hands and the digging of the heels into her flesh.

"You're hurting me, please ..."

He pressed her back again and this time she felt the

sharp heels digging into the flesh at the tops of her thighs. He forced her head down and she took his cock again, sucking it and licking it in panic, hoping that he would ease his grip and relieve the pain from the sharp heels. But he pushed the heels of the red shoes even further against her flesh and they turned inwards until she felt them pressing against the filmy gusset of the thong and digging into the soft flesh of the edges of her cunt. The tips bit into her wet labia and she tried to pull herself away but he forced his cock deeper into her mouth and pushed the heels up until they dug into the entrance to her wet vagina. Again she managed to pull away, choking and coughing, but he was too strong for her to resist and, as he pressed her down, she found her mouth enclosing the stiff cock again as the heels penetrated her vagina and pulled at its swollen sides.

Suddenly he grabbed her feet and twisted her over, rolling her on her side and causing her to gasp for breath. She struggled and tried to crawl away from him but he held her feet together, pinching her skin and digging his nails into her ankles. He held her there with one hand while he reached over to his bag with the other, pulling out a piece of rope and quickly tying her feet together. He got up and dragged her across the room to the coat hanger by the curtain and lifted her feet up to it. He wrapped the loose ends of the rope around the hanger and hoisted her feet up to it, suspending her upside down with her head well off the floor.

Her head pounded and the sharp heels of the red shoes dug into the wall as she twisted and turned on the tightly drawn rope. She felt the tension in her body as it stretched downwards under her weight; her breasts tightened against her ribs and the swollen folds around her naked cunt drew up around the tight-pulled gusset of the thin, white thong. The flesh of her wet cunt was pressed so tightly against the thin material that it revealed the darker pink of her inner labia and the entrance to her vagina and her red, throbbing clitoris was outlined by the raised material as it stuck out from the front of her squeezed-open crack.

The man pulled a long roll of kitchen film from his bag and drew it back behind his head as he twirled Barbara around on the rope and pressed her face-forwards against the wall. Then he brought the heavy cardboard roll down across her taut buttocks with a sickening thud.

Thud!

The heavy, film-covered roll fell across her upturned bottom and she gasped as the breath was knocked from her, then he brought it down again and she was smashed against the wall by its weight.

Thud!

The cardboard roll struck her again with a heavy, bruising shock and she felt her head flopping backwards as her neck muscles could no longer take the strain.

Thud! Thud! Thud!

Every time the heavy cardboard roll smashed down she tensed and held herself tightly against the rope around her ankles, then as the deep, shocking pain eased she dropped back and gasped for breath until the next one. Gradually her head hung back further and further and, as he continued to beat her, she found herself staring at the ground and watching a long dribble of spit running from her gaping mouth and trailing into a pool on the floor. Her head spun and her eyes bulged as the shocking blows set up a continuous throb throughout her whole body, then it stopped and straight away she felt the man wrapping something around her legs.

She had not got the strength to look up and see what was happening but she felt a clammy heat against her skin as he wound the transparent film tightly around her calves. He pulled it hard, passing the roll around her legs and bind-

193

ing her tightly as he moved from her ankles down to her thighs. She tried to struggle but she was weak and could only hang there feeling a hot stickiness between her legs as the heat from her skin was caught behind the tight wrapping of the wide film.

She flushed with fear as she realised she could not move her legs at all and the heat of her panic caused her legs to stick together even more. He grabbed the gusset of the white thong and ripped it away from her cunt; she shrieked as it pulled her labia sharply and cut into her buttocks as it came away. He wrapped the film around her hips, up across her stomach and over her breasts, pulling it tightly around her neck and finally wrapping it around her face.

For a moment she hung motionless, completely encased in the shiny film, unable to move and sweating across the whole of her body with the trapped heat that burned from her taut skin. She gasped for breath and felt the film pulling against her open mouth then, as she realised she was getting no air, she gasped again but the film just pulled more tightly across her gaping mouth. She flushed with terror and the heat of her fear sent a wave of sweat across her whole body as she gulped in frantic disbelief. She could see the man reaching out and twisting her on the rope and she spun around, desperate for air and struggling to stay conscious.

The man poked his fingers against the stretched film that covered her gaping mouth and it broke with a crack. She gasped in air and gulped and heaved but she had not got her breath back properly before her mouth was plugged by his stiff cock. He thrust it in, plunging it to the back of her tongue, and finished in strong pulsating spurts down her throat.

She coughed and choked noisily as the spunk trickled stickily back into her mouth and ran over her lips onto the floor. She watched it dripping in a gummy stream from her sore mouth as she felt the red shoes being pulled from her feet. She turned slightly and glimpsed the man zipping up his bag, getting dressed and leaving.

Suddenly, she was seized with another panic as she realised that she was alone. She squirmed on the rope at her ankles and felt a shocking pain as they twisted against her stretched skin. She twisted again then suddenly she felt the heat in her legs turning to cold wetness as someone slid a pair of scissors down through the tightly wrapped film.

She felt the transparent film falling away and a cold shock of air made her shiver as her wet body was exposed, the her ankles were released and she dropped heavily to the floor. She lay with the tattered film hanging from her legs and face. She felt desperately humiliated and wanted to cry out for mercy, she wanted to beg to be released and she wanted to hide herself in shame. She looked up at the man, he was young and well built but as he caught her eye she saw in him only anger and purpose.

He bent down and dragged her to her feet, pulling her wrists high and tying them to the curtain rail above the window to the street. She was aching all over and completely exhausted as he stretched her face-forwards against the window. He pulled her legs out and tied her sore ankles to the pipes of a radiator, pulling them wide and drawing the ropes against the deep indentations that were already there.

She hung against the window, staring out into the narrow street, unable to believe what was happening to her. A man stopped outside and looked at her as she hung pinioned against the glass, naked and filled with fear. He stood and stared at her nakedness and put his hand to the glass where her cunt pressed against it. She looked down at him and watched his fingers moving against the glass, fondling her cunt without touching it and poking into it without penetrating it. He pressed his fingers harder and she felt s sudden surge of wetness inside her cunt. She was giddy with exhaustion and yet the exposure at the window and the man's hand pressing against the glass was releasing a wave of desire that was overcoming all her pain and anxiety.

She bent her head and pressed her mouth against the glass. The sticky spunk was still on her lips and she ran her lips around the glass, smearing the semen onto it and rubbing her wet cheeks against it. The man kept pressing his fingers against the glass and Barbara pressed her hips forward until the front of her naked cunt was squashed and opened by the pressure against the transparent surface.

Then she felt the man behind her opening her buttocks and she pressed them back to let them open wide. He pushed his fingers against the back edge of her cunt and prised them inside her swollen outer labia. She let them in then pressed forward again, imagining the man outside probing her around her engorged clitoris. The man behind opened her cunt wider and thrust his fingers deeply into her vagina. She sank back onto them as they went in then she pulled them forward as she pressed herself against the window again, looking at the man's fingers and wanting them inside as well.

She felt the fingers in her cunt come out and slip up her arse. She drove back onto them and sucked them in up to the knuckles then started moving up and down them rhythmically. She pressed herself against the glass as another two men stopped in the street and looked at her stretched, heaving body. Their gaze caused a wet surge in her cunt and a trickle of moisture to run down the insides of her thighs. As the man behind her withdraw his fingers from her arse, she pressed forward towards the men in the street, opening her mouth wide and smearing the spunk that still ran from it in broad circles against the glass, then she felt a cock against her arse and she rose up to take it.

The man behind her forced his cock in past the dilated ring of her anus and deeply into her arse; she felt it going in and squeezed against its veiny sides as it penetrated her as far as it could before plunging down onto it for more. She looked out into the street and saw that others had gathered around. She felt so exposed, so abused and humiliated and yet she felt inflamed by the exposure and set on fire by the abuse that ignited the heat of a building desire. She wanted them all to watch her being fucked up the arse, she wanted them all to gather around her and watch her anus tightening around the man's cock as he plunged it in, she wanted them to wank all over her and fill her mouth with spunk and she wanted to show them how she could swallow it and feed on it and plead for more.

As the cock in her arse began to throb with the coursing semen that flowed up its engorged and pulsating shaft, she felt the heat of her own orgasm burning deep inside her flesh. She desperately wanted her cunt filled but the exposure to the men in the street was enough to make it flow and she reared up against her bonds, jerking fitfully as she was consumed by a throbbing and convulsive spasm of ecstasy. Her pounding head spun giddily as her body thumped down on the spurting cock then she fell back onto it, her eyes filled with flashing lights and her chest tightened by the pressure of her seizure.

The next thing she knew she was lying on the floor alone with her legs spread wide and her arse dribbling with spunk; her orgasms had passed and now she felt only distress and exhaustion. She tried to move but she felt racked with pain and could only roll over onto her side. As she pulled her legs together she felt the edges of her distended cunt squeezing together and dribbling with wetness; her anus was sore and suddenly, she felt engulfed by a wave of desperation and hopelessness.

Slowly, she pulled herself painfully across the floor to the window. Condensation and smeary swirls of wetness covered the glass and she could hardly see the street outside. She hauled herself up against the sill, stretched out her finger and watched it moving shakily as she scrawled out her desperate message, 'PLEASE SAVE ME'.

She dropped her hand and looked feebly at the small dribbles of water running from the bottom of the letters and gathering in little pools on the wooden sill. Then she heard someone tapping on the glass and, as she rubbed the condensation away with the flat of her hand, she stared through the window in disbelief as the Ringmaster grinned at her menacingly. She drew away in fear and crawled behind the red curtain, pulling the cover off the bed and holding onto it desperately.

Barbara cowered by the narrow bed as she listened to the Ringmaster arguing with Ramon and Carlo. There was a lot of shouting then the Ringmaster appeared at the door, his face red with anger and the blood vessels standing out in his temples and neck. He pulled the red curtain aside and stood over her as she crouched on the floor, clutching the bed cover across her breasts. He did not speak as he grabbed her and hauled her roughly out of the building and into a waiting taxi.

She looked up occasionally and saw the high buildings of the narrow Amsterdam streets flashing by but mostly she stared down to her naked knees as waves of shame and fear spread over her and made her feel sick. She was bundled out of the taxi and soon found herself again lying on the sawdust floor of the Ringmaster's circus.

"On your podium my little bitch!"

The Ringmaster stood above her with his long whip

trailing along the sawdust floor of the big cage. The monkeys screamed and clung to their bars and the multi-coloured parrots flapped wildly in their cage that was drawn high up to the ceiling.

"Get up, girl, or you will have a taste of this."

He drew the long whip back and cracked its slit end just above her face. She pulled away as a puff of smoke flew from it and she scuttled obediently across to the metal rostrum. She climbed up its sides and crouched down on the platform with her arms pressed down between her open legs and her palms pressed flat against its swaying top.

"Mercedes! Release the wolf!"

Barbara glanced across in fear as Mercedes came out of the shadows and walked over. The grey wolf padded around in circles and dropped its drooling jaw menacingly as Mercedes flung back the iron grill to its cage. From the side of the cage, she pulled down a long pole with a heavy iron ring on its end then lassoed the wolf tightly by its throat. The wolf reared up on its hind legs and pulled frantically against the iron noose but Mercedes guided him out of the cage and brought him to the entrance of the sawdust covered circus ring.

Mercedes guided the wolf into the ring then snatched the noose from around his neck. He jumped back, shaking himself free as the noose came away, then ran to the back of the ring and padded back and forth, staring all the time at the Ringmaster.

"Come down here bitch, I've got a treat for you."

The Ringmaster flicked the bull-whip back and cracked it close to Barbara's face; she shrunk back in fear but obediently climbed down from the podium.

"Here!"

The Ringmaster pointed to his feet.

"Here!"

Barbara looked over at the padding wolf and nervously started to make her way over to the Ringmaster. As soon as she moved from the base of the podium the wolf lunged towards her, snarling and dribbling saliva from his dangling tongue. She froze in fear but the Ringmaster cracked the whip again and the wolf leapt back against the iron bars and Barbara scuttled forward.

"On all fours bitch!"

Barbara knelt down obediently. She felt overcome with despair and hopelessness and lifted her bottom automatically as she felt the Ringmaster kneeling down behind her. She felt the hot end of his cock pressing against her wet cunt and as it slid in she began to fuck him like an animal.

As the Ringmaster fucked her cunt from behind the wolf moved towards her and looked into her face. She stared at the long tongue that hung loosely from his salivating mouth, then suddenly she remembered the picture she had seen in the shop window of the girl being fucked while she sucked the dog's huge, red cock. She tried to look away but all she could see was the image of the wolf's cock deep inside the girl's ravenous mouth as he thrust it frantically between her clasping lips. Barbara shivered all over then her eyes widened in fear as the wolf lurched forward and reared up in front of her gaping mouth.

21

Barbara awoke to find herself naked and curled up against a heavy, wooden door frame. She stretched herself and felt stiff all over.

"Is that you Barbara?"

Barbara had not heard her name for ages and she looked

around to see who was calling her. There was no one in sight and she thought she must be dreaming or imagining it.

"Barbara, is that you? Please come in won't you?"

A man's voice was coming from behind the door. She listened as he called again and she thought it seemed familiar.

"Barbara, what are you doing, come along we've got things to do."

Barbara reached up to the door handle and slowly turned it. The door swung open and she saw Mr Simms sitting behind his desk.

He jumped up and rushed over.

"What on earth has happened to you my dear. Here, let me help you."

He reached his hand down and lifted her to her feet.

"Where are your clothes? What has been going on?"

"Oh Mr Simms! At last! You've managed to save me!"

"My dear Barbara, what do you mean?"

"Oh Mr Simms, it has been so awful, so dreadful, I never thought I would escape, I never thought you would find me."

She looked down and suddenly realised that she was naked.

"Oh Mr Simms I'm so sorry, I feel so ashamed, so embarrassed, what must you think of me. Please forgive me, please, please, forgive me."

"It's alright my dear, sit down and relax, it's all over now."

Barbara sat forward with her hands across her knees in the chair on the opposite side of the desk to Mr Simms. Although she was naked, and it seemed so puzzling to be back in the office with Mr Simms, she felt overwhelmingly relieved that at last she was safe. Now, sitting in Mr Simms' office she did not even know if all those terrible things had really happened or whether it had just been a dream or even whether she had imagined it. Whatever it had been it was over now and she was safe again.

"Oh Mr Simms I'm so grateful. How did you find me? It doesn't matter, you did and you brought me back. Oh thank you Mr Simms, thank you."

"Tell me my dear what has been happened. It will help you feel better."

Barbara took a deep breath and began to tell her story. She stopped every now and again because she had forgotten some details but Mr Simms gave her time to collect her thoughts and waited patiently while she worked her way through all the things that had happened to her. When she finished she sat back on the chair and relaxed, draping her arms on the side of the chair and opening her knees slightly.

She felt so much better and even though she was naked in front of Mr Simms she still felt relieved and glad that it was all over. He passed her a cup of coffee from a flask on his desk then offered her some sugar but as she was taking it she dropped the spoon down between her bottom and the chair. She lifted herself up slightly and pushed her hand down to retrieve it but could not find it. She twisted her hips and lifted her bottom even more then, when she looked down to see where it was, she saw the deep red mark on her buttock where the Master had branded her with the hot iron. She froze, not daring to move then, as the memory of the pain flooded back into her mind, she felt a sensation of wetness around the soft edges of her naked cunt.

"I'm so pleased you are safe now my dear," said Mr Simms, walking around his desk and standing at her side. "You need not worry any more."

He put his arm around her shoulders and patted her with his hand.

202

"Oh Mr Simms!" she cried out as she turned and flung her arms around his waist. "How can I thank you?"

"Your safety is enough my dear."

She squeezed her arms tightly around his waist and felt the heat of his body against her flushed face, then, moving her hands down, she pressed her palms against his buttocks. He tried to pull back but she held him firmly and moved her hands further down until they folded against the insides of the tops of his thighs. He seemed flustered and embarrassed and pushed his hands down to try and push her away.

"Please," he said, "you mustn't, really you mustn't."

She held him tighter and pressed her face against hard against the front of his hips; she felt so grateful to him for saving her. Telling him about her suffering had somehow caused her to want more; her admission of the terrible things she had experienced brought them freshly into her mind and she wanted to do his bidding and she wanted to be punished for everything she had done.

"Please Mr Simms, I'm so grateful, please let me give you something in return, please, you must."

She released her grip on his legs and moved her hands to the front of his trousers. He tried to pull back again but she held the zip at the front between her fingers and it was enough to keep him there. She pulled the zip down slowly and pushed her hand inside the opening; she felt his thick cock, lying flaccidly inside his underpants and wrapped her fingers around it.

"Would you like me to suck it?"

Again he tried to pull back but she squeezed his cock through the material of his underpants and ran her fingers along its soft, weighty length.

"Please Barbara, there is no need, it is enough that you are safe."

203

"But I would like to, I want to thank you."

She lifted her hand and undid his trousers, then she ran it inside the front of his underpants and took hold of the soft cock. She squeezed her fingers around it and pulled at the loose skin that folded over the end of his glans. She lifted it gently and with her other hand pulled his underpants down, exposing his soft cock and holding it in front of her mouth. She put her mouth around his foreskin and gripped it between her teeth, biting down onto it and stretching it forward. She felt his cock swelling in her hand and she let go of the foreskin as his glans engorged and emerged, pink and throbbing from the loose flesh. She licked it and made it wet then, as it grew, she sucked it in slowly between her lips. She pressed her tongue against the underside of the swelling shaft and felt the veins hardening against its surface. She wrapped both her hands around its base and pressed against the throbbing shaft, squeezing it rhythmically as it grew larger and filled her sucking mouth.

Suddenly, as if only then realising what she was doing, he pulled back and stepped away, his cock dripping with her spit and rising and falling with heavy, pulsating throbs.

"You mustn't, please Barbara, you mustn't."

He sat down on a chair and she looked down, her face flushing red with embarrassment and shame. She wanted to please him and now she felt so guilty she just wanted to be punished. She got up, her mouth still open and her lips wet with spit, and went over to him. She bent down across his knees and stretched her hands out to the floor. She felt the heat of his throbbing cock against the side of her hips and she pushed against it to feel it more.

"Spank me Mr Simms, please spank me for being so bad."

She stretched her bottom higher, opening her thighs so that he could see her shaved cunt between the dark triangle of taut flesh at the base of her buttocks.

"Look at my cunt and spank me while you watch it. I have been so bad, so naughty, you must spank me, please Mr Simms, spank me as hard as you can."

She lifted herself up and moved her cunt above his cock, then she dropped herself back down and squeezed it between the tops of her thighs.

"Now!" she said.

"Barbara, please, you must stop this."

"Now! Spank me!"

Spank! Spank! Spank!

His hand came down repeatedly across her buttocks, scorching them with heat and making her gasp for breath as she tightened her thighs against his stiff cock and felt it throbbing against the wet, open flesh of her cunt.

"Spank me harder!"

Spank! Spank! Spank!

The pain of his smacking hand seared through her and her flesh tingled all over with heat and anguish but the more her bottom burned with the heat of his blows the more she wanted. She wanted to be spanked until he could do it no more, until her was exhausted and could no longer lift his hand, and she squeezed his cock against her cunt tighter with every blow.

Smack! Smack! Smack!

She stretched out her hands as far as she could and pushed her legs out stiffly behind her, prising her toes against the floor and digging her nails into the carpet.

Smack! Smack! Smack!

The blows fell harder and harder but she still wanted more. Then she felt his stiff cock throbbing against her cunt and through the soft folds of her wet labia she sensed the coursing of his semen. She gripped hard against the pulsating shaft, waiting for his spunk to spurt up and fall across her bottom.

Smack! Smack! Smack!

She tensed herself and suddenly she felt it come. It shot in flooding gushes from the tip of his swollen cock and splashed back down against her reddened buttocks, running down into the crack between them and streaming against the back of her open crack.

Smack! Smack! Smack!

He kept finishing as he smacked her harder and harder. His hand splashed across his still spurting spunk and it sprayed up onto her back and down the backs of her stretched out thighs.

He stopped when he could smack her no more and she rolled off his knees and onto the floor. He got up and stood above her, his stiff cock still glistening and with beads of spunk dripping from its end.

"Give me more," she said, rolling onto her back and opening her legs. "Please Mr Simms, give me more."

He bent to the desk, brushed a pile of magazines and papers off its top and pulled out some short pieces of rope from a drawer. He held out an upturned palm above the desk and obediently, she got up, went over to it and laid herself down across its leather covered top. He bound her ankles and wrists tightly then pulled the dangling ends of the ropes around the four legs of the large, leather-topped desk. As she lay spread-eagled with her head craned back over the edge, he picked up one of the magazines from the floor, rolled it up tightly and brought it down on her splayed-out bottom.

Whack! Whack! Whack!

The rolled-up magazine struck her heavily and she gasped as it sent a flood of pain through her body.

Whack! Whack! Whack!

Three more heavy blows and she dropped her head forward over the edge of the desk and desperately gulped for air.

Whack! Whack! Whack!

Her bottom stung from the punishing blows as he beat her and she wanted to scream for him to stop. But she knew she must let him carry on until he had punished her enough, and she did not know how much that would be, she could only hope that she was strong enough to take it.

Whack! Whack! Whack!

She fought for breath, gasping in before each blow and coughing out a spray of spit as it landed. As she coughed she watched spit run from her swollen lips and dribble in sticky threads onto the carpeted floor of the office.

Finally, he stopped and undid the ropes from the legs of the desk. She bent back to get up but he grabbed her wrists and pulled them back, squeezing her shoulders tightly and painfully behind her. He grabbed the ropes at her ankles and yanked them forward, pulling her legs back until her feet were drawn up against her hands. He tied her wrists and ankles together and she lay, bent backwards like a bow, on the hard surface of the desk. He took the rolled-up magazine that he had spanked her with and pulled it across her gasping mouth. Her eyes widened in terror as he tied it behind her head with two pieces of rope, pulling them as tight as he could and drawing the rolled-up magazine painfully against the sides of her wide-stretched mouth.

He tore the red satin cover from a cushion on the settee and pulled it roughly over her head, tying it with more rope tightly around her neck. She shook her head from side to side as she tried to breathe; she could see nothing through the material of the cushion cover and she opened her eyes wide into the claustrophobic darkness. In panic she pulled at her wrists but they were bound too tightly to her ankles and as she tugged at them they cut into her skin. She threw her head about and tried to get her mouth free of the rolled-up magazine but it was forced in too tightly; she could only bite down onto it and squeeze it together with her teeth so that a trickle of air came past its wet, glossy edges. As she sweated inside the heavy material, the air got hotter around her head and when she did breathe it scorched her dry throat and made her heave.

As she threw herself about he gripped her hips and dragged her to the edge of the desk top, the outstretched mound at the front of her crack scraping painfully against its surface. She thrashed her head about but she banged it on the wooden top and made herself feel giddy and sick. She thought she was going to vomit and another flood of panic streamed through her. She felt him gripping her hips and cutting into her skin with his fingernails, then she felt him opening her thighs wide. Her cunt felt exposed and she tried to pull her legs together but she did not know where she was as the darkness engulfed her and the hot air and spit rushed over the bitten, mushy magazine that pulled her mouth out so painfully.

She felt his cock against her cunt and she bit down hard onto the magazine as he thrust it in and fucked her roughly. Her hips smacked against the edge of the desk as he pounded deeply inside her. He lifted her hips up higher and the strain against her wrists and ankles sent shocks of pain into her arms and legs. She felt herself being dragged further back until she thought she was only resting on the desk top by her shoulders but she could not properly tell as he gripped his nails even deeper into her hips then plunged his cock in and held it there until his spunk had all run out.

When he had finished completely, he dragged her from the desk top and threw her down heavily onto the floor. She bit down onto the rolled-up magazine in agony as she landed in a heap and rolled over painfully onto her back, her arms and legs pulling behind her and sending waves of pain into her tortured body. She rolled about disorientated and gasped desperately for breath inside the darkness of the cushion cover that was still pulled tightly over her head, then she felt a heavy lash across her breasts and stinging pangs of agonizing pain rushed through her chest.

Lash! Lash! Lash!

She could not breathe any more and felt her teeth loosening their grip on the rolled-up magazine as she licked at it to force an airspace at its edges.

Lash! Lash! Lash!

He beat her mercilessly across the breasts and her nipples hardened against the flailing rope as it left red weals across her taut skin.

Then, as he continued to flog her, she felt someone else pressing the insides of her knees wide apart and exposing her cunt to the lashing blows.

Lash! Lash! Lash!

The scourging rope cut across her flesh and snatched at her swollen labia, tugging the soft folds and drawing them out in wet puckers. Her legs were pressed wider and, as her cunt was exposed even more to the vicious rope, she felt her inner labia distending and spreading and she wanted more.

Lash! Lash! Lash!

The soft skin of her cunt burned as the rope thrashed her but she felt its wetness sticking against the flail and holding onto it before it was taken away. Each time it tugged at her soft flesh, she felt it widening and heating with increased desire.

Lash! Lash! Lash!

This time she forced her legs wider without any pressure from the unseen hands; she welcomed the heavy, stinging blows and she lifted her hips so that they would find the centre of her moist, sensitive flesh.

Lash! Lash! Lash!

The thrashing rope penetrated the opening to her vagina and she rose up as a rapid swell of heat coursed through her, gripping her innards and burning her all over as it spread through her stretched arms and legs and into her reddened face. She imagined the red stripes that laced the insides of her thighs and the angry weals that were raising up around her cunt and she strained back as the seizure scorched her again and she writhed in a confusion of darkness, punishment, pain and desire.

She lay there gasping and jerking as involuntary spasms ran through her veins. She was hardly aware of her bonds being undone but she felt her muscles relax when her arms and legs were freed. Her legs dropped open until her knees touched the carpet under pressure from the hands that were still against them and she stared into the darkness and felt relieved that at last it was over; her pain had finished and she was satisfied and safe. She moved slightly against the pressure from the hands at her knees as they ran down the insides of her thighs and rested just below her swollen cunt.

She felt the cushion cover being pulled from her head and her feeling of safety evaporated as she saw the Ringmaster bent between her legs and staring down at her still dilated cunt. Still with the rolled-up magazine pulled tightly across her mouth, she screwed up her eyes in disbelief and horror as he stood up and whacked his short riding crop against his black leather trousers.

"Stupid bitch, did you really think you were safe? Look out of the window. Go on, look out of the window!"

Barbara struggled to her feet and sidled nervously towards the window. She stared down anxiously and saw the tall buildings on the opposite side of the narrow alley and realised that she was still in Amsterdam. Her soul flooded with fear as she looked down towards the doors of the houses opposite and saw Ramon talking to someone. He was holding a picture and pointing to it as he asked questions and made gestures. The man he was talking to pointed to the building she was in and she ducked behind the white, lace curtain that hung loosely across the deep window. Suddenly, she realised that he was searching for her and he must have got a photograph of her; but from where? She felt ridiculous as she turned back into the room and saw Mr Simms laughing and joking with the Ringmaster.

"Yes, you stupid bitch, we've still got you, and of course if we get tired of you," he walked to the window and pointed down to Ramon, "we can always let him take you back."

They both laughed loudly and she dropped down onto a small settee and hung her head in shame. She could not believe how they had manipulated and tricked her and she thought that now she would probably never escape their clutches, and even if she did then her fate would be even worse.

The Ringmaster sat down on a chair and whacked the riding crop against the leg of his black leather trousers.

"Come here bitch and bend over!"

22

Still with the rolled-up magazine pulled securely across her mouth and with her eyes tightly closed, Barbara bent over the Ringmaster's knee and stretched her hands to the floor. Her heart was pounding in fear and yet at the same time she was overcome with an uncontrollable eagerness for the beating. She felt her bottom rising to receive the punishment that she knew would be too painful to suffer. She waited expectantly for the sound of the whip being drawn back and stretched herself flat against his knees to show that she was ready. She wanted him to see her glistening cunt and she wanted him to know that the whipping she was to get was her only desire. She heard the whip being drawn back then she felt the tension against the small of her back as his hand pressed her down firmly. She started to push back against the tension of his hand, wanting to feel the control that he was exerting, but then the whip lashed across her bottom and she tightened with pain.

Whack!

She opened her eyes widely as the agonizing blow scorched her taut skin. As she looked down to the floor she saw a magazine spread open at his feet and, as she gasped for breath and waited for the next smack, she stared incredulously at the glossy pictures that lay before her. She saw an image of herself, spread-eagled on her back with two men caning her breasts. She could not believe it but as she looked more intently and saw her face grimacing in agony, her mouth screwed up tightly and her eyes ablaze with terror, she knew it was her. There were thin red marks lacing her skin and a dribble of spit ran from her tight-pulled lips. She saw how wide her cunt was and she could not stop her eyes following the angry red stripes that were laced across her stomach, inside the tops of her thighs and along the edges of her swollen labia.

As the Ringmaster raised the whip again, she moved her hand towards the magazine and nervously flicked the page over, then she felt the tension of his hand again in the small of her back and the whip smashed down across her bottom for a second time.

Whack!

She bit into the rolled-up magazine in her mouth and it split under the pressure from her teeth. She gulped in air as it fell down soggily against her chin and she shrieked and howled in a spasm of relief and suffering. Spit burst from her gaping mouth but she was unable to take her eyes from the picture that lay on the floor below her. She could see herself again, tied up with a metal bar clamped between her legs and strung to the ceiling by a rope around her neck. Her eyes were black and her cheeks flushed red as two men beat her with canes as she spun dizzily on the rope. She looked as if she was barely conscious with only a glimmer of white showing from beneath the rims of her heavy-lidded eyes.

She knew it was her in the picture but she could not remember it being taken and worse still, she could not remember the incident. A wave of panic ran across her skin as she wondered what else had happened, what other terrible things had been done to her that she had forgotten? There had been so many punishments she had suffered, so many humiliations, so many beatings and she had been made to have sex so often in so many different ways, she could hardly imagine that there were other, even darker things of which she was unaware. There was so much she could remember but the knowledge that she had suffered even more violation, that she had taken part in even more humiliation, was more than she could bear. Her spit dripped down onto the glossy paper as she turned the page and the whip came down for a third time.

Whack!

She bit down onto her lips as the her body convulsed with the scorching pain from the whip. Her eyes remained fixed on the picture that lay open before her and even though she was knocked forward by the force of the blow she did not let them stray. She could not keep her lips together and, as she opened them, an involuntary scream burst out as if she was a trapped and petrified animal. Spit streamed from her mouth and she writhed across the Ringmaster's knee as she stared at the terrible picture that confronted her. As her screaming eased, she dropped her head and her wet, tousled hair fell forward in heavy swirls across her face. The picture lay close to her eyes and she mumbled softly in a shaky and terrified voice.

"Please save me, oh someone please save me ..."

But her words were drowned by the explosion of screaming and spit that burst from her mouth as the whip crashed down again. She tightened in a seizure of agony as the whip sent a deeply penetrating pain through her body, consuming her feelings of horror, desperation and self-disgust and transporting her into a world flooded with obscene desires, images of bestiality and never-ending willingness.

As usual we start the bonus pages with an extract from our next book, SINFINDER GENERAL. by Paul Tremayne:

A woman is not truly conquered until she has been taken like a dog.

Jed and Sam knew that.

Maybe even Lucinda Drake knew it as she ran from them, stumbling through the dense woodland. The snapping of twigs, the thudding of her riding boots against the sodden earth, the grizzled growling of her pursuers, all combined to panic her, so that the noise of her flight was nearly drowned by the sound of her feverish panting.

Her white blouse snagged against a low-hanging branch, the material ripping to expose a frantically bouncing breast - nipple big and pink; hard, like a bullet. Her long blonde hair snagged too, until she tore it free and stumbled onwards. She staggered against a crumbling log and fell head-first into the damp moss.

From a distance, Jed and Sam saw her tumble. Her body descended and her aristocratic bottom flashed into view.

They stumbled on eagerly, fingers tingling with the need to grope her fleshy buttocks, cocks throbbing with desire for her. The mistress had been promised a fuck in her bottom and a fuck she would get.

Lucinda had squealed and run, horrified at the thought of the crusty old men stripping her buttocks clear of her clothes and taking turns to enter her back-passage with their disgusting cocks.

She'd heard the master - her husband to be - heard him laughing as she'd fled across the fields towards the woodland. She'd heard him urging his two rough farmhands after her, and as she ran, she wished she'd let him have her that morning. John was a cruel man - a man who thought nothing of letting his servants use her.

It was too late for Lucinda now. Her fate was sealed. No

amount of pleading would save her from her punishment. Her only chance was to run, and hope against hope that Jed and Sam would give up chasing her. She stumbled through a thicket of brambles, wincing as the sharp thorns scratched her soft skin. There was no chance of them letting her go. No chance at all. They had to catch her, to have her as they had been commanded, if they wanted to keep their jobs.

John wouldn't tolerate failure...

Lucinda tore free of the dense woodland and lurched into a yellow field. Jed and Sam were at her now, like unruly dogs snapping and scratching at her quivering flesh. Jed was behind her, holding her still while Sam ripped away the shredded remains of her blouse and mauled her naked breasts. His fat fingers squeezed the soft white flesh and twisted her big bullet-head nipples.

Lucinda tried to pull away, thrusting her bottom backwards into Jed's stiff groin. "Get off me!" she squealed, and raked the heel of her boot down his shin.

"She's a wild one!" Jed laughed, unperturbed by the sudden pain in his leg. "I'm looking forward to bum-fucking the feisty little bitch and that's a fact!"

Sam tore at her jodhpurs, wrenching them to her knees. Jed dragged her big white pants down, baring her so that her thick pubic bush sprang out towards his accomplice and her round aristocratic buttocks wobbled cheekily, daring Sam to part them and penetrate the tight brownness of her bum-mouth.

"Let go of me!" Lucinda wailed, twisting and turning frantically as she attempted to free herself from their attentions. "I'll have you both soundly flogged for this outrage!" She tried to kick, but the tangled trousers wrapped around her knee-high boots acted as a restraint. "I'll have the skin flogged off your hides!"

Jed and Sam gurgled and laughed again, baring rows of none too white teeth. Sam persisted in his rough massage of

216

Lucinda's succulent breasts. Jed continued to hold her still, with one strong arm wrapped around her stomach, clamping her to him. His other hand folded around the fleshy mound of her left buttock, teasing it away from its mate and opening the deep sweaty cleft that cleaved her cheeks.

"Mistress Drake's all hot and wet from riding that horse of hers this afternoon," he growled, fingers dipping into the clammy crack. His fingertip pressed against the moist ring of anal flesh that throbbed wantonly and Lucinda squealed as the thick digit dug into her.

"I think she's ready for a good hard arse-fuck," Jed declared. He tickled at the rubbery walls of her back-passage, delighting in the resulting whine that emanated from her lips.

Lucinda heard the sound of a zipper, felt Sam press himself into her breasts and take a firm hold of her arms to restrain her, and then felt Jed's hands roughly wrench her buttocks wide apart. Fresh air kissed her anus for a brief second, then she felt the hot, bulbous head of Jed's penis nuzzle against her.

A good hard thrust and Jed was within her, thick cock ploughing forward against the moist walls of her rectum, plugging her up.

"That's nice, Mistress Drake," he whispered. "Now hold nice and still while I give this arse-crack of yours a good hard fucking!"

The farmhand's penis felt like a thick trunk inside Lucinda's bottom, throbbing and hot, stretching her tight brown hole until it was the size of a pink cunt. Jed began to thrust in and out of the mistress's bum; long, firm strokes that sent his sex muscle deep into the darkness of Lucinda's most shameful hole. He admired the brown flesh of her distended anus as he hammered away at her.

Lucinda found herself grasping Sam for support as her bottom was ravaged. She was clamped between the two rugged, ugly men, their breath slaked with the sweet aroma of cider, their hands rough and hard.

"Go on!" Sam urged, clutching her to him, "poke her arse good and hard! Give that tight brown hole a good fuck!"

Lucinda clenched her teeth as the old man thrust himself in and out of her rectum. If only she'd acquiesced with John's wishes; if only she'd let him take her that morning. The constant thrusting and withdrawing of Jed's sex muscle was serving as an excruciating reminder of her foolishness. She was certainly paying a heavy price for her mistake...

Here are this month's excerpts from Stephen Rawling's VICTORIAN SCRAPBOOK, vignettes from a sterner age. Stephen Rawlings is the author of JANE AND HER MASTER (his version of Jane Eyre) and the forthcoming PRIDE AND PERVERSION (no doubt you can guess that one!)

1 - ABUSE IN GERMANY.

At the beginning of Victoria's reign what we now know as Germany was still split into a vast number of more or less independent States, some small, some large. By the end of his life Bismark had extended the power of Prussia to weld them into one powerful whole, but before that the individual Princelings often behaved with absolute cruelty to their subjects of every degree. The following is an imaginary scene from such State:

In a small German Principality, let us call it Rohenstock, Amelia, a Countess in her own right, has aroused the jealousy of the Graf's wife, since both married women share the same lover. When Amelia is trapped into a political offence, the Grafin persuades her husband to condemn her to a House of Correction for female offenders, where the whip is used freely, and all inmates are branded on arrival, to mark their criminality. The Graf is the more ready to grant his wife's desire for revenge as Amelia has been very reluctant to allow her husband the use of her anus, despite his well known preference for buggery, and the two men are close cronies. The Grafin has come in person to gloat over her fallen rival:

"Strip!"

So now it was here. The moment she had been dreading, when she would have to submit to being marked, permanently. Not just marked, but burnt with hot iron, her flesh seared until it bore a permanent scar, a token of her disgrace that would not go away once she was free of this nightmare. Worse still was to have to suffer this torture and humiliation under the gloating eyes of Charlotte. She vowed she would go through with it without giving the bitch the satisfaction of hearing her scream.

She crossed her arms before reaching for the hem of her simple robe, drawing it up over her head, and discarding it on a bench. Not the bench destined for her though - that stood dark and bizarre to one side of the room, a strong timber structure, like a low trestle with, fixed to its top, what she could only think of as an inverted flat iron, a steel triangular shape covered in short stiff bristles, shorter and harder than a scrubbing brush, facing upwards. She had guessed its purpose, the moment she had entered the room. Its shape, and position off the ground made it obvious, knowing what was to happen to her here.

The man in charge grunted something unintelligible, then made an unmistakable gesture with his hands, miming what he required. She had come bare footed to the chamber, and now stood clad only in her stays and cambric drawers. She sucked in her breath and undid the tapes of her pantelettes, peeling them off her ample hips and discarding them. The dress already lay to one side. As the thin material peeled away from her moist crotch, a thick black bush of wiry hair sprang into prominence, a lush growth appropriate to her vibrant femaleness. Her half-naked breasts were lifted and displayed by the lacy cups of the stiff boned corset and its constricting pressure about her waist threw her lush buttocks into even greater prominence.

Charlotte was at her elbow.

"Bend, Amelia darling," she said softly, for her ears only, "Bend and show me your flesh. I'm going to have you marked as boldly as any woman who's passed through this room. Deep and long, so that you'll never lose your badge of shame. Bend and let me touch you, so you'll know just where the iron will bite."

The older woman shuddered, but would not give the other the satisfaction of having her plead. She bent with surprising suppleness for her build. Her buttocks tautened. She flinched as she felt her enemy's fingers stroking over the rounds, seeking the lower part, under the highest swelling.

"Here, darling, and here," pressing at two points a couple of inches apart on her left cheek, "then he'll reheat the irons and put them here and here." The fingers moved to her right cheek, still in the underhang of the meaty buns.

Amelia hissed through her clenched teeth.

"Get on with it, you cruel bitch," she choked. "Stop tormenting me like this."

"What! All hot for the iron's kisses? Well I won't keep you from it!" The Grafin stood back from her victim, gesturing to the executioner to proceed.

Following his signals, the condemned woman advanced to the bench and looked at it for a moment, working out what was needed next. Hands thrust her forward, puling up one leg. She could see now what they were after, and mounted the bristle decorated triangle as if it were a saddle, which it did slightly resemble, though much narrower and smaller than any normal saddle, cut away at the back, with the top curving up like a crescent moon and pointing to the rear of the apparatus, Gingerly, she lowered her mons onto the rough surface, wincing as she felt the prickles in her tender flesh, giving a small squeak as two fibres, longer and more intrusive than their fellows, found her clitoris and punctured the delicate membrane of its tip.

The hands continued to pull, and she found herself lying forward on the narrow padded platform ahead of the 'saddle'. Her hands were drawn down, and put together beneath the pad, so that she clasped it like a pillow. She gave an involuntary shudder as she felt the chill of the broad leather strap that was passed over her waist, securing her to the block, cold and clammy from the sweat of fear and agony deposited by the endless column of other women who had preceded her on this apparatus for the marking of females, and the infliction of unbearable anguish inherent in the process of branding flesh with white hot iron.

The bristles were pressing in her pubes now, pricking and stinging. She moved her hips about, trying to settle herself in the least uncomfortable position she could find. Her generous haunches undulated as she tried to adjust, but the short stiff spikelets were designed to prevent a woman moving to avoid the heat of the iron when it was presented to her flesh, and held her fast. Those damned needle-like points, that had found her bud, would not be dislodged, and she squirmed with the constant pricking in her most sensitive female part.

Now the assistants were tugging at her legs, forcing her knees apart and forward, under her, until they were in an approximation of the kneeling position. They were secured, straps holding them firmly in place beneath her. With the 'saddle' under her groin, her buttocks were splayed open, the whole under-side displayed from the rear, the flesh vulnerable and poised for the branding.

She was a well built woman, not fat, but big, and with the generous flesh to the buttocks that maturity and maternity bring. As she settled herself, the well formed thighs showed as meaty columns, the nates as fleshy moons, pale but firm, perfect pages on which to print her fate. Between, the cold air reminded her, her moist and pouting vulva was totally vulnerable in its exposure. Oh God, surely even Charlotte would not order the iron to be touched to a woman's sex.

Their preparations complete, the men did not delay. The great dumb ox of a Polish Executioner grunted something to his assistants, who seemed to understand, though Amelia could not make out his fractured and accented German, there was a rattling of coals on the hearth and, suddenly, she could feel heat near her bare flesh. Suddenly atrocious agony burst on her bent left buttock. As she drew in her breath in a strangled grunt, she heard the Grafin's voice intoning, slowly, "One!"

As she writhed and hissed in her pain, the count continued, its slowness as agonising as the assault on her defenceless bottom. The iron wrought its horrid work in her smoking flesh, her head came back in an arc of pain, she beat on the padding of the bench with clenched fists, all the while uttering a weird whining through clenched teeth as she fought to survive the atrocity that was being inflicted on her. The Grafin looked on, her teeth bared in a grin of triumph, savouring the sight of the heavy iron in the brute male's hands, pressed against the full buttock, eating its way into the smoking flesh. She completed a full count of ten, before she gestured to the executioner to take away the brand, and replace it with a fresh one.

Again she intoned the snail-paced count as Amelia heaved and bucked on her bristly perch, the mere puncturing of her clitoris long forgotten in the red haze of pain in which she

222

swam. When it was over the letters P R, Palgrave Rohenstock, two inches high, were etched permanently into the fatty tissue of her left buttock, and the irons were back in the fire, being prepared to repeat the torture on her right cheek.

When it was done, and the smell of burnt meat hung heavy in the chamber, the cruelly branded woman slumped on the trestle. She was not sufficiently conscious to hear the Grafin's ironic farewell, but she was wide awake, even though her buttocks throbbed and ached, when her enemy returned to visit her in her cell the next morning.

"You have been sentenced to hard labour, and labour you shall," the Grafin assured her. "The road gang for you, slut, breaking stone all day in the open, and you'll do your stint in the mill as well, with a hook up your arse. And, when you come back, all spent and sweaty, your muscles aching, your nails broken, your skin caked with dust and grime, washed into crevices by the stream of your perspiration, when all you want is to be allowed to get under the pump, sluice off the stench from your stinking body, then fall onto the straw in your cell, you'll have to do your exercises." She laughed evilly. "Your husband particularly mentioned your reluctance to give him your bum. I'm going to make sure you go back stretched and trained to give the best buggery in Europe."

Germany had long been the home of the finest clockmakers in Europe. The Master craftsmen of the town had made many fabulous automata for the Grafin's entertainment and now she had a clock maker construct an ingenious machine, powered by powerful weights, like those used to drive the spits in the kitchens of great houses, or the hands of the great clock in the Cathedral square. The motion of a wheel drove a plunger, to which dildoes of various sizes could be fixed, in and out of the victim's anus. The Countess was forced to grease her own fundament, then mount the frame, where she was secured by straps. Once up, the machine was adjusted to bring the head of the phallic cylinder to touch

223

her shrinking rosebud, which she had to impale on the massive prick, gasping and wincing as she forced it through the reluctant opening.

Once in place the true ingenuity of the device came into play. The motion of the weight driven wheel first, drove it deep into her rectum, then withdrew it until the nose just nuzzled inside her sphincter. If there was sufficient resistance to the withdrawal, a spring loaded mechanism within the plunger extended a metal finger to strike a clock mechanism, recording a valid stroke on the dial. On the next in stroke, if the artificial prick encountered any resistance, compression of another spring caused the finger to extend again, cancelling the stroke.

"Now darling, you can learn to service Heinrich as he deserves. Grip tight as it pulls out, then relax, and let it enter you freely. You've a hundred strokes to score, before you can come off and go to your cell. Best get working, or you'll be here all night. You're getting it easy the first time. It will be two hundred in future, and the springs are set low to start with, they'll be set tighter as time goes by, until you can pull on his prick like a milkmaid on a teat. Happy buggery darling."

Night after night, desperately tired and working her butt to the bone, she fought to grip the slippery shaft, as it withdrew from her distended rectum, then let her anus flower like a rose to accept it back again, thrusting deep into her sore hot bowel, dreading all the time to hear the mechanism click, denoting another stroke cancelled, and all her straining in vain. Back and forth, back and forth, clench down on the rod with aching muscles, then try and relax, let her sphincter uncoil, her stomach muscles go slack, open herself to the impalement, if she wanted to get off this dreadful machine in time to get some rest before the dawn start to the section of highway, where, naked under the sun, or lashed by bitter rain, she would smash one rock against another, until the splinters were small enough to pass through the riddle, squatting uncomfortably to keep her poor ravaged bottom off the ground.

Nor was the machine the only phallus to bugger her sore behind. After she had been at her exercises for ten days or so, the Grafin, who came every other night to gloat over her in her discomfort, announced she would has a treat the next night.

"No horrid piece of steel up you, tomorrow," she announced, "You can have a rest from Herr Feldnicht's technological triumph, and his ingenious wheel."

It was a cruel deceit. She had staggered in from the gang, the sweat running off her, her limbs full of hurt, her fingers and feet bruised from the heartless stone, only to be put on a leash by an attendant, and taken to one of the tower rooms by the main gate. There she was made to anoint her fundament again with tallow, and bend over a groove cut in a board that ran across the room at waist height. When her middle rested firmly in the groove, the matching half, which had been hinged up towards the ceiling, was lowered, completing the encirclement of her waist. Moreover it totally shut out the light from behind her and, since the only windows were in that part of the room in which her bent buttocks stood, she was in near total darkness, quite helpless, though she was not secured in any other way.

She had guessed what her fate was to be, when the Grafin had smirked at her, as she had stuffed the rancid tallow up her anus, encouraged by the attendant's crop across her thighs, but she still flinched, and cried out in protest, when she felt something hard and hot pressed against her cringing arsehole. The partition was very solid, the fit around her waist tight and sealed. suddenly there was a tiny chink of light as a small spyhole was opened beside her. The Grafin spoke.

"Work your arse, as you've been taught, slut. If the man complains, it won't count, and you'll get the crop across your fat arse. You have to satisfy at least ten men, before you'll be released, so I would advise you to try hard."

2 - TIGHT LACING VICTORIAN UNDERWEAR

With the brassiere not yet invented, the principal items of a Victorian lady's underwear were her chemise or shift, her drawers and her stays or corset. There is little to say about the first. It was a simple garment, only differing in the quality of its material and decoration, which could vary considerably.

Drawers only came in with the new Queen, English women of all classes going about 'bare-arsed' up to that time; indeed, at first, the wearing of drawers was greeted with the same shocked indignation and concern for the morals of young women who would resort to such garments, as the lack of them in later times might induce. The new is always shocking to some.

Stays have a longer history. Throughout historical times women cut their garments to support and emphasis the delights of their bodies, seeking to show off a trim waist and shapely breasts. At first just a cleverly cut bodice, with front lacing to draw up the bosom, and nip the waist: by the time of the first Elizabeth a stout board had been inserted in the stomacher to press on the belly and flatten it, while the top end reinforced the bodice, to thrust up and separate the breasts. These boards, or busk bones, were often elaborately hand-carved, usually by the ladies' admirers, this being a slightly daring, though allowable, intimacy, speaking as it did of close contact between the lover and the loved one's breasts, belly and mons veneris, for some of them came down this far, imposing a rigid posture on the wearer.

By the next century that garment had been extended to wrap round the body and stiffened all over, not just down the front, first with more wooden strips, like the busk bone, then with the newly introduced whalebone. Women began to appreciate the effect and feel of tight lacing. One Noblewoman of the period complained it made her stomach ache and remarked, as her sisters were to do down the ages in their millions, 'It pinches so beneath my arms, and makes my waist sore, but one must pay pain for beauty'. Not all saw it as unmitigated discomfort.

By Victoria's reign the corset was King or, rather, unrelenting tyrant, and no woman from the highest degree to the lowest would appear in public without her stays. They were now made with strips of whalebone, later steel, set tightly one against another to form a continuous carapace about the female form, compressing it into the shape that fashion dictated. So relentless was this compulsion to acquire the perfect figure that healthy girls, with well developed lungs and rib cages, submitted to their lower ribs being broken by blows of cloth covered mallets, after which they were bound, and then encased in corsets while they healed to the shape dictated by the tight lacing. It is even said that some actually submitted themselves to the surgeon's knife to remove the lowest ribs on either side. Paying pain for beauty indeed!

Girls were put into stays from an early age, and those who had not started their training by the time they entered their teens were thought in grave risk of being unable to attain the standards required - the elusive eighteen-inch waist. At the boarding schools for young ladies they were put into stays on first arrival, figure training being a principal ingredient of such 'finishing'. There are records of establishments where the girls were sealed in their stays on Monday morning, wearing them day and night, even in bed, until the following Sunday, when they were let out for an hour, for their weekly ablutions.

Nor was pregnancy an excuse to avoid this relentless embrace. The young matron was expected to hide her condition for as long as possible, and special corsets were made with slits over the lower belly, and over each breasts, the openings being furnished with laces of their own, which could be let out gradually as the belly swelled, and the breasts filled, though always exercising tight control. There could be no exuberant show of flesh to witness to the growing babe in the belly.

Strangely the Victorians, while shocked by the glimpse of a slipper beneath a skirt, let alone an ankle, permitted the nudity of arms and shoulders literally as far as the nipples. The tightness of the corset below the breasts forced them up in exuberant mounds of white flesh, nestling in the lacy trim of the garment, where they were recorded as perpetually threatening to spill over into public gaze. In a well known museum of costume in the North of England, the curator proudly displays corsets of the period with small hooks sewn into the half cups in which the breasts lay. She explains that some women of the period, in order to push this licence for nudity to the limit, wore rings in their pierced nipples, which engaged the hooks and ensured that a sudden movement did not lead to embarrassing exposure.

This insistence of tight lacing and steel boning survived right up to the first world war, after which it disappeared with remarkable rapidity, as the 'flappers' tasted their new found freedom.

Not everybody welcomed their passing. One young woman remarked: "Tight lacing produces a delicious sensation, part pleasure part pain." Another: "It is an ever present reminder in directly bidding its wearer self restraint. It is evidence of a well disciplined mind and well regulated feelings." Indeed, there are women today, young attractive women, who still wear strict stays; not the elasticated basques and waspies of the upmarket lingerie counters, pretty though they are, but implacable corsets with steel 'bones' and laces drawn tight as bowstrings, obtaining the same satisfactions as their grandmothers quoted above.

America, always more prudish and conservative in the matter of women's underwear, whatever they may put on top, was last to go - it kept the memory in the form of the universal girdle until modern times. It is only in the last few decades that the American woman has been persuaded that her buttocks come in two halves!

3 - SEXUAL MORES IN VICTORIAN SOCIETY.

While the conventional picture of the Victorians as sexually repressed is generally true, especially as the Queen began to exercise influence on the generals public, there was a seething mass of sexuality beneath the surface. The Queen herself enjoyed sex so much she seemed to think it too good for the lower classes, and seemed under the impression that she and dear Albert invented the whole thing for themselves.

The generations immediately preceding hers though were any thing but repressed and expressed their sexuality boldly and publicly.

There was a class element in all this and the aristocracy continued to hold to their traditional attitudes, which were mainly concerned with not inflaming the lower classes by allowing their affairs to become public knowledge outside their own charmed circle.

Within that magic almost anything went. As Lady Elizabeth Melbourne, the mother of Victoria's favourite Prime Minister, and a notorious bed hopper, informed Lady Caroline Lamb, her daughter-in-law, and rival for the attentions of Lord Byron, the even more notorious poet and libertine, 'all a wife owes her husband is one male heir. After that she is free to choose who shall share her bed'. She certainly made it her own motto and, after the obligatory heir, had children by at least four other men, including the future William IV.

One of her lovers, Lord Egremont, acknowledged father of the Prime Minister, 'bought' her from a rival for £15,000, her husband taking a commission on the deal.

Moreover the bride did not necessarily come to the marriage bed totally inexperienced and unprepared. Although brides were generally very young, sixteen or seventeen being very common, and virginity was outwardly the general rule, there was a long tradition in the underground literature of the nubile daughters of the aristocracy being 'put to the prick' in preparation for marriage, being 'broken-in' by some older man, usually a relative, although sometimes a stranger or else disguised, or the girl hooded, so that she might not know who had used her. The rational behind this bizarre rite was to ensure harmony between bride and groom, since she would not shrink from him, or hold her pain and disgust at her first deflowering against him, while the groom received a willing and co-operative bedfellow.

There was another, darker, side to the sexual initiation of young women of the aristocracy. Theirs was a very small closed world, where their class consciousness made it difficult for many to have sexual relationships with common women. Of course this was far from general, the majority of males in the big country houses of the landed gentry considering the females employed there as chattels whose bodies could be used at will, but there were many who did not stoop to what they considered tainted meat. For them incest was always a temptation, and daughters and nieces were sometimes coerced, sometimes entered willingly, into relationships with their close kin. Tradition had it that, to avoid the embarrassments that swollen bellies might provoke, buggery was the usual practice, this also being held not to affect the girls notional virginity.

Now for Erica, or rather Balikpan, not part of our published series. We shall not be able to follow her much further now, but Balikpan can be downloaded from our web site:

At Bangkok airport, a massively busy super-glossy place on several floors, I was given back the control unit, but, due to our late arrival, we were immediately hustled towards the special check-in for Balikpan, and there was no chance to use it.

A few eyebrows were raised at Erica by the friendly smiling Thais, but we got there without incident.

Security at the Balikpan check-in was very high indeed. As soon as an outer lounge hid us from the rest of the world we were ushered through another door into an inner lounge where our papers were scrutinised and our names checked in a register before we could pass yet a third door, a massive one guarded by two alert soldiers with guns.

I think the plane had been held for us - at any rate, there were no other passengers still checking in.

Apparently the airline was run by the military, and it was a soldier who stood at the desk and put our luggage on the scales. After weighing it he gestured to Erica to stand on the scales.

"She's with me," I said. "I have her passport here."

"But she baggage, Sir."

"Baggage?"

"Yes, Sir, woman is baggage, you reclaim with luggage please."

Erica looked at me in dismay, but obviously we had to go along with local ways of doing things. I gestured to her to do as the soldier ordered, and in a trice she had been weighed.

"Just fill in this label please". He handed me a large sticky label with weight and flight number filled in. I soon completed the section marked 'Property Of'.

When I handed it back to him he passed it to the soldier

231

who had weighed Erica, and he turned her round, tucked her little skirt up into her belt and slapped the label on her bottom.

She started to protest, but the soldier merely hoisted her over his shoulder, giving me a great view of her bare backside as her legs kicked harmlessly in the air.

"The snake, Uncle," she shouted. "Turn off the snake!"

But before I could get the control unit out of my pocket and activate it she was gone. She had been squirming quite deliciously for some time, and I looked forward to our next meeting!

After the short flight from Bangkok - about an hour - a splendid verdant island appeared below us, fringed with white surf. The plane made a wide sweep as we turned in towards the runway, which was built out into the blue sea, with a range of hills for a back drop.

The Airport itself turned out to be quite a surprise. It was not very large, but it was modern and extremely well equipped, clean and apparently run very efficiently.

"Now Sir, it will be a an hour or so before the baggage is ready for collection." The man at immigration stamped the passports and handed them back to me. "There is a lounge over there. I advise you to wait there and have a drink. Collect your baggage at leisure, Sir: there is no air-conditioning in the baggage area, so it is better not to go there too soon."

It was in the complimentary cocktail lounge that I got my first sight of Balikpan women - all of the splendid barefooted oriental-looking waitresses wore similar short tunics. Although there were several different colours they all seemed to be of exactly the same length, sashed at the waist.

The tallest girls were in greatest demand - as they took orders and carried drinks round the crowded little room they came in for more than their fair share of groping from the new arrivals, as it was obvious that they wore nothing at all except the tunics. One could have quite an erotic holiday without venturing beyond the arrivals lounge!

I got into conversation with a very interesting fellow. He described the girl he had entered into the obedience trials at great length - in fact in the end he got to be a bit of a bore about how sure he was of winning with her. Apparently she had come in third at last year's trials and he had worked hard on her since. It seemed he visited frequently, and had her trained locally. She wouldn't dare not to win this time, she just would not dare! I tore myself away at last without any regrets.

In the baggage reclaim, the sight of Erica sitting on my suitcase was quite a tonic. It was gratifying how some of the other visitors lingered to admire her. Specially, perhaps, her squirm! I noticed that some, presumably those who had been to Balikpan before, had no hesitation in fingering her, although after I arrived none did so without asking me first.

"Come," I said, "let us see what Balikpan has to offer."

"The snake, Uncle? What about the snake?"

"Don't fidget," I said. Everyone was admiring her squirm, and I suspected it was imagination rather than actual pain that was causing it. "I put the control in my bag, I'll see to it when we get to our apartment."

The real surprise - perhaps culture shock would be a better description - came when Erica and I reached the concourse. The exit to this was through one of a number of elegant archways, each with a language written above it.

Immediately through the 'English Speak' archway we were confronted with a desk at which sat a young man, slanted eyes that were a dark lustrous brown, black hair, slight figure, smiling face. In other words, as we soon came to realise, a typical Balikanese male.

"Saawatdi krap," he said, holding his hands together under his chin with a slight bow, a gesture I had only read

233

about, but recognised as a wai. "Please, the Kingdom of Balikpan honours its distinguished guests. Please to accept a porter with our compliments." He snapped his fingers and a young woman ran to us. Also obviously Balikanese, she wore a brief tunic of the same standard length and design I had seen in the cocktail lounge, but with words stencilled on it in the strange hieroglyphics of Thai (also the language of Balikpan) and repeated in English: 'AIRPORT PROPERTY Not to be taken away'.

"Saawatdi kaa". She made a much deeper deep wai than the man had done. "I take cases please?" Her voice was very pleasant, low and singsong, with a distinctive accent

"What does that mean, Airport Property?" I asked, in somewhat of a daze, for nothing I had read had prepared me for this. The noise and bustle all around was staggering.

"Me belong airport just like -" She pointed to a trolley. "Like tlolley."

Well, I had read about Balikpan, of course, but reading is one thing, seeing is another. And, obviously, most of what is written about Balikpan is highly censored. Whatever they have read, any outsider who visits this strange Kingdom, so barbaric is some ways and yet so technically advanced in others, is in for a big shock!

It was difficult to know how to answer the porter girl. "I didn't expect such good English," I said feebly.

"Please, we are teach much language at school. English is velly difficult."

"Velly? You can't say 'r'?"

"Not if it is stlong." She was very agitated at my innocent query and even seemed to go a little paler, though it is hard to tell with those delicious brown skins. "Oh Sir, do not complain, please! None of us can say them velly well."

"What if I complained?"

She dropped to her knees and kissed my feet: I learned later that kissing feet is among the most degrading things

234

for a Balikanese to do, feet being very low. "No, please, no!" I had had no intention of doing so, but as she rose gracefully to her feet and lifted the case again, it burst open, spewing out its contents on the smooth tiles of the airport floor.

"Look at that!" Erica turned to the man at the desk. "See what this clumsy little cow has done!"

At once the girl prostrated herself at Erica's feet, trying to kiss them. But the man behind the counter came out and seized her by her long straight glossy black hair, dragging her away across the polished floor and bowing to me.

"She shall be punished, you shall see, please, insulting tourists is not permitted, please, come."

He pulled down two strands of rope from a crane-like apparatus beside his desk. Each ended in a loop which he tightened round the girl's ankles as she lay on the floor. Then he pressed a button. There was a faint whirring sound and she was hoisted into the air. Her tunic fell over her head from where it was belted round the waist and she hung upside down, only her long hair and finger-tips touching the smooth floor.

Like the waitresses, she wore nothing beneath the tunic.

He offered me a riding-crop.

"Please," he said.

"No, really," I started to say. The situation was so bizarre. But Erica snatched the crop from my hand and started to thrash the hanging girl in a savage attack.

This was something new, an Erica I had never seen before - she was enjoying being the one to inflict punishment! I stood back and watched as the smooth brown body twisted and jerked about, writhing under the assault as the girl doubled up and straightened out but could not escape the crack crack crack of the crop.

When at last Erica's sudden fury had blown itself out, a man who had been watching took over. Apparently the girl's position was an open invitation to any spectators, and quite a few had gathered round.

"For how long should she hang, please?" asked the official.

"Enough already," I said.

"No!" Erica put a finger to my lips and I didn't have the heart to disappoint her. The tip of her tongue was between her lips as she watched the figure of the girl swinging and twisting from the ropes. "Can I say an hour?"

The man looked at me. I nodded and he shrugged his shoulders. "If it is the wish of Sir. We always do as tourists ask."

"Two hours then!" Erica was really excited, and again I nodded in support of her. She went over and lifted the girl's tunic to look into her anguished face. The arms hung down beside it, fingers opening and closing. "I'm giving you two hours, of this, you clumsy little bitch!" The girl made a pathetic little upside down wai as the assault on her bottom from the rapidly growing queue continued.

Erica's eyes were gleaming in a way I had never seen before as she stepped back to watch the increasing contortions of the dangling body. The queue to thrash what was visible of it continued to lengthen.

"Why doesn't she cry out?"

The man resumed his seat. "It is not permitted." He snapped his fingers again and another girl came forward instantly. This one was shorter, and the tunic covered her sex, though I supposed that like the others she wore nothing under it. She also was brown and very very pretty, and obviously extremely apprehensive. She wai'd to me with great respect - the lower the wai, it seemed, the greater the respect.

"Master want taxi? This way, please."

As soon as we left the airport concourse a blast of hot air hit us and the cultural shock continued - was reinforced, indeed. A man shouted to us from a booth at the side of the road:

"Guide? You want guide?"

Behind him was a raised platform, and on it were several girls. They wore similar tunics to that of our porter, and rather fetching little caps with writing in various languages.

"Angrit," said our porter, and two girls immediately ran to us. They stood before us, wai-ing and smiling. The man came forward, rubbing his hands. "She talk English. You like?"

One of the girls did appeal to me more than the other, and the man saw my eyes on her. He gestured to her and she slipped the tunic off. She looked rather succulent in just a cap, small but very well rounded - none of the girls I had seen so far had shoes. "You like, please?" She revolved like a mannequin. "Nice, yes? She guide you, she do anything for you. Four hundred baht a day. You take, please?"

"What do you mean, anything?" I asked.

"Guide, cookie, fuckie, anything. You not like, you beat. You ask money back, I beat, OK?"

"Oh Uncle Rex, do let's have one!" Erica sounded really keen. "You could afford one each for us, couldn't you? And look, there's plenty others to choose from."

I looked round and realised that this was only one of several booths.

"Maybe we'll come back," I said.

"OK, OK, three hundred baht, if you not like I exchange."

I shook my head and heard a little cry as he cuffed the girl back to her place.

We walked to the next booth.

There was only one girl in that, naked. A big man with a cigar was examining her, pushing his fingers into her sex, pinching her nipples, opening her mouth. He seemed well satisfied.

"Six hundred baht," said the stall holder.

"Right!" The man, an American I rather fancy, had obvi-

237

ously been over-charged, but it was no business of ours. Besides, it was very hot out here, beyond the reach of the air-conditioning. We strolled on, followed by our porter.

The flood of arrivals was drying up now, and as we arrived at the last booth the girls in it were reduced to only two hundred baht a day, according to the spiel of the salesman. About five pounds sterling. At the same time he removed their tunics and piled them on a chair. Then he handcuffed the girls wrists to a bar that ran high across the top of the front of the booth.

Business picked up immediately!

Here it was better to be tall than short - one, a plump little thing, dangled, her toes barely brushing the ground, and because of that, I suppose, became the object of more fingering than all the others, though nobody took her. She was rather appealing, actually, the usual lovely liquid brown eyes, very frightened, high firm breasts moist with sweat. The proprietor was down to three girls now, settling for a hundred and fifty baht without too much haggling as the customers from the flight dwindled. Within minutes all were gone except for the plump one.

He flicked her bottom with a riding crop, his usual way of attracting attention to his wares, and her legs kicked out violently.

"This one new. You want this one?"

I shook my head.

"She velly young. One hundred only."

"No thanks."

"Fifty? Reduced. Too much fat but she velly young make a good fuck!" He lashed out at her in fury and she shouted out: "Yes, yes, me make good fuck."

Resisting Erica's unspoken plea, I turned away from the jerking body, the sweat drying on it as the sun cleared the canopy and shone fully on her.

"Pah! The meanness of you tourist pigs!" He put the padlock key in his pocket in disgust and placed a stool under her dangling feet before swaggering out, ignoring her despairing shout, which sounded to me like 'water'. As we reached our taxi I looked back and saw some lads who had been fooling about with a football abandon it in favour of the girl. The last thing I saw, one had appropriated the stool, climbed upon it and started to pinch her.

I hesitated. "When is the next arrivals flight?" I asked our guide, as she loaded my bags into the taxi.

"Airport not busy tomollow, Master. Maybe he come back." She didn't sound too sure. "Next day busy. He like girl more slim, I tink."

The taxi driver cut in. "You want girl, I take you girl market, many there, better better, that one no good."

In any case I couldn't undo her handcuffs. I put my arm round Erica and settled back in the taxi for a drive through Balikpan City.

She was squirming most deliciously, but the time had come to turn off the heater in the dildo, or the battery would run down. She sighed with relief, but it was quite a while before she was to stop her squirming...

TITLES IN PRINT

Silver Moon

Silver Mink

UK £4.99 except *£5.99 --USA $8.95 except *$9.95